SCORPION'S FURY

SCORPION'S FURY

METAL LEGION™ BOOK ONE

CH GIDEON   CALEB WACHTER   CRAIG MARTELLE

DISRUPTIVE IMAGINATION®

LMBPN Publishing
PMB 196, 2540 South Maryland Pkwy
Las Vegas, NV 89109

First US edition, December 2018
Version 1.03, December 2020

We can't write without those who support us
On the home front, we thank you for being there for us

We wouldn't be able to do this for a living if it weren't for our readers
We thank you for reading our books

SCORPION'S FURY TEAM

Thanks to our Beta Readers

James Caplan
Kelly O'Donnell
Micky Cocker

Thanks to the JIT Readers

John Ashmore
Angel LaVey
Crystal Wren
Kelly O'Donnell
Nicole Emens
Peter Manis
James Caplan
Misty Roa
Paul Westman
Keith Verret
Kelly Ethan
Terry Easom

If I've missed anyone, please let me know!

Editing services provided by LKJ Bookmakers www.
lkjbooks.com

ELVIRA

Humanity reached for the stars, but then did what humans do best. They disagreed and went their separate ways. The Terran Federation and the Solarians. The Solarians did their thing. Terra did another. The Terran Federation negotiated with the aliens and signed treaties so they could use the wormholes. Then the aliens reneged and showed up in warships filled with soldiers...

The deck bucked beneath Xi Bao's pilot chair violently enough to jostle her neural link, temporarily interrupting *Elvira*'s data streams and giving Bao a wave of intense vertigo before the links were restored.

"Kill that fucking nest, Podsy!" Bao snarled as she struggled to keep *Elvira* stable. The fifteen-meter-long mech's six spider-like legs scrambled to stay upright amid the hail of ordnance coming from the enemy position, a bunker *Elvira* had stumbled upon seconds earlier.

"Give me a quarter-second firing window," Podsednik snapped back, his voice transmitted via the mech's hard-lines.

In spite of the rounds hitting the armor, and the impacts disrupting the ground beneath its legs, she managed to steady the ungainly mech. Just as Xi opened her mouth to rebuke her engineer-turned-gunner's tardiness, he sent an archaic fifteen-kilo slug, *Elvira*'s second-most-potent weapon, into the enemy's nest.

Even with the short-range 'soft-loaded' ammunition, the sound was terrifying, and the recoil doubly so. *Elvira*'s front legs lifted a full two meters off the rocky ground as every kinetic compensation system kicked in to counteract the force of the blast. Where the enemy-filled nest had been, nestled beneath the surface of the volcanic rock-field, now a smoking crater lined with shrapnel and charred lumps of flesh remained. Nothing, not even a Marine in state-of-the-art armor or a mech like *Elvira*, could survive a point-blank hit like that.

After the mouth of the subterranean 'nest' was silent for a few seconds, Xi Bao breathed a sigh of relief. "Lucky shot," she snorted as she processed a stream of damage reports from *Elvira*'s active compensation systems.

"You're a real bitch, you know that?" Podsy retorted.

"Takes one to know one."

"Oh, fuck off," he snorted. "And don't do it up there, that's not why they call the manual controls 'joysticks.'"

"One for you, Podsy," she laughed before an alarm went off on her HUD—her heads-up display. "We've got a blown stabilizer on five," she said, transmitting the relevant information to Podsy's console.

"Probably just the hydraulic safety tripping again," he said confidently after a rapid perusal of the data. "I'll reset it."

"Copy that," she acknowledged as she swept the nearby area for more contacts and found none, not even the humans which should have been in range of *Elvira*'s thermal imagers. "Where the hell is our infantry, anyway?"

Podsy used the crawlspace between *Elvira*'s segments to get to the panel where he could manually reset five's safety circuit.

"Captain Murdoch said the force was exposed, so he pulled them back to the center. He must have been confident that we'd have things covered over here," Podsy drawled. "Frankly, with your winning personality, I'm amazed they didn't go AWOL and plaster themselves as meat shields on *Elvira*'s armor to defend your virtue."

"*Captain* Murdoch. Like we needed a ground pounder rank between Lieutenant and Lieutenant Commander, but there it is."

She snorted with derision before addressing Podsy. "If the rock-biters counterattack during this push—" Bao grimaced, ignoring his dig at her notorious prickliness. "—we're going to be stuck out here on the flank with no support. I haven't registered a drone sweep through our quadrant in the last forty minutes. Mechs aren't designed to operate solo, especially not mechs with systems that are as old as our great-great-grandparents!"

"I think you underestimate our girl," he replied and drifted off as a new stream of data came pouring in through his helmet's HUD. "Is five showing online?"

Bao checked the stream and nodded in relief. "It is. Good work. Now get us off the skyline."

Podsy scampered back to his position.

"What," he quipped, "I'm not *lucky* this time?" *Elvira* started flexing her legs, preparing to navigate the rubble of her last engagement.

"It's better to be lucky than good," Bao riposted.

"Maybe, but it's best to be *both*."

She had no comeback for that. After testing the five legs' systems, she resumed her trek across the blasted wasteland of the volcanic planet, which for the last three weeks they had called home.

"Get back on the fifteen," she urged, referring to the cannon Podsy had cleared the enemy nest with. "This whole area's riddled with caves and shit. There could be a zillion more bunkers out there."

"On it," he replied, moving to his second position and quickly strapping himself into the gun's control pod.

Normally the mech's pilot, Bao, would directly control the weapons and wouldn't need a gunner. But half of *Elvira's* control systems had failed shortly after arriving in the combat zone. That meant while she controlled *Elvira's* movement and anti-personnel systems, she was forced to rely on Podsy, her engineer, to man the heavier weapons until they received replacement components.

Like that was going to happen any time soon.

Elvira was a two-hundred-year-old relic, pulled out of some godforsaken scrapyard, or, more likely, a collector's showroom, and approved by a panel of boneheads back at Fleet Command for active duty, despite missing a quarter of her onboard systems. With less than a weeks' training with the rusty bug, Bao and Podsy had been dropped behind enemy lines as part of the aptly-named Operation Spider-Hole.

Just two months earlier, Bao had been training at HQ with an eye toward an official posting later in the year. A mech Jock by training, her unorthodox career had nearly been derailed by run-ins with superiors at nearly every stage of that training. She had resigned herself to serving as some other Jock's Monkey, the backup to every other job, and generally considered the most expendable member of a mech's standard three-person team. But when Commander Jenkins' new unit presented the opportunity for her own rig, she had leapt at the chance.

In hindsight, she wondered if it wouldn't have been better to wait, cooling her heels as some other Jock's Monkey rather than taking a museum piece into combat.

The Terran Republic had declared Durgan's Folly a potential host planet and that meant it had to be cleared the old-fashioned way. No nukes from orbit. No high-intensity, high-damage weapons. Only a quick clearing operation of the estimated small number of Arh'kel. But Xi knew better. The op had gotten her out of jail first and foremost even though she already knew that

4

nothing was quick or easy so expected the battle to go sideways. They always did.

"You know," Podsy observed, seemingly reading her mind, "this would be a lot safer with a dedicated Monkey aboard."

"I thought you Wrenches all started off as Monkeys," she retorted while guiding *Elvira* across a particularly deep, narrow chasm, stretching the mech's legs to their maximum in order to cross the deadly crack in the blasted surface of this hellish world. "You should be right at home hotfooting it from one job to another."

"Nice. Thanks for not dropping us into the pit of doom," Podsy noted, eyes locked on the screen showing the mech's external view. *Elvira's* twin fifteens swerved back and forth to reduce reaction time in case of an ambush. His goal was to shoot more while getting hit less. He and Bao had the same goal: survive. He also refused to take anything too seriously. "*I* thought you Jocks all had decent interpersonal skills since they're kind of helpful in command positions," he fired back. "So much for thinkin'."

Bao deepened her voice in blatant mockery of their division commander, Commander Jenkins. "Fleet Command needs to field the maximum number of platforms with the minimum number of crew. This is a fast-track opportunity for anyone bold enough to seize it. We achieve our objective in three months or less and every Jock, Wrench or Monkey in the division earns a ticket to promotion or back to whatever shit-stain of a world was misfortunate enough to have birthed you. Your choice."

"Which will it be for you?" Podsy asked as Bao finally guided *Elvira* away from the deadly chasm.

"What's that?"

"You going for the promotion or kicking out of the service after we turn these boulders into gravel?" Podsy clarified.

In truth, Bao hadn't given it much thought, at least not since arriving on rock-biter central. She'd been too focused on staying alive, which she suspected would be all the reward she could reasonably hope for as an unfortunate participant in Operation Spider-Hole.

"I doubt we'll live long enough for my preference to matter," she said dismissively.

"Maybe," he allowed, "but me? I'm calling it quits after this. Getting that 'time served' stamp on my jacket three years into a fifteen-year sentence is looking pretty good. I might even be able to get my old job at the plant back and have something approaching a normal life."

"Remind me again what you got clinked for, Podsy?" she drawled. She could almost hear him wince and snarl.

"Stuff it up your..." he began, only to be cut off when the ground beneath *Elvira* gave way and the mech tilted dangerously.

"Shit." Bao gritted her teeth, struggling with both the neural and manual controls as the ground before them gave way.

Fanning out in front of *Elvira*, the formerly-solid ground of the flat plains fell away in a spectacular cascade of brittle volcanic rock—spreading out in a crescent before the mech and exposing a massive cavern with the floor many times *Elvira*'s height. The roof of the cavern crashed into the floor, the mech's six legs lost traction, and she started to slip down into the now-bowl-shaped depression like a bug caught in an antlion's pit-trap.

"Shiiiiiiiiiiiit!" Bao called out, fighting desperately to keep the mech upright while they slid toward the depression's center.

"Commander, I'm picking something up in Grid Three Two," reported Styles, a battalion high-altitude drone operator.

Commander Jenkins turned, his stomach clenched in a sudden knot. "Aren't we a little thin there?" he asked, moving toward Styles' workstation.

"Yessir, just one Scorpion-class in a two-click radius of the event," Styles reported as he maneuvered his drone to get a better look.

"One Scorpion with attached infantry…it's light, but it might be enough to secure an access junction," Jenkins' brow lowered darkly as he recalled his numerous rejected requests for reinforcement. Fleet Command had pled poverty, as usual, leaving him and his battalion of forty-four mechs, manned by mostly criminals and reprobates, the unenviable task of soaking up however much of the enemy's vigor as possible before the *real* soldiers moved in to execute the main phase of Operation Spider-Hole. "Get the *Monsoon* and *Babycake* on the line; they need to be ready to move to support our Scorpion in Grid Three Two if I give the word."

Jenkins had been painstakingly surveying areas like Grid Three Two for days in an attempt to find a mainline passage into the enemy's underground facilities, but had met no real success. Every time they got close to a tunnel large enough to move armor down, the enemy would collapse it, willing to blow the passage up rather than see it fall into human hands.

When the commander moved diggers in to clear the rubble, the enemy's efforts were at least a step ahead of their excavation efforts. Division HQ had made clear they could not afford to fight a war of attrition down there: they needed to strike at the enemy's bases of operation quickly or they risked losing what little support they had thus far received.

"No infantry showing in the area, sir. The mech is out there solo," Styles said grimly.

Jenkins' eyes narrowed, "Who the hell authorized a Scorpion to hold down the right flank of this advance without infantry support?"

A pause. "It looks like Captain Murdoch gave the order twenty-eight minutes ago to re-deploy that mech's infantry complement to reinforce his company's Mobile Command Platform."

"Make a note of that," Jenkins said grimly as the first mid-resolution images of the event came across the viewer, images which made his narrowed eyes widen in a mix of surprise and horror. Without delay, he snapped off orders, "Orbital, I need every piece of hardware in the area to re-orient onto that location. Comm, get everything that rolls, marches, slithers or crawls diverted into those tunnels ASAP. Styles, establish contact with that Scorpion," he said, watching as the giant mech somehow, against all odds, managed to keep its feet as it skittered to a halt at the center of the largest subterranean transport nexus yet unearthed on this hell-hole of a planet. "Tell them reinforcements are inbound, and they are to hold that position and prevent a coordinated cave-in of the main arteries leading out of there," he ordered, watching with a thrill of satisfaction as the Scorpion's fifteen-kilo slug thrower annihilated an enemy vehicle before it could flee down one of the fifty tunnels leading away from the nexus.

Acknowledgments streamed in from the various recipients of his orders, and he watched as the Scorpion's flank-mounted anti-personnel arsenal unleashed a storm of fire on the enemy stirring from beneath the collapsed roof.

It soon became clear from the thermal feeds that there were *thousands* of the damned things climbing up through the rubble.

At its current rate of fire, *Elvira*'s pilot would exhaust her Scorpion's maximum ammo supply in less than three minutes.

Reinforcements wouldn't arrive for another six minutes.

"I can't establish contact with *Elvira*, Commander," Styles reported, the tension in the command center thickening with each passing second. "I've got a pair of air units inbound, ETA five minutes."

"A surrounded Scorpion can't hold that long…" he muttered under his breath, recalling a similar situation he had once narrowly survived during his third tour as a mech pilot. He gripped the rail as he leaned intently toward the nearest video feed display, which showed the aged Scorpion pivoting in preparation to fire one of its chem-driven fifteen-kilo cannons. "Make each round count, rookie..."

Elvira's fifteen belched righteous fury, thundering into the far side of the now-open-air cavern and destroying two more of the fleeing enemy tanks, or whatever these rock-biters called the large, lumbering hunks of mostly iron that served as their heavy unit transports.

"Good shot, Podsy!" Bao cheered as she pivoted *Elvira* on her two remaining left legs.

The front-left leg had been snapped off at the nearest joint, leaving the mech badly-crippled but still able to fire her main guns, for now. Thankfully, the rest of the mech's limbs were functional; she could still maneuver her big guns into firing arcs that would keep the worst of the enemy off them as long as their supply of close-range rounds held.

"Side-up against the wall," Podsy suggested just as she had the inkling to do precisely that. "We can cut our fire to just one flank's machine guns and maybe stretch the ammo out for another minute, minute and a half."

The downside to his suggestion, of course, was that they would be conceding the possibility of escape. Using the wall for cover would make certain this would be a fight to the death, since the enemy would cut them off from the rubble-strewn slope down which they had arrived. But it was an easy call to make. Bao had no illusions about the fact that they weren't *already* in a fight to the death, and clearly Podsy felt the same.

"Good call," she agreed as she walked *Elvira* toward the nearest cavern wall while pouring hot rounds point-blank at an enemy that seemed to ooze out of the rubble.

They were made of the same stuff as the stone that had temporarily buried them.

Rock-biters. The Arh'Kel.

Silica-based life forms were nothing new to veterans of the Fleet, but this was Bao's first combat deployment and her up-close-and-personal look at non-humans. These ones were short, squat, three-legged things with a trio of 'arms' that were apparently identical to their 'legs' because, in actuality, they were. Without any recognizable head, the creatures' locomotion consisted of them 'rolling' along like a cross between a slinky and a caltrop, with each limb taking a turn as a leg before rotating upright once again and becoming an arm.

They were big, too, over three meters tall when fully extended. Each of their limbs was half a meter thick, and they moved with greater speed than most creatures of their mass, an average of three-quarter metric ton apiece, seemed physically capable of.

Still, like anything with a skin, the bastards bled just as freely as humans when *Elvira*'s machine guns delivered the most intimate of greetings.

The ammo bars on Bao's virtual HUD steadily dropped as she lashed out, precisely delivering short bursts into the encroaching hordes. *Elvira*'s comm antenna had been damaged during the fall, which meant Bao and Podsy were among the unlucky few who, no matter how effectively they fought, would know exactly what the inside of their final resting place looked like.

A pair of enemy 'infantry' came dangerously close to breaking through *Elvira*'s machine gun arc, but two thousand hours in the targeting simulator paid off as a burst of three rounds struck the rushing enemy twice apiece. Four hits with three shots, at this range, had to be some kind of battalion record.

Not that anyone would ever learn about it. Even though the mech recorded all data streams for later review, and its data storage systems were hardened against EMP interference, the old-style silica boards in *Elvira*'s computer systems were like candy to the rock-biters who stripped every last trace of silica from any piece of hardware they'd yet captured.

She and Podsy were going to die here, surrounded by rock-biters in a six-legged metal casket. She had already made peace with that.

The only question now was how many of the bastards they took with them.

Fire spat from *Elvira*'s right flank, downing over a hundred enemy soldiers before the right side's ammo broke into the red zone. "Turning," she barked, knowing that Podsy would need to make the most of his next shot with the fifteen.

As the Scorpion-class mech pivoted, round after round of enemy fire slammed into her badly-perforated armor. But it was all small arms fire, miniature plasma launchers and coilguns not much different from their human infantry counterparts in terms of destructive force, so the punctures in the mech's armor were shallow. *Elvira* would hold together against such weaponry long enough to empty her guns.

Beyond that...

As Bao pivoted *Elvira* clockwise, Podsy sent a soft-loaded fifteen-kilo shell into the far side of the cavern mere seconds before an enemy railgun was brought to bear on them, a railgun she had not been aware of until Podsy had obliterated it.

"One shot, one kill," she joked, silently cursing herself for missing the railgun's presence. She soon completed her turn, and promptly vented her indignation upon the approaching wave of enemy soldiers, tearing them limb from rocky limb as they tumbled toward *Elvira*'s position.

"No luck, all skill," Podsy approvingly finished the much-maligned poem for her. "I'm reading an overload in the number two power coupler," he reported more seriously just as her neural linkage indicated the same via her HUD. Number Two powered the fifteen's ammo feed system. Without it functioning, they would be down to *Elvira*'s missile launcher.

Firing the soft-loaded fifteen at point-blank range in unstable terrain was risky, to be sure. But firing the ballistic missile launcher closer than a kilometer?

That was straight-up suicidal for more reasons than Bao could list.

"Shut it down and reroute through Number One," she grunted, swaying *Elvira* aside an eighth of a second before another enemy railgun appeared at a larger tunnel and spat fire at them. The hypervelocity projectiles tore clean through *Elvira*'s right middle leg, cleaving it roughly in half. Bao felt a surge of feedback akin to pain as the neural interface fed damage reports directly into her brain.

Spraying *Elvira*'s machine guns in tightly-grouped bursts, Bao put another fifty of the enemy infantry down while Podsy worked furiously to re-align the mech's failing power grid. They were at risk of a cascade failure if he couldn't get it under control, which meant their remaining lifespans likely stood at less than a minute.

A flicker of movement from a nearby tunnel showed another railgun platform emerging. Followed by another, and another. It was over. They'd fallen into the heart of the enemy and were about to pay the price for nothing short of bad luck.

"Fire the pulse warhead!" she growled, re-orienting *Elvira* toward the open ceiling as the enemy railgun set up for a second shot. As last words went, Bao knew those left a lot to be desired, but there was no way she would go down with unspent ammo in the can.

"Firing," Podsy acknowledged, his voice filled with resignation as he unleashed the fury of the million man-hours of blood, sweat, and tears which had gone into building the high-precision pulse warhead, a weapon designed to create a powerful EMP capable of knocking just about any electrical system offline, at least temporarily.

The missile fired off its launcher, propelled by chemically-driven rocket engines. It hurtled up toward the sky, passing from view as Bao turned *Elvira*'s machine guns toward the horde of rock-biters.

A time-to-impact countdown appeared on her HUD, signaling they had just six seconds before the pulse warhead completed its turn and went off a few hundred meters above their position.

Her right machine gun ran dry at the three-seconds-to-go mark, prompting her to stomp *Elvira*'s front-right leg with such perfect timing that it flattened an inbound soldier breaking through the breach in her defenses. His flanking allies cart-wheeled in their odd fashion past his ruin and moved with plasma torches burning, their intentions clear.

She kept firing the left guns, watching the countdown clock draw steadily nearer to zero. While she did so, the infantry began cutting into *Elvira*'s armor with their torches. Apparently, they were considered standard sidearms by the rock-biters.

"Back to the stone age, assholes," Bao snarled as the clock reached zero, and the soft glow of the enemy railgun preceded what would certainly be a fatal shot on *Elvira*'s ruined hull.

Dying with a pun on her lips was about the last way she had envisioned going out, and as the world exploded with hellish light, all Bao could think about was how much worse those 'last words' had been than their predecessors.

"Detecting a targeted EMP, Commander Jenkins," Styles reported grimly after his drone's video feed went dark. "The pulse warhead went off eighty-three meters above the surface."

Jenkins released his death-grip on the rail, straightening as he nodded curtly. "Understood. How long until our aerial units arrive?"

"First unit intercepts in twenty seconds," Styles replied promptly.

No one could survive an EMP's explosive generator at that range, especially not while riding an old rust bucket like a Scorpion. Those things, even in their heyday, had been designed more for show than proper warfare. The human aversion to insects, coupled with the constant need for engineers to constantly reinvent the wheel, and topped off by the bureaucratic insistence on spending government funds on boondoggles, had resulted in the old Scorpion and a handful of similarly bizarre designs being approved and built.

Thankfully, until now, they had never seen anything approaching real combat. Pulling them out of mothballs had been entirely Jenkins' plan, and now that plan had cost at least two of his mech crewmen their lives. Given the last few weeks' results on this dump of a planet, Jenkins was giving serious consideration to leaping off the wagon and finding a deep, dark bottle to crawl inside.

"Gain altitude and achieve overwatch outside of the biters' small arms range," Commander Jenkins ordered. "Our land units will need as much intel on that hole as possible when they arrive. Every byte of data matters here; keep that bird in the air as long as possible."

"Moving to overwatch," Styles acknowledged.

"Have *Monsoon* and *Babycake* formations group at Rendezvous Point Charlie," Jenkins continued. "We're scrapping the reinforcement op and adopting a fast-attack posture in the hope we can get there before they collapse all of the tunnels. Establish overlapping fields of fire from the depression's rim to prevent..."

"Sir!" Styles interrupted, more than a little uncharacteristically. "You need to see this!"

Jenkins ground his teeth and glowered in Styles' direction, "What is it, Mr. Styles?"

"The hole…it's clean," Styles reported eagerly as he threw data streams up on a nearby display for Jenkins to peruse. "No movement, limited EM activity. The thermals clearly show where the rock-biters went down, but…"

"But they're not moving," Jenkins interrupted as he realized what Styles was showing him. The rock-biters were not, in fact, completely motionless, but they were moving sluggishly and without any of the coordination they had displayed in previous engagements. They were either stunned or dying.

This was the opportunity of a lifetime: the chance to actually breach the enemy's line before Jenkins' battalion was battered to a pulp!

"Rescind my previous orders," he snapped anxiously, turning to his comm operator. "*Monsoon* and *Babycake* are to move with all speed to secure that location. Every second counts!" he barked, and the warrant quickly went to work relaying his orders.

"Without their infantry," Styles observed, "they'll be as exposed as *Elvira* was, Commander."

"The difference here is that *Elvira* was facing an enemy stronghold at full strength," Jenkins said, offering a silent prayer of thanks to the fallen crew in the downed Scorpion-class mech, the wreckage of which sat near the edge of the collapsed cavern. "*Monsoon* and *Babycake* will be more than capable of securing the area, especially after the hell *Elvira* gave them. And in eight minutes," Jenkins added, "*Silent Fox* and *Blue Balls* will reinforce their position. Let's get in there and grab these sandy bastards by the stones!" he exclaimed with relish, and it was obvious from the postures of his command center's crew that they shared his enthusiasm.

"Copy that, Commander," Styles said with an eager nod, and sure enough, the overwatch drone soon spotted the quadrupedal

Babycake as it approached the crater, while the bipedal, but six-armed, *Monsoon* followed some twenty seconds later. *"Babycake* and *Monsoon* have started securing the area," Styles reported unnecessarily as *Monsoon* began to pour anti-personnel fire into the cavern from the edge, while *Babycake* slowly wended down the treacherous rubble-strewn slope that *Elvira* had fallen down earlier.

The grisly work was done well in advance of the mechs' attached infantrymen, and soon human soldiers were moving in teams down the rockslide to secure the mouths of each major tunnel leading out of the unthinkably vast transit hub, a hub which stretched a full kilometer from one end to the other at its longest.

Overwatch was established two minutes later, as another quartet of mechs arrived, but the good news was far from finished, streaming continuously into the command post.

"Commander," Styles muttered in an awestruck tone as he looked up wide-eyed, "they survived..."

"Who, the rock-biters?" Jenkins demanded, the hairs on the back of his neck rising as he wondered how the damned rock-biters could have made it through the hell his people had just poured on them.

"No... Lieutenant Xi and Chief Warrant Podsednik, sir," Styles clarified, *"Elvira's* crew...they survived!" Jenkins blinked in stunned confusion for a moment before Styles continued, "I've got a team of corpsmen reporting Xi is in critical condition. They're requesting immediate medevac."

Surprising no one more than himself, Jenkins pumped his fist victoriously as the command center erupted into a chorus of cheers. "Deploy the medevac, priority one," he barked, trying to rein in his enthusiasm and retain the dignity of his position. "Yes!" He raised his voice above the hoots and high-fives around the command center as he declared. "It looks like this battalion just produced its first heroes. Keep them alive, Styles. At all costs, keep them alive. They've done the battalion's heavy lifting. Now it's our turn to carry them."

Judging by the mood of his people, he had finally, after six months of working with the dregs and castoffs of every other unit in the armed forces and scraping together every mobile platform which could remotely be considered a combat mech, managed to produce a fighting force worthy of taking the field.

It was a good feeling, being proud of his people and their accomplishments, and in the grind of the military, good feelings were usually few and far between. He was going to savor it as long as possible.

But he still had an invasion to spearhead, and he had every intention of achieving his objective before the so-called *real* soldiers arrived.

MAXIMIZING INITIATIVE

"1st Company, throttle up and follow *Roy* at best possible speed," Lieutenant Commander Jenkins barked over the local comm, "we've got to link up with 2nd Company and move into that hole before the rock-biters close it. Break formation and move out at max-burn."

"Orders acknowledged. All units show five-by-five, Commander," Warrant Styles reported as *Roy*'s engines ran near the red line, driving the six-man-crew vehicle across the blasted glassy plains.

Roy was Jenkins' Mobile Command Center, and the only proper super-heavy vehicle in the battalion. With a quad of individual motive units, each at the end of an extendable limb capable of stretching ten meters out in a ninety-degree range from its joint with the rectangular hull, it was capable of greater speed than any other vehicle under Jenkins' command.

Jenkins' battalion was little more than two full companies of loosely termed 'combat-ready' platforms, plus a pair of support mechs used for shuttling damaged gear from the engagement zone for repairs. Those mechs were nearly as fast as *Roy* and had remained in tight formation with Jenkins' mech since the battalion's arrival on this contested world. But as *Roy*'s engines spun up to maximum output, driving their leg-mounted bearing-style rollers to their rated limits, Jenkins soon left the relatively-fleet-footed recovery vehicles chewing his exhaust.

The landscape was dotted with meter-deep craters broad enough to fit whole mechs and crisscrossed with fissures deep enough to spell certain death for any vehicle unfortunate enough to fall down them. Some of those crevices were even large enough to swallow *Roy* with the wrong misstep.

But Jenkins' pilot, Chris 'Chaps' Harbaugh, was one of the best.

Extending and flexing the mech's front and rear limbs in a perfectly-coordinated display of hard-earned skill, Chaps made traversing ten-meter-wide fissures seem like child's play, and he did it without *ever* throttling back.

As *Roy* tore across the blasted volcanic glass-field, barely registering the depressions it easily crossed, the vehicle came to a twenty-meter-wide fissure. Rather than slow down and look for a path around the two-click-long ravine, Chaps adjusted the mech's posture and took it to max accel. Jenkins gripped the nearest rail, noting his crew doing likewise, as Chaps angled *Roy*'s legs at the last second. The cabin pitched back, then forward, then back again like a galloping horse before the ultra-heavy vehicle launched across the divide with less than a meter to spare.

Roy landed with a deck-shaking clang, the edge of the ravine crumbling into a slide of rubble that fell away into the chasm while *Roy*'s momentum carried it forward. With every second precious, Jenkins bit back the rebuke that he wanted to deliver. With 2nd Company already at the rendezvous point, Jenkins needed to get to the breach with his lone assault-grade mech if they were to have any chance of penetrating the tunnels.

"Mind the paint, Chaps," Jenkins remarked with forced calm.

"Sure thing, sir," Chaps acknowledged tersely. The uncharacteristic dribble of sweat running down his pilot's temple told Jenkins he should let him focus. Reviewing two thousand hours of Chaps' training records with this specific mech had taught Jenkins everything he needed to know about performance limits, both the pilot's and the mech's.

Chaps didn't sweat unless he was already balls-out.

"Must be the heat," Chaps muttered, wiping the runnels away as he reclined in the pilot's chair.

"I'll see about adjusting the AC," Jenkins said with a knowing smirk.

"Thanks, Commander."

"Sir," Styles called from his station to Chaps' left, "only our two Owl drones are capable of subterranean flight. Our Vultures would never be able to maneuver their way through the tunnels that I'm seeing on the early seismic scans. They grow too narrow in too many places."

Jenkins leaned over Styles' shoulder, and after a moment's perusals he agreed with his subordinate's judgment. The tunnels were wide enough for the vultures, but their sharp twists and turns made it impossible for the all-purpose Vulture-class drones to maneuver at the speeds necessary to stay airborne. Even the Owls were hardly designed as subterranean flyers, but they could serve as advance scouts as the mechs descended into enemy territory.

"All right…run a test flight no more than two hundred meters down," he decided, "but wait until we've formed up before proceeding."

They finally arrived at the edge of the collapsed cavern, where Captain Murdoch's 2nd Company mechs had assembled after securing the site of *Elvira*'s epic stand.

He noted two Monkeys working alongside the corpsmen to secure Xi's limp body to the undercarriage of one of the Vulture-class drones. The drone was a fixed-wing, long-range, multi-purpose platform that had earned its nickname after use in this precise fashion: shuttling wounded off the line. The reason for the nickname was typical for military monikers: most of the passengers tended to be dead meat by the time the Vultures got through with them.

Of course, that was due more to the circumstances surrounding Vultures being employed in that capacity. Their long-range capabilities, coupled with the fact they were unmanned, made them the top choice for the most dangerous medevac missions.

Fortunately for Xi and Podsednik, there were corpsmen present to stabilize them before loading them onto the Vultures for their trip back to base.

"How are *Elvira*'s people, Doc?" Jenkins asked over the corpsmen's dedicated channel.

"Podsednik is already back at base being treated for minor electrical burns," the corpsman, David 'Doc' Summers, replied as *Roy* descended the treacherous, rubble-strewn slope *Elvira* had impossibly navigated during the collapse. Even *Roy* had difficulty maneuvering down the now-stable rockslide.

In Jenkins' view, Xi's talents as a pilot, and his faith in her, had just been proven beyond all doubt.

"Slippery slope…" Chaps grunted, wincing as he nearly lost *Roy*'s footing during the descent.

"How's our pilot?" Jenkins asked after Chaps finally got through the worst of the slope.

"Physically, she's stable," Doc Summers replied, "but she got a wicked e-mag spike that shorted out some of her implants. I'm surprised she's alive, Commander."

"Recovery?" Jenkins pressed.

"Too early to tell, sir," Doc said firmly, and through *Roy*'s cameras, Jenkins saw the Vulture bearing Xi lift off and hurtle away from the assemblage of war machines. "Biologically, there's nothing wrong with her. If they can repair the damage to her neural linkage and reset her neurotransmitter levels before any long-term damage sets in to her brain, there's a chance for full recovery."

"Good work, Doc," Jenkins said approvingly. "Stay here and help the recovery teams prep *Elvira* for transfer back to base. When they're done, hold this position and wait for further orders."

"Understood, sir," Summers acknowledged. Everyone knew what was about to happen: they were preparing to besiege the enemy where they lived. Before this was over, there would be a whole lot of bodies on and under the ground.

Jenkins took a deep breath and raised Captain Murdoch's direct line, "2nd Company, report."

A brief but telling delay preceded Murdoch's reply. "All mechs but *Elvira* are present and accounted for, Commander. We're ready to advance on your orders."

Jenkins' lip twisted into a faint sneer before clarifying, "Condition of mechs acknowledged. Finish your report, Captain."

A second delay. "All squads of infantrymen stand ready to advance, Commander Jenkins."

"I want a count, *Captain*."

Yet another delay, this one more pointed than its predecessors. "Twelve squads of sixteen infantrymen, totaling one hundred, ninety-two, present and awaiting orders...*sir*."

"One nine two..." Jenkins repeated, adding a deliberate pause of his own, one intended to convey his displeasure at Murdoch's reassigning *Elvira*'s infantry detail, leaving her vulnerable. Murdoch's selfish short-sightedness, pulling *Elvira*'s troops to protect his *Flaming Rose*, had ultimately led to *Elvira* launching a dangerous close pulse missile strike. "Copy that, Captain. Form up on *Roy*; we'll lead the column down Bravo Tunnel." As tunnels were marked on the map, *Roy* automatically labeled them and updated the information slaved to the mechs. Having readily identified geo-references was critical in combat.

"We'll have your back, Commander," Murdoch acknowledged

as *Roy* rolled its way toward the only tunnel large enough for the entire column to move down.

2nd Company's three roughly-humanoid mechs, *Monsoon*, *Kamehameha*, and *Paul Harris*, would have difficulty moving down the tunnel given the variability in roof height, but the rest of the units would have no problem. Bravo Tunnel, along with five others, was tall enough to permit a vast array of alarmingly large gear to be transported underground. Fleet Command had already relayed the sudden appearance of anti-orbital artillery being set up so quickly they couldn't coordinate strikes before coming under fire.

Neutralizing those guns was a primary objective of Jenkins' mission, and he knew that every minute he delayed down here was another potential shot sent Fleet's way.

"Styles, put our birds five hundred and three hundred meters ahead of *Roy*," Jenkins ordered. "Have *Silent Fox* continuously run its seismic sensors to detect any potential activity adjacent to Bravo Tunnel."

"Owls deployed, Commander," Styles acknowledged as the two drones' icons appeared on the main tactical plotter in *Roy's* command center. Speeding ahead of the column, the drones flew down the surprisingly straight tunnel before assuming their respective positions. "Drones in position. *Silent Fox* reports seismics are online. Continuous data feeds coming in from the rest of the column should cancel out our noise well enough to detect vehicle movement."

"Understood." Jenkins nodded. "Roll out."

Roy moved forward, followed by the recon mech *Silent Fox*. Murdoch's *Flaming Rose* was next, with the rest of 2nd Company in trail. A hundred and forty infantrymen rode the mechs down the dark, foreboding tunnel on a mix of dedicated and improvised seats. The rest brought up the rear of the formation on foot.

"You're clear, Podsy," declared the battalion's chief medical officer, Dr. Nick 'Strange Bed' Fellows. He was all right in Podsy's book, apart from the whole patient molestation thing which had landed him in the clink for a quarter-century. But Fleet reported that he was fully reformed at release time. "We'll give you another dose of burn gel before wrapping your hands in healing bandages, but you'll be fit for light duty in another three hours."

"What about Xi?" Podsednik asked as a corpsman went about administering the gel, which burned ten times worse than the damned wounds themselves!

"She's not out of the woods yet." Fellows shook his head grimly. "The neural feedback caused by the pulse missile's EM spike shorted some key neural link components. Normally that would have shut the whole system down, but the spike locked a few neurotransmitter lines open long enough to put her into a coma."

"How long will it take to bring her out?" Podsy asked grimly. He didn't want to lose her, especially not after the rough patch they'd just been through together.

"We're not a neuro unit here, Podsy." Dr. Fellows shook his head again. "I'll be happy if she eventually recovers without permanent cognitive deficits. I'm not equipped to try to revive her here, especially not with all the junk that leaked into her cerebrospinal fluid. It's safer to shut her down and prevent any further damage until we can get her back up to Fleet Medical."

Podsy gritted his teeth. He knew he was lucky just to make it out of that kind of SNAFU, but it had been Xi's quick reactions and decisive nature that had saved them. Had he been the one making the call, he would have waited too long to fire on their own position, and they'd both be dead.

He owed her his life, and he needed to make good on that debt.

"Come on, Doc." Podsy held Fellows' eyes. "Unlike most of us mooks, you were top-drawer back in the world. I read your file:

two dozen research papers focused on neurophysiology, which is why the commander tabbed you for this unit. You can do *something*."

Fellows met Podsy's gaze unyieldingly. "I can, but it goes against the first bit of the Hippocratic Oath. And you're not in a position to authorize such drastic measures..."

Podsy produced a small polymer card and thrust it into Fellows' face. "Durable power of attorney, Doc. She gave me total control over what happens to her if she went down and had a questionable recovery timetable, up to and including giving her a dignified death."

Fellows' brow lifted in surprise as he examined the card, plucking it into his fingers before flipping it over and examining it for authenticity markers. He nodded after a quick perusal. "Seen enough of these to know it's genuine."

"She told me she'd rather take a ten percent chance of a full recovery than a ninety percent chance of coming back a fraction of what she was," Podsy pressed after Fellows handed the card back. "She also told me if it was a choice between getting back on the line or pulling back for recovery, she'd choose the line every time. So be straight, Doc," he said, tucking the card back into his pocket, "what can we do?"

Fellows nodded slowly. "We'll need to keep her under for another two hours, during which time I'm going to need to tap you for some of your spinal fluid."

Without hesitation, Podsy nodded. "How much?"

Fellows gestured to a nearby medical table. "Pretty much all of it."

Podsy was concerned, but he didn't delay in undoing his trousers and lifting his shirt before sitting on the edge of the table. "Don't I...umm...need to keep at least a *little*?"

"Not really." Fellows smirked. "You'll be fine with a regular saline transfusion, but Xi's implants require the real thing or they won't operate. Her current CSF is flooded with neurotransmitter waste products that will lock those implants off for at least a week as they clear her system, assuming I can even revive her with the meager means available to me here. But if she really would want to get back in a mech, this is the only way I can make that happen." He emphatically wagged a syringe with a particularly long needle attached. "Let me be clear: I'm not guaranteeing anything here. This will be risky for both of you, though obviously more so for her since she might die from anaphylaxis, meningitis, cerebral hemorrhage, serotonin cascade, or a dozen other potentially fatal conditions. The worst you'll get is a headache and some vertigo. If you really want to go through with this, lie down on your side and pull your knees against your chest. I'm going to need this suite empty when those casualties start coming back, so the sooner we get started the better."

Podsy complied, and the doctor began swabbing the base of his spine with a cold sterilizing pad. He breathed heavily through gritted teeth and urged, "Let's do it, Doc."

LANCING A BOIL

"Enemy contact," Styles reported urgently an hour into the column's descent into the dark, increasingly humid tunnel. Jenkins moved to his side as the Warrant Officer continued, "Owl One was just engaged by enemy infantry."

The video feeds from Owl One were erratic as the drone juked and spun, all while returning fire to at least six of the rock-biters that had engaged with small arms. A lucky shot managed to hit the pickup, causing the feed to go dark.

"Pull Owl Two back," Jenkins commanded. "Have it establish contact with 1st Company. And signal the rest of the column: prepare to engage the enemy," he said with satisfaction. "Infantry to remain with the rear of the formation until we've secured the tunnel."

"All units acknowledge orders," Styles reported promptly, and the tactical plotter began to fill with deploying infantrymen as they streamed out, or off, of their assigned mechs. Despite their environmental suits, which permitted them to retain secreted bodily fluids for later recycling, the infantry would become dangerously dehydrated after two hours of fighting.

As was so often the case in situations like these, speed was critical.

"Move *Silent Fox* to the rear of the column," Jenkins ordered. "Fire lance formation."

"Fire lance formation, yes, sir." Styles nodded, and after a few seconds, the column confirmed his orders by adjusting posture behind *Roy* as it drove deeper into the darkness.

Roy's headlights stabbed into the slightly foggy tunnel, illuminating the triangular passageway as it bent gently to the right. Owl Two zipped past *Roy* as it retreated to the relative safety of the rear echelon, and soon the wreckage of the other Owl came into view.

The rock-biters who shot it down were nowhere to be seen.

"Anti-personnel only, Chaps," Jenkins urged, "but kill anything that moves and keep pressing the advance. The rest of the column can deal with your scraps."

"Yes, sir." Chaps grinned fiercely as *Roy* came to a sharp turn in the tunnel, and immediately came under intense plasma fire.

Chaps unleashed *Roy*'s forward-facing anti-personnel coil-guns, laying four hundred rounds into the enemy infantry squad in just under a second. After the brief-but-hellish firestorm abruptly ceased, the headlights illuminated silica-based gore spattered across the walls and floor of the tunnel.

It took several seconds for *Roy*'s computer to reconstruct the scene of the crime and feed the data to Styles' station. "Fifteen rock-biters neutralized, sir," Styles reported clinically.

Jenkins let a thin smile flash across his lips. "You're a greedy boy, Chaps."

"Sorry, sir," Chaps said with patently false contrition. "I'll leave some for 2nd Company next time."

Roy rolled over the mass of rock-biter carcasses, some of which were still twitching when they were crushed beneath the command vehicle's leg-mounted rollers, and continued down the tunnel.

"Where are their railguns?" Jenkins muttered as they rolled for two kilometers—or in military parlance, two clicks—without seeing a single sign of the enemy. "They should have fortified this position by now. It's been over an hour since *Elvira* breached their tunnels."

"There was no immediate traffic in this tunnel, Commander," Styles suggested. "It's possible we went down an empty hole."

"This tunnel's the largest artery feeding the surface chamber." Jenkins shook his head firmly. "Something important is down here."

"Or *was* down here," Styles observed, and Jenkins found himself equally impressed and dismayed by the Warrant Officer's suggestion. "Contact," Styles called out.

"I'm not seeing anything," Chaps snapped.

"I'm picking up radio signals ahead consistent with Arh'Kel comm chatter," Styles clarified.

"Hold up, Chaps," Jenkins commanded, and *Roy's* pilot complied. "We must be right on top of them," the commander muttered, subconsciously, and uselessly, quieting his voice. "We lost contact with the surface one click down."

"And the interference has only gotten worse as we've gone deeper," Styles agreed as he worked to isolate the signal.

"What are we looking at?" Jenkins pressed after several silent moments had passed without an update.

"I can't be sure, sir," Styles said with evident frustration, and the tension in the command mech grew thicker by the second as the mostly-green crew prepared to engage the enemy. "It looks like five or six heavy platforms and a few hundred soldiers."

Jenkins was ambivalent at hearing that. He had hoped to land on a central nexus and enemy supply depot, which should have been much more heavily-guarded than by what Styles was seeing. "Inform the column we're about to engage. Make sure the infantry hangs back while we clear a hole. Let's go, Chaps," he urged, and *Roy* resumed its trek down the dark, dank tunnel. "Don't stop till we've hit their teeth."

As they moved, Styles' station became increasingly active, and icons popped up one-by-one on the tactical plotter as *Roy*'s sensors made positive ID on as-yet-unseen enemy targets.

Five distinct heavy weapon platform icons appeared, surrounded by a cluster of four hundred enemy soldier signatures. Those five heavies soon became ten, then fifteen, and by the time they were halfway to the cavern's entry, there were twenty icons and over a thousand soldiers.

Twenty quickly became thirty, and one thousand enemy troops became *four* thousand before *Roy* finally caught a glimpse of a cavern so vast it could have only been artificial. Measuring six kilometers on a side and nearly fifty meters from floor to ceiling, the chamber before them was over ten times the size of the junction *Elvira* had fallen into.

And it was *crawling* with rock-biters.

Roy's coilguns tore into a pair of Arh'Kel formations flanking the cavern's entrance. Two thousand rounds shredded their rock-hard skins and decorated the cavern walls with rock-biter innards in a handful of seconds, causing their fellows deeper within the cavern to return harmless fire with small arms.

A flare from the far side of the cavern preceded a direct railgun hit to *Roy*'s forward armor. The enemy heavy weapon's tungsten pellet splashed as superheated, hyper-velocity plasma against *Roy*'s robust defenses, turning the impact site a fiery red.

"Armor's holding," Styles reported as *Roy* drove over the ruined enemy position. No sooner had a fresh wave of Arh'Kel soldiers revealed themselves than Chaps lashed out with the forward coilguns. Twenty enemy troops fell with *Roy* never breaking stride as the battlefield behemoth tore through their meter-tall rubble barricade, a wall likely intended to slow Jenkins' advance.

The rock-biters had clearly never seen assault-grade Republican armor in action.

Blowing through the pile of loose rock like it was made of sand, Chaps extended *Roy*'s legs and raised the mech's main chassis while raking left and right with his coilguns. Another flash from the far side of the chamber preceded a second impact, this one turning *Roy*'s forward armor a furious yellow-white.

"Forward armor's down to seventy percent," Styles reported.

"Silence those heavies, Chaps," Jenkins commanded.

"On it," Chaps replied tersely, activating *Roy*'s primary targeting system and zeroing in on the fortified railgun mounts. Chaps unexpectedly piped his normally-private music into *Roy*'s overhead speakers. The song was *Exciter* by Judas Priest, which in recent weeks had become something of a company anthem, though Chaps' favored version was a cover by Gamma Ray.

Jenkins felt like he should object, but he'd always had a soft spot for the classics, so he let it slide. There was nothing like heavy metal while riding in heavy metal in the middle of a firefight. Or anytime. Jenkins shook his head. He was growing soft. Or metal hard.

"On the way," Chaps called out with relish, and *Roy*'s pop-up missile launchers sent six armor-piercing rockets streaking toward the enemy railguns.

The rockets skewered their targets, flinging them apart in a shower of jagged debris which sprayed a hundred meters in all directions. The far side of the cavern erupted into a raging inferno as some of that debris touched off a hydrocarbon fuel tank, and soon the cavern was filled with choking, black smoke.

Jenkins gritted his teeth as *Roy* continued to charge across the huge cavern, laying into enemy infantry formations as the command mech pushed ever-deeper into the fight. They had cleared the mouth of the cavern of hostiles and were continuing toward the center of the chamber, blazing a trail through fighting positions and makeshift barricades as they went.

"Local air supply," he grunted as *Roy* shook from another railgun impact, this one to their left flank.

"Copy that: local air supply," Styles replied before relaying the shorthand order to the battalion's infantry. With all the smoke in the cavern, they would need to use rebreather masks when they arrived. Styles and Jenkins had developed a good working rapport while building the unit, which was an invaluable asset in battle.

After the order was acknowledged, it was 2nd Company's turn to join the fray.

Captain Murdoch's eight-legged *Flaming Rose* burst into the cavern, banking right and laying into the enemy as soon as its pilot sighted a rubble wall hiding a dozen enemy soldiers. More short-legged octopus than spider, 2nd Company's command vehicle still struck an imposing figure as it lurched forward, trampling the enemy barricade with its front legs. Sweeping left and right with those legs, Murdoch cleared the enemy position without firing a single shot, until he spat white-hot plasma fire on the enemy's trampled remains to ensure the threat had been neutralized.

The position dealt with, *Flaming Rose* moved fifty meters wide-right of *Roy*'s path before turning and running a parallel course to Jenkins' mech.

While the eight-legged *Flaming Rose* went right, the task of forging the left-hand path fell to the track-mounted *Rammer*, a throwback vehicle with a low, wide profile, four distinct tracks on each side of the chassis, and a fifteen-kilo cannon as primary armament to go with two chem-fueled chain guns and a bizarre, wedge-shaped ram on the prow.

Rammer's chain guns whirred to life, each spitting a hundred rounds per second as they sprayed projectiles into a nearby formation. Splitting a stone barricade with its namesake, *Rammer* charged through a dozen enemy soldiers hunkered behind the shattered rampart. Some were cut in two by the razor-sharp ram's lower edges, others were crushed under the ancient war machine's legs, and still others were flung aside like grass through a lawnmower.

Despite its archaic design and badly-outdated arsenal, *Rammer*'s armor had been upgraded during its refit and was theoretically able to withstand multiple direct hits from a high-powered railgun.

That theory was soon put to the test.

An enemy railgun sent a bolt of hyper-velocity tungsten straight into that upgraded armor on the upper-glacis, the left portion of its angled armor. Had Jenkins not insisted on *Rammer*'s armor being upgraded, which came in spite of Fleet Command's stated priorities, the venerable mech would have been destroyed outright by that first shot.

As it was, it took *two* shots to put the old tank down.

From the far side of the cavern, a second railgun sent a hyper-velocity projectile into *Rammer*'s right flank. The tracks on that side were obliterated, and the mech's forward momentum halted completely. Its three-man crew died before they knew the second shot hit them, and *Rammer*'s flaming remains were scattered as ammo quickly began cooking off from inside.

Without missing a beat, the four-legged *Babycake* moved from its position on the formation's centerline to replace *Rammer*. Stomping past the exploding wreckage of the ancient vehicle, the relatively high-profile *Babycake* was one of the few multi-role vehicles in Jenkins' battalion. It was equally at home wading into the enemy as it was standing off at ten clicks and delivering ballistic strikes on hapless targets.

With a coilgun situated between each of its legs, it raked nearby unarmored rock-biters with savage ferocity. Delivering vengeance for its fallen comrade, *Babycake* swiveled its top-mounted artillery gun to the right side of the cavern and sent a fifteen-kilo slug into the mobile railgun that had killed the ancient *Rammer*.

Flaming Rose and *Babycake* widened the spearhead, paving the way for the rest of the column to clear the cavern in an ever-expanding fan formation. As the rest of 2nd Company supported the initial gains, *Roy* barreled across the cavern's mid-point and tore down another railgun mount with a trio of AP—armor-piercing—rockets.

"Commander," Styles called out, "I'm receiving word from 1st Company. They've engaged the enemy in Bravo Tunnel."

"How?!" Jenkins demanded, knowing that without 1st Company to reinforce in the next sixty seconds, he would risk being surrounded. The fire lance formation required two groups, the tip and the shaft, in order to take-and-hold a position like the cavern. 2nd Company was the tip, with 1st Company adopting the role of the formation's shaft. Without the support of 2nd Company, 1st might shatter on the enemy's inevitable counterattack.

"A cave-in four hundred meters up-tunnel from the cavern," Styles explained. "*Blue Lotus, Priscilla,* and *Forktail* are on this side of the collapse. *Racetrack* was trapped under the rubble, and the rest of 1st is on the surface side of the barrier."

Jenkins bit back an angry retort and gritted his teeth. "2nd Company: execute final protective fire and reverse course six seconds after my mark. Mark!"

"Orders acknowledged," Styles reported as the quickly-erected countdown clock reached two seconds left. Then, with a measure of precision which would have struck terror into any sane soldier, Jenkins' mechs halted their advance in perfect unison. Their weapons, which had been firing precisely and in short bursts, began spewing fiery wrath in all directions ahead of the column.

Tens of thousands of anti-personnel rounds spat from dozens of mech-mounted guns in five seconds' time, laying waste to anything that moved, and then some. Even one of the railgun platforms was taken down by a concentrated barrage of chem-

rounds, but most of the ammunition tore into the cavern's walls. Man-sized slabs of stone fell free from the walls, and ceiling, as the granite cavern was shattered by the onslaught.

Then the artillery thundered, sending fifteen-kilo slugs into suspected enemy heavies. Rockets screamed from launch tubes, their impacts causing two smaller tunnels on the far side of the cavern to collapse entirely. Even *Kamehameha*, the battalion's lone railgun-armed mech, added to the devastating barrage.

Standing upright in its humanoid configuration, *Kamehameha*'s twin railgun arms sent slivers of hyper-velocity tungsten into the stream of enemy units emerging from one of the mid-sized tunnels on the cavern's southern edge.

At least four more enemy railguns were taken down by the high-output barrage before, moving as one, Jenkins' column reversed course at maximum speed and withdrew behind the cavern's mid-line.

Then the rock-biters counterattacked.

A dozen enemy railguns spat from positions nestled within adjoining tunnels. *Triple Threat*, a dedicated artillery mech near 2nd Company's rear, lost one of its three legs from a direct hit. The crippled mech tilted and fell toward the cavern floor. Before it landed, its central chassis was skewered by railgun cross-fire and exploded.

Paul Harris, a mech of similar design to *Triple Threat* but with close-range flamers and chain guns instead of artillery, took rapid-succession railgun impacts to its central hull. One of its legs flew off and its external flamer tanks lit off, spraying burning fuel across the cavern floor. *Paul Harris'* crew fought desperately to withdraw with the rest of the company, dragging the crippled mech on two legs toward Bravo Tunnel, while dozens of rock-biters cartwheeled toward it, in their peculiar way, faster than it could withdraw.

Jenkins gritted his teeth so hard, he chipped a molar. There was nothing he could do for them but divert *Roy*'s coilguns toward the encroaching enemy infantry. Chaps was already doing so without needing to be ordered. He sent every possible anti-personnel round *Paul Harris'* way, but it was a foregone conclusion made official a few moments later: the *Paul Harris* was dead.

Babycake was struck in the forward hull by a hypervelocity dart, and her robust armor held while flaring an angry orange. *Monsoon, Jammer,* and *Blue Balls* also suffered hits, but were able to maintain course and speed as the company withdrew to the mouth of Bravo Tunnel.

"Target those railguns!" Jenkins snapped just as those very weapons thundered into *Roy*'s front and flanks with lethal precision. "I'm authorizing use of *Roy*'s HE rounds in the next barrage to fire on my mark," he added as warning lights appeared all around the command center.

Using HE—high explosive—ordnance underground was dangerous in the extreme, but the enemy was dug-in better than he expected and 1st Company had been cut off from the advance. What might have been a textbook sweep across the cavern had turned into a messy, bloody affair when the enemy demonstrated they were far less disjointed than they initially appeared.

So the choice was simple: use ordnance, which was nearly as dangerous to Jenkins and his people as it was to the enemy, or let the affair devolve into a process of attrition where his hope for victory, let alone survival, was pinned on him having more material to lose than the enemy.

To Jenkins, or any other warrior fit to bear arms, that was no choice at all.

After *Roy*'s AP ammo had been swapped out with HE, Jenkins gripped the rail before him and barked, "Fire, fire, fire!"

Guns thundered and rockets screamed, filling the cavern with a deafening barrage that struck every enemy-occupied edge. Thousands of enemy infantry died and a dozen railgun platforms were scrubbed as the column's fury was delivered like a steel-toed boot to the teeth.

The cavern went quiet, and none of the cave-ins on the far side had caused damage to his people as they withdrew. But in spite of the relative calm following the HE barrage, Jenkins knew there were plenty more Arh'Kel down there.

The only question was whether or not he would be ready for them when the rock-biters regrouped.

BACK IN BLACK

Xi awoke to a blinding light and instantly clamped her eyes shut. "Fucking rocks!" she snarled, reaching out for the manual controls and finding her arms somehow restrained. "Fire another pulse missile, Podsy!" she screamed, thrashing against the straps around her wrists. "What the hell?!" she cried in alarm, forcing her eyes open and looking down at her arms.

"Bao, it's me," she heard Podsy say, and felt a hand on her wrist. "Calm down. We're at Battalion HQ."

"Battalion HQ?" she repeated, squinting to protect her eyes as she tried to focus on his badly-blurred features. "What the hell are we doing there?" she demanded before screaming at the top of her lungs and straining with all her might against her wrist-cuffs. "AND WHY THE FUCK AM I TIED DOWN!?"

"You just got out of major surgery, LT," Podsy explained calmly, and as she blinked away the blurriness, she saw he was white as a sheet. "The pulse missile worked," he said, gripping her hand tightly in his own. "We held the breach long enough for the commander to arrive and move down with the rest of the battalion. They've been down the hole for over an hour now."

She shook her head, feeling a strange wave of numbness wash

41

over her. It was similar to the sensation she experienced when linking with *Elvira*'s systems, but there was none of the endorphin rush which usually accompanied that process.

"We...we held?" she asked disbelievingly. "*Elvira?*" she pressed hopefully, prompting Podsy to shake his head.

"She's counted out," he replied grimly. "Most of her peripheral systems were fried by the e-mag pulse. She's not going to fight any time soon."

She heard a soft snort from behind her, and Bao craned her neck to see the unit's lone physician stroll into the room. "Good, you're awake. That means we can get you out of that bed."

"Why did you restrain me?" she demanded.

"I had to chemically-induce a number of mild seizures to revive you on short notice," Dr. Fellows replied with a smirk. "You would have hurt yourself worse without the restraints than you did with them," he explained as he undid her left wrist's cuff, revealing a raw and bleeding ring where the metal cuff had bit into her skin. "This way, you'll be able to get back out there, if that's what you *actually* want," he added with a pointed look in Podsy's direction before undoing the other cuff.

She took the doctor's meaning plainly enough and nodded affirmatively, "You did the right thing. When can I move out?"

"Physically, aside from these abrasions and a few torn muscles, you're fine." Fellows shrugged. "I wouldn't recommend initiating another neural link any time soon, though," he warned half-heartedly. "We managed to reset your implants, but your neurochemistry is badly imbalanced. Another spike like the one you experienced, or even half as bad, would be fatal on the spot."

"Good." She nodded, ignoring everything after 'you're fine' and swinging her legs over the edge of the bed. Before she could stand, a sudden wave of vertigo washed over her and stopped her from standing.

"Easy there," Fellows deadpanned, "you just got a full CSF transfusion and your meninges are a little stiff from the high-dose epinephrine and hyper-oxygen treatments. Any sudden head and neck movements and you'll risk serious injuries, including a subdural hematoma."

Xi steadied herself for a second attempt at getting out of bed. With Podsy's assistance, she managed to stand on wobbly legs before nodding curtly. "Thank you, Doctor, but I need to get back in a mech."

"Don't be foolish." Fellows snorted derisively. "You've done your part. The way I hear it, you two are lucky your mech was positioned beneath the remains of the cavern's roof. Without that extra protection, the e-mag would have killed you *both*."

Xi jutted her chin defiantly. "The commander led the battalion down that spider-hole and they've been out of contact for an hour. That means they're operating in enemy territory; they need every last Jock and Wrench they can get."

"Your mech's out of commission," Fellows observed, and Xi thought she saw the hint of a smile playing just beneath his eyes. "What's your plan, to throw rocks at them? Obvious irony notwithstanding, I don't..."

"*Devil Crab* is the same design as *Elvira*," she interrupted, "and with just a few transplants of *Elvira*'s hardened components, we could get her back up under manual control. But it's going to take time, time the commander doesn't have, so if you don't mind..." She made to push past Dr. Fellows, but Podsy surprisingly restrained her.

"Calm down, Xi," her teammate urged.

"I will *not* calm down!" she snapped. "The commander is out there bleeding right fucking now, and you two cowards have the audacity to tell me I should calm down?!"

Fellows stifled a laugh, which led Podsy to do likewise.

"What the hell is so funny?!" she demanded, tearing her arm free of Podsy's grip.

"You are, LT." Podsy grinned as Fellows erupted into a mocking belly laugh. "Before operating on you, Dr. Fellows

43

ordered Koch to bring *Devil Crab* to the cavern instead of bringing *Elvira* here. The transplants should be mostly completed by the time we arrive in the Vultures," he explained, popping open the APC-turned-field-hospital's door and gesturing outside to the two landed Vulture-class drones.

Xi went red from the collar up, realizing she'd just been played by both of them as they continued their laughter at her expense. She bitterly schooled her features. "I hope you two got your money's worth."

"We did," Fellows assured her, "but in truth, I also needed to assess your neurological function with a series of responsive tests, and you passed, barely. Now get the hell out of my hospital." He waved his hand dismissively. "I've got work to do, as do you two."

Xi nodded, feeling a thrill as she and Podsy made their way to the Vultures. Each one had a wingspan of three-and-a-half meters and was fitted with vertical take-off or landing, VTOL-capable turbines. Situated beneath the Vulture's spindly landing gear struts was a coffin-like basket. Podsy helped strap Xi into one basket before a corpsman did likewise for him, and soon the duo lifted off aboard the remote-controlled drones.

The trip to the collapsed cavern was faster than Xi expected. As soon as the Vultures touched down, she was extricated from the thin metal pod by one of the Wrenches assigned to Lieutenant Billy 'Big' Koch's retrieval-and-repair team. Koch was the head of the unit's battlefield repair crew, and normally traveled alongside Jenkins' *Roy* with the battalion's two recovery-and-repair mechs: *Kochtopussy* and *Murphy's Ointment*.

The naming conventions in Jenkins' battalion were reflective of the unit's colorful personalities and generally rebellious natures. Three in four of Jenkins' people, Xi and Podsy included, had been recruited directly out of prisons. The rest were castoffs and washouts from various military branches. As people like Captain Murdoch incessantly reminded them, 'the cream of the crop, you were not.' It was in no small part due to Murdoch's snide attitude that the various crews had named their mechs so colorfully, in open defiance of conformity.

In keeping with that non-conformist tradition, Xi had named *Elvira* after a striking personality she had encountered while perusing a collection of ancient video files. As a teen, Xi had seen the Elvira character as strong, intelligent, and feisty, but above all, she was unafraid to act like a woman when it suited her. That character had been something of a guide-post during Xi's formative years, as she had grown up in one of the most creatively-oppressive regimes in the Terran Republic.

Xi was taller than most women, not lean and not heavy. Growing up, she had often gotten into fights with young men and, much to their chagrin, won her fair share of those engagements by being better-prepared and trained in hand-to-hand combat. She'd left too many broken noses, and hearts, in her wake during her teens, and looking out into the collapsed cavern littered with broken rock-biter corpses and equipment, she felt grim satisfaction at seeing yet another job well done.

Then her gaze fell on *Elvira* and she winced despite herself. The mech lay in a crumpled heap, her central chassis resting lifelessly near the pile of rubble Xi had narrowly skated down during the cave-in. Two of her legs were completely destroyed, her hull was riddled with head-sized pock-marks made by small arms fire and plasma cutters, and her fifteen-kilo gun looked to have been torn off its mount sometime after she lost consciousness.

In her current shape, it was hard to see the old Scorpion-class mech ever fighting again. But in that moment, Xi was glad to have chosen *Elvira* over the generally-superior *Babycake* back when she had won top honors among the Jocks in their training camp. *Babycake* was the sweeter ride, no question, but *Elvira* had a major advantage which was now about to come into play: she was the exact same model as *Devil Crab*.

Koch's people had somehow brought *Devil Crab* down the scrabble onto the cavern floor, where his people worked frantically to bring her online. *Devil Crab* was missing a primary control module, having come from a civvy-owned military museum on Mars, but *Elvira*'s systems were completely interchangeable with *Devil Crab*'s. Even the neural linkage system, if it could be salvaged post-EMP, could be transplanted from one to the other.

But that transplant process would take days of work by a full-time crew, so for now, Xi was going to pilot her backup mech manually.

From the corner of her eye, Xi noticed Lieutenant Koch overseeing work on *Devil Crab*'s flank-mounted machine guns. "How long until she's ready?" Xi asked, tearing her gaze away from *Elvira* to focus on her new ride.

"Motive systems are online, and she's fully-fueled," Koch replied without looking her way. "Machine guns are armed and ready to sight in. All we're missing now is to load her heavy weapons and..."

"Seismic alert!" called out one of the infantrymen standing guard at the upper edge of the depression.

"Confirmed," a second trooper shouted from a position on the other side of the depression. "We've got inbound!"

Xi shared a brief look with Podsy, and his expression confirmed he was as ready as she was. "Looks like it's time to sight in those guns, Lieutenant Koch," she said as she rushed toward *Devil Crab*. Alarms went off along the perimeter. The sixty-four infantrymen assigned to the R&R mechs were locked and loaded and hunkered down. Incoming heavies didn't bode well for humans in the open.

"Button her up!" Koch barked, prompting his people to close the machine gun mounts while Xi and Podsy made their way into *Devil Crab*'s cabin. "Get the *Puss* up on that ridge!" he snapped just as Podsy yanked the hatch shut.

Xi strapped into the pilot's seat while Podsy ran the minimal series of diagnostics on the power system. While keeping his attention on the streaming information, he asked, "Are you sure you're good to go all-manual?"

"Just get the weapons online, Podsy." She smirked as *Devil Crab*'s power core audibly thrummed to life. She lifted the central 'carapace' of the mech off the cavern floor and using the admittedly complicated manual interface, she slowly walked the Scorpion-class mech up the scrabble. "Let me worry about the sticks."

As they crested the edge of the depression, Xi noted six separate nests the infantrymen had established. With combined RPGs, mortars, machine guns, and even two flame-throwers set up behind rubble barricades, they were ready to receive the enemy. All they lacked was heavy artillery, which *Devil Crab* unfortunately also lacked.

A flicker of movement half a click off preceded an upward burst of rock, showering like a fountain as rock-biters streamed out of the newly-made hole. Dozens appeared in the first seconds, and the horde soon became hundreds.

Then the first of the enemy vehicles appeared, bearing the signature railguns that the Arh'Kel deployed on this volcanic world.

"Where are our Vultures?" she demanded, unable to get anything out of the comm system when she tried to feed a tactical update to her display.

"Reloading at Battalion HQ," Podsy replied after a moment's hesitation. "I've got a link established with my personal unit, but it can't directly relay tactical feeds to *Devil Crab*."

"Verbal updates it is," Xi acknowledged as she crouched and pivoted *Devil Crab* so her right flank machine guns were on-target. "We need those Vultures' Hellraisers right about now," she muttered.

"They're saying they got *Generally*'s fifteen-kilo guns working," Podsy said, jerking with surprise. "They're asking for target coordinates," he said, even as she threw the relevant data to his screen.

"Relaying..." he replied, and a few seconds later said, "Receipt confirmed. They're sending a ranging shell to get the magnetics aligned."

"Of course they are." Xi smirked as a total of three railgun mounts emerged from the enemy hole in the glass-field.

"Vultures inbound. ETA fifteen seconds," Podsy reported.

"All right," Xi grunted as she armed her right flank machine guns, "let's put these stoners on their heels."

Her twin machine guns blazed, spitting twenty rounds apiece which raked the ground midway between *Devil Crab* and the enemy line. Biting her tongue in annoyance, Xi ceased fire and adjusted her targeting algorithm. Adjustments made, she fired another short burst, which slightly overshot the enemy position.

"Third time's a charm," she muttered, unleashing another short burst that partially hit the enemy line. A handful of rock-biters fell while some of her rounds went high and others went low. Frankly, she was amazed she could land more than ten percent of her rounds at this range and without proper alignment of her weapons' rotary barrels.

"Hellraisers away. Time-to-impact is three seconds," Podsy reported as the rock-biters began cartwheeling toward them far faster than seemed possible given the physics involved.

Those three seconds seemed like an eternity, during which time it was all Xi could do to refrain from unleashing her guns on the approaching horde.

But when the Hellraisers finally struck, it was well worth the wait.

Streaking in at a low angle, the missiles landed with near-perfect unison and the field erupted into a raging orange wave consuming the rock-biter position. A nearly two-hundred-meter-long fireball rose to the sky, dragging columns of black smoke up with them. Visualizing through the smoke-field was impossible, but Xi knew that any humans caught in that blast would have been instantly killed. Hellraisers were old-school incendiaries with limited value against armored targets, but seeing the enemy position consumed by the inferno would bolster the surviving ground pounders' morale. Or give them something else to bitch about.

Then the rock-biters emerged from the cloud, cartwheeling at full-speed like nothing had happened.

"Damn," she grunted before unleashing her right flank machine guns on the approaching Arh'Kel troops. Her flanking infantrymen did likewise, firing well-aimed rounds at a rapid rate and adding mortars to the machine gun fire.

A dozen Arh'Kel fell in the first seconds of fire. A handful fell to mortar impacts, the explosions blowing them apart, limb from rocky limb. *Devil Crab*'s machine guns were the most effective weapons, sawing down dozens of cartwheeling rock-biters as they emerged from the smoke.

The infantrymen got their licks in too, grimly holding the line.

Spraying controlled bursts, the unarmored human warriors sent round after round down-range. Even at three hundred meters, more hit their targets than missed. With practiced poise and fearless focus, the men and women of the Terran Fleet Ground Forces executed according to their training. Aim and fire. Aim and fire. Reload. Hold the line. Fire and fire again.

And the rock-biters kept coming.

Hundreds of the silica-based, six-limbed creatures rolled limb-over-limb at an average speed of nearly eighty kilometers per hour. The nearest of them were only two hundred and fifty meters away when a telltale whistling sound filled the air above.

Inbound ordnance.

"Incoming!" someone shouted, loud enough to echo from the chamber walls.

A violent explosion shattered the ground about two hundred

meters from the smoke-covered Arh'Kel formation. A geyser of glossy black rock and dust erupted, but not even the debris reached the rock-biters as they drove steadily toward *Devil Crab* and her flanking FGF troopers.

Xi forwarded her console's telemetry on the range-finding round's strike point, and Podsy soon acknowledged, "Got it. Forwarding now."

The rock-biters broke the two-hundred-meter mark, tearing forward with a single-minded purpose toward *Devil Crab*'s position.

Kochtopussy and *Murphy's Ointment*, silent until that moment, opened fire with four machine guns identical to *Devil Crab*'s. Their accuracy left plenty to be desired, showing less at two hundred meters than *Devil Crab* had shown at three hundred. But the added weight of fire began to take its toll, cutting down entire lines of Arh'Kel infantry. But they kept coming, a fearless tidal wave of alien soldiers.

The FGF troops fired with increasing intensity with every meter the enemy covered. By the time the rock-biters crossed the hundred-meter mark, the Pounders' weapons were sending ammo down-range as fast as their feeders could load it.

Then the Arh'Kel railguns made their presence known.

Kochtopussy was struck by a pair of hypervelocity projectiles, sheering off one of the grappling arms it used to load and secure damaged vehicles. *Murphy's Ointment* took a direct hit to one of its tracks, blowing it completely off in a shower of molten metal. One of those fragments careened into an FGF nest, killing its occupants and cooking off the mortar rounds they had been steadily feeding into the enemy line.

The nest nearest that one was shaken, with two Pounders leaping over their makeshift barricade to avoid a similar fate. After a few seconds, its remaining occupants resumed pouring fire into the advancing enemy, and the briefly-scattered soldiers returned to their posts.

"Where the fuck is my artillery?!" Xi screamed, and not two seconds later, in the form of a distinctive whistle, she got her answer.

Like a thunderbolt hurled by the hand of God himself, a fifteen-kilo range-assisted HE round fell upon the rushing enemy horde. Twenty Arh'Kel died instantly, and dozens more were thrown bodily backward by the shockwave and debris.

But the rest rolled on.

"Transmit the railgun coordinates relative to that impact point," Xi barked, ceasing fire while she forwarded the info to Podsy. She wasn't *positive* about the locations she had keyed in, but they were close, and right now that was the best they could hope for. Time was critical. If wasted, they'd die again, within spitting distance of where they'd died before.

Xi screamed her war cry in fury and frustration. Today was not a good day to die.

Again.

"On it," Podsy acknowledged as Xi pivoted *Devil Crab* to present her left bank's fully-loaded guns. Once oriented, she unleashed them and sent hundreds of rounds into the rock-biter formation before the second artillery strike landed.

Another plume of rocky debris shot skyward, this one from the railguns' target coordinates within the slowly-dispersing smoke cloud. She hooted victoriously when her instruments positively confirmed that one of the three enemy railguns had been neutralized.

Its fellows soon made their displeasure known.

Devil Crab was rocked by a pair of direct railgun strikes to her left flank's armor. One of her machine guns was scrubbed completely, and warning klaxons went off within the cabin.

Pivoting the mech yet again, Xi snarled in frustration before letting loose with her right-side weapons. The closest enemy were now thirty meters from the line, and as they crossed that threshold, they were greeted by a wave of Pounders' RPGs. Of the ten grenades sent, only one missed its target. The rock-biters swayed under the fusillade.

The rock-biter wave had been thinned significantly, to be sure. No more than thirty of the leading edge had survived the charge, less than ten percent of the number that started the race to meet the humans.

But those thirty soon proved their mettle against the FGF.

Firing their bizarre slug-throwers after reaching point-blank range, the Arh'Kel warriors sent single shots into their targeted nests. Each round delivered more kinetic energy than even *Devil Crab*'s machine guns. The incendiaries took their toll and this time, the infantry suffered mightily.

Each FGF nest erupted with white-hot clouds of phosphorous. Dozens of those brave Pounders died in the first wave as the mechs' machine guns fought back against an enemy that had gotten too close. No matter the amount of fire, there would be no respite for the Pounders. Every man and woman was in a fight for their lives.

Some of the rock-biters pulled a bizarre braking maneuver, planting four of their limbs against the ground while flattening their bodies. Precisely two Arh'Kel did this before reaching each of the nests' rubble ramparts erected by the FGF, and when the skidding rock-biters collided with the rubble walls, they blew through them like freight trains through sand berms.

Chunks of stone weighing hundreds of pounds were flung into the air when the rock-biters slammed into the barricades. Smaller bits of rubble became deadly projectiles, some of which claimed the lives of Pounders hunkered down near *Elvira*'s wreckage fifty meters away.

Another artillery strike, courtesy of *Generally*'s crew, blew apart a second railgun mount. Xi was surprised at their accuracy but was too focused on the fight at hand to spare it much thought. She cut down two rock-biters with her lone left-side machine gun as they cartwheeled past the FGF nests. Unlike their skidding fellows, who had apparently been tasked with breaking the FGF line, these rock-biters seemed determined to breach the depression.

The *Ointment* and *Kochtopussy* put down several of the would-be intruders as they dashed past the line. Two of those silica-based soldiers exploded far more violently than should have been possible, even with lucky hits to their sidearm mags. Little was known about the Arh'Kel, but suicide attacks had not once been mentioned in the pre-op intelligence briefs.

Despite the mechs' best efforts, a handful of Arh'Kel infantry slipped through the line and began tumbling down the depression's slope, where they were greeted by the gentle sigh of Pounder RPGs. Despite taking a heavy toll on the FGF troops top-side, not a single rock-biter survived from that first wave, though parts of six rock-biter corpses did come to tumbling stops mere meters from the FGF's final stand at *Elvira*'s wreck.

Another artillery strike landed near the last remaining Arh'Kel railgun. Returning her focus to the remnants of the approaching horde, Xi was bitterly disappointed to find that the latest strike had missed the mark by at least thirty meters.

"Nobody's perfect," she grunted, deciding it was time to push the offensive as she drove *Devil Crab* out from the line toward the approaching enemy, "especially not me."

Crab-walking side-on to the enemy in order to keep her two nearly-depleted machine guns on target, Xi quickly counted no more than fifty rock-biters remaining from the original several hundred. But instead of retreating, as any sane unit would have done in their circumstance, the remaining Arh'Kel continued cartwheeling toward the line. Their impressive, and patently suicidal, determination was met with a steady diet of depleted uranium slugs. Slowly but surely, the horde of enemy soldiers was cut down with none reaching the shattered remnants of the FGF line.

Devil Crab lurched violently to the left from another railgun strike, whiplashing Xi badly enough to make her temporarily black out. As her senses quickly returned, she became aware of another artillery strike on the Arh'Kel railgun's position. The mushroom cloud and debris cleared, showing that the final railgun had been silenced forever.

Xi shook her head vigorously on instinct, causing a wave of nausea which overcame her and emptied the meager contents of her stomach onto her lap. As she regained control of herself, she was glad to find Podsy had not leapt to her aid and was instead working to put out several fires along their badly-damaged left flank.

Wiping her mouth disdainfully, she activated her comm-link and set it to the position's assigned frequency. "This is Lieutenant Xi. Good work, people. I want readiness reports in three minutes and anyone capable of turning a wrench to help get the rest of *Devil Crab*'s weapons online. Everyone else, assist with the wounded until the corpsmen have it under control."

She cut the line and made to get up, but another wave of vertigo swept over her. She fought down the urge to dry heave and was about to try standing again before Podsy placed a firm hand on her shoulder. "They've got it, LT. Stay in that chair or I'll tie you to it."

Xi shot him a bitter look before seeing his lopsided grin. She smiled tightly before grunting, "You'd like that, wouldn't you?"

"Not my type, babe." He wagged a finger before heading back and popping the hatch so he could assist with getting their big guns online.

QUICK THINKING

Forty-nine minutes had passed since Jenkins had cleared the cavern of hostiles. *Roy's* limited seismic scanners detected enemy activity within several connecting tunnels, but until he rejoined 1st and 2nd Companies, he lacked the mechs to secure all points of the cavern.

His remaining mechs had spread out across half a kilometer of the cavern's edge near Bravo Tunnel. Their AP ordnance was nearly half-spent after the advance-and-withdrawal of nearly an hour earlier, which only increased the urgency to regroup.

Unfortunately, the harder they worked to clear the rubble, the more the enemy counter-tunneled. The Arh'Kel had already erased their progress in clearing the rubble three different times, but without an accompanying counterattack, it was clear they were merely buying time for their own forces to rally.

"Sergeant McNaulty reports the next round of demo charges are set. Infantry have taken cover," Styles reported.

"Blow it," Jenkins commanded, and the charges exploded in rapid succession. Tons of granite were cast from the collapsed tunnel's mouth in a long and low rumble, and when the dust settled, a sliver of blue light poked through the upper quarter of the rubble pile. That light swept in and out of the gap cleared by the demo charges, signaling it was from 1st Company's mechs.

Then, just as before, the enemy counter-blew from directly above the momentary breach in the barrier. Hundreds of tons of rubble fell, with a few boulders slamming into some of Jenkins' mechs. Jammer suffered minor tread damage, but other than that, the unit remained intact, and cut-off from 1st Company.

"Dammit," Jenkins swore. "They must have prepped a dozen of these collapses at each tunnel." Jenkins needed to reconnect with 1st Company, soon, or the enemy's inevitable counterattack would see them fighting with their backs to the wall. Hardly ideal for any military formation, but for a unit like Armor, which relied on mobility and range, it was a worst-case scenario.

Fleet brass had known that this would be a subterranean engagement and had sent Jenkins' unit in well in advance of the Marines and other ground-force elements. If he was being charitable, he'd say the admiralty was stress-testing his unit. If he was being cynical, he would say that he and his people, consisting mostly of convicts and castoffs, were being served up as fodder, thinning the enemy ranks to make it easier on the so-called A-Team. Not the Marines, they could hold their own and were probably miffed at not being first.

First to fight was their motto. They probably wouldn't join the fight at all. Sloppy seconds wasn't their style. Fleet Ground Force's main body. Those guys would arrive en masse and clean up the scraps, claim victory, and give themselves medals for their bravery.

All the while, Jenkins was knee-deep in dead bodies and rubble, his retreat cut off.

"Seismics are picking up increased activity from the northern rim of the cavern," Styles reported urgently, snapping Jenkins' attention back to the moment. "Enemy platforms detected four hundred meters from the northern tunnels."

"Chaps, load HE shells," Jenkins barked. "Close those tunnels off, now."

"HE up," Chaps acknowledged, and a moment later declared, "on the way."

Roy's cannon spewed hellish destruction, sending a rocket-assisted HE round screaming across the cavern.

When it hit, it delivered like the Founders' Holiday.

A riot of flame signaled a direct hit on an enemy fuel supply, one which was likely attached to a railgun platform. The tunnel behind the explosion collapsed, though not as spectacularly as the Arh'Kel counter-tunneling efforts which kept 1st and 2nd Companies separated.

"More seismics, sir," Styles said calmly. "The southern edge… Echo Tunnel."

"Reiterate our stance to the enemy, Chaps," Jenkins ordered.

"HE up," Chaps acknowledged, "on the way!"

Another high-explosive round belched forth, this one to the opposite side of the cavern. Unfortunately, even Chaps' superior targeting solutions were unable to send this one all the way to Echo Tunnel. The shell exploded midway to its target, bringing a shower of granite collapsing from the cavern's roof.

Jenkins instinctively sucked in a breath, knowing even as he did so that it was a fooling gesture. If the cavern was unstable enough to be caved-in by a few high-explosive shells, the Arh'Kel would never have used it for a major transit hub. This planet had an extremely active tectonic plate network, resulting in frequent and major volcanic eruptions. This strata of bedrock was incredibly resilient after enduring millions of years of violent earthquakes.

Still, regardless of what the science said, it was unwise to send explosive shells into the roof of a cave one was trapped in. But when faced with making a possibly unwise decision or no decision at all, Jenkins opted for the former every time.

"Two platforms emerging from Echo Tun…" Styles began, but

was cut off when *Roy* rocked viciously from left-to-right. Even the mech's robust shock-absorption systems, normally used to counteract the mech's artillery recoil, was unable to keep two of *Roy*'s crew from snapping against their harnesses.

"Return fire, Chaps!" he snapped. "2nd Company: fire all rockets at Echo Tunnel."

"On the way," Chaps snarled, and after walking *Roy* a few dozen meters to the right, he was able to send an HE shell downrange. It missed the tunnel's mouth by thirty meters, but the wave of HE and AP rockets which soon followed filled Echo Tunnel. Anything which had thought to emerge was annihilated, but Jenkins knew he could only send another volley or two of that intensity before 2nd Company's supply of rockets would be exhausted.

Caved-in roof in front. Cave-ins behind. Ammunition was critical. And a determined enemy was coming. It was the textbook definition of a shit sandwich.

Two railgun mounts had managed to clear the tunnel before the rocket barrage effectively closed it, and those railguns spat fire into the *219*, a mobile SAM—surface-to-air missile--platform with limited complementary armaments. Both railguns struck true and the *219* exploded, but thankfully, her ordnance did not.

The humanoid *Kamehameha* took aim with its own railguns and returned fire, skewering the left railgun mount through its capacitor bank. The enemy vehicle died without so much as a whimper, reminding Jenkins yet again just how badly he needed to update his battalion's arsenal.

Fighting with two-century-old weapons left a lot to be desired.

"Kill that second railgun, Chaps," Jenkins growled.

"On it, sir," Chaps replied, sending one of his last HE shells into the enemy vehicle. It was no bulls-eye, but even an indirect hit with explosive shells was enough to scrap the Arh'Kel railgun.

"Anything on the seismics?" Jenkins asked.

"Nothing at the moment, sir." Styles shook his head. "But our sensor range is limited without a link to *Silent Fox*'s suite. I can only see them when they're a few hundred meters from the cavern."

"Do what you can to clear up the readings," Jenkins said, knowing that if Styles couldn't do it then nobody in the battalion could. He was a good officer. Smart, ambitious, and possessing the rare ability to know when to seize the initiative. The only reason he'd fallen into Jenkins' lap was because he had the wrong last name, not that Jenkins would ever complain. He could never have gotten the battalion any further than a back-of-the-napkin dream without Styles' help.

"Commander..." Styles said hesitantly. "I'm reading something..."

"What is it?"

"I...I'm not sure..." Styles replied in frustration. "There's a signal down here. At first, I thought it was local EM interference, or maybe some kind of feedback from our own comm systems. But now...I think I've found some sort of enemy comm channel."

Jenkins' brow furrowed. "Arh'Kel don't make a habit of hiding their comm chatter."

"I know, sir." Styles shook his head as he methodically worked the controls of his station, "But I swear I've seen this type of wave form before. It almost looks..." he trailed off before shaking his head bitterly. "I'm sorry, Commander."

"Record everything you're reading," Jenkins ordered, knowing that it was unlikely Styles would bring something trivial to his attention in the middle of an engagement. "Maybe we'll be able to sort it out once we get back to HQ."

"Yes, sir," Styles nodded.

"In the meantime, get more demo charges placed on Bravo Tunnel," Jenkins barked. "The rock-biters aren't going to give up that easily. They probably don't know how little ammo we've got left. If their next attack is anything like their previous, we'll have a rough time of it. Redeploy the column while the Pounders set the demo," he continued, glancing at his wristwatch and seeing that the infantry only had another two hours of local oxygen left in their personal air supplies.

The choking smoke that filled the cavern was going nowhere, which meant that the only open passages leading out of this cavern went deeper underground instead of to the surface.

If they didn't get out of here in the next two hours, his FGF would suffocate and die.

Minutes steadily ticked by, and soon the demo charges were set. But before Jenkins gave the order to blow Bravo Tunnel yet again, Styles' board lit up like a Christmas tree.

"Multiple contacts!" Styles reported in surprise.

Jenkins instinctively checked the seismic sensors, finding nothing on them. "Show me," the commander urged, moving to Styles' side.

"I localized that signal I found, sir," Styles explained, adjusting one of his displays to show an overlay of the cavern and its adjoining tunnels. The battalion's armored units showed up as green triangles, the FGF infantry as yellow dots, with both allied forces tightly clustered near Bravo Tunnel.

Every other tunnel, however, was soon filled with thousands of tiny red dots and larger, blue squares—enemy railgun mounts.

"Holy hell," Jenkins muttered, "are they advancing?"

"Negative, sir." Styles shook his head in confusion. "They're moving, but not toward the cavern. They seem to be milling around, even the HWPs are just moving back and forth."

"How did you find them?" Jenkins demanded, his eyes snapping across the tactical plotter as he realized the magnitude of what they had stumbled upon. This was nothing short of an enemy headquarters complex. Fleet Intelligence had estimated Arh'Kel strength on this planet at no more than fifteen thousand infantry and two hundred railgun mounts, with a dozen anti-orbital platforms capable of sniping anything smaller than a dreadnought as far out as high orbit.

Jenkins' battalion had already uncovered at least half that many enemy units during *this advance alone.*

"Fan out the column," Jenkins ordered. "We can't let them catch us in another crossfire. Move *Sword of Damocles* and *Monsoon* to the northern and southern flanks respectively, then take *Roy* north and *Babycake* south to support them and maximize our artillery's effective range. Cluster the rest of the battalion inside, centered on *Kamehameha.* Those railguns are our best weapons down here and can reach any point in the cavern, unlike our fifteens."

"Orders acknowledged," Styles confirmed.

"You found them by monkeying with that signal," Jenkins concluded as *Roy* began rolling to the northern flank in support of the *Sword of Damocles.* "Show me what you've got."

"It's some sort of distributed, P2P comm network, Commander," Styles explained. "In fact, the reason I recognized it is because it bears striking similarities to the Solarians' One Mind network."

Jenkins snorted derisively at the mention of the Solar humans, a branch of humanity which the Terran Republic had little practical relationship with these days, "The Solarians?"

"Yes, sir." Styles nodded. "The Solarian system connects nearly every human mind on Earth, forming a kind of gestalt intelligence system..."

"I'm aware of the framework, Chief," Jenkins interrupted. "I'm also aware that such direct links are strictly regulated in the Terran Republic for security reasons, no matter what our 'enlightened' Solarian cousins think."

"Of course, sir." Styles nodded sheepishly before rallying. "But I was studying the system's architecture back at the academy, and the similarities between this Arh'Kel system and that one are obvious now that I cracked the code. The rotating frequencies used to encrypt all data transfers, the procedurally-generated data nodes, even the self-limiting blockchain appear to be similar to the system used in Sol."

"How did you crack it?" Jenkins asked warily.

Styles hesitated before making pointed eye contact. "I've got friends who theorized about a potential way to hack the One Mind gestalt."

Jenkins' eyes snagged on the tactical display as *Roy* finally arrived at its position in support of *Sword of Damocles*. Thankfully, the Arh'Kel did indeed appear to be stationary. "These friends of yours," he mused aloud, taking Styles' meaning clearly enough, "they didn't happen to give you a copy of their work, did they?"

"Not a complete one, no," Styles replied with a tight grin, "but with a few days' study of their transceivers, I could probably come up with an approximation."

"Every Arh'Kel has one of these?" Jenkins pressed.

"It appears that way." Styles nodded. "But if they're anything like the Solarians' devices, they'll be rendered inert after their bearers' vital functions cease."

"Fine." Jenkins nodded. "Order the Pounders to examine rock-biter corpses near Bravo Tunnel. Tell them what to look for and see what they come up with. But first, they need to blow that..."

"Movement!" Styles interrupted. "Rock-biters in the western tunnels are advancing in force."

Jenkins nodded, watching as the enemy consolidated and advanced with mechanical precision on the cavern.

"Signal the column," Jenkins barked, "prepare to receive the enemy. Concentrate railgun fire on the western tunnels. I want *Kamehameha* cycling its capacitors no more than twelve seconds apart. *Roy* and *Babycake* are to focus artillery on the north and south. The rest of the column is to hold fire until eight of the railguns are in range before clearing all AP rockets. Once the APs are gone, load HE and await my order to fire."

Styles related the commands before reporting, "Orders acknowledged. Arh'Kel will breach the cavern in fifteen seconds. Twenty railgun mounts and four thousand infantry inbound."

Jenkins grimaced. "Have the Pounders blow the tunnel, now, then order them to hunker down behind their barricades. This is about to get messy."

"Five seconds," Styles called out. Despite the mounting tension in *Roy*'s cabin, Jenkins was pleased to find everyone attending to their duties with a high level of professionalism. Concern and sweat, but no one had lost their nerve.

"Here we go," he grunted as the first icons streamed into the cavern's opposite side six kilometers from Bravo Tunnel. That tunnel exploded with the last batch of demo 2nd Company had at its disposal, and before the dust had settled, the two sides were furiously exchanging fire.

Kamehameha stabbed a pair of railgun bolts into the emerging railgun mounts, scratching one and damaging the other's drive system. Four more railgun mounts drove through the western tunnel, callously brushing past their predecessors before unleashing fire on Jenkins' mechs. *Roy* took a thunderous hit to its forward armor, which thankfully held, while a second strike struck one of *Roy*'s four legs. Alarms went off on Chaps' station, but it seemed they had weathered the first strike.

On the other end of the crescent formation, *Babycake* fared worse. Taking two direct hits to its armored left flank, the mighty mech was nearly toppled as its crew struggled to turn its relatively fresh right face to the enemy.

Arh'Kel units soon began pouring through the northern and southern tunnels, and when eight railguns were in firing range, Jenkins gave the order, "2nd Company: empty launch tubes at your assigned targets."

A devastating wave of eighty-three AP rockets tore across the smoke-filled cavern. A line of Arh'Kel infantry advanced a few dozen meters ahead of their railguns. Considering fifteen of the

AP rockets struck rock-biters, one could be forgiven for thinking the Arh'Kel were throwing their bodies in the way of the barrage. But Arh'Kel reflexes and senses were no better than that of humans, so it was merely a numbers game as thousands of rock-biters advanced ahead of their heavy weapons platforms, the HWPs, faster than any human soldiers could move without mechanical assistance.

All eight railguns were torched by the rocket barrage, which was the last 'safe' salvo Jenkins' people could deliver. At least ten more rock-biter HWPs were moving into the cavern, which meant that he'd soon be rolling the dice on HE shells.

"Commander, I've got a theory," Styles said urgently.

"Let's hear it." Jenkins nodded as a horde of cartwheeling rock-biters drew nearer.

"I think the pulse missile *Elvira* launched in the collapsed junction shorted out the rock-biters' P2P comm network," Styles explained. "The EMP was more powerful than anything we can generate down here, but if I'm right about this network's architecture, we might be able to generate something practically comparable."

"*Elvira* was armed with our only pulse warhead." Jenkins shook his head grimly, recalling just how difficult it had been to sneak that one missile into his battalion.

Styles nodded. "I understand, sir, but *Kamehameha*'s got an old-style micro-fusion generator that could produce an EMP if overloaded. The mech would be destroyed, but it looks to me like we would render the remaining rock-biters as lethargic and confused as the ones *Elvira* hit with the pulse missile."

Jenkins sucked in a breath. Decisions between 'bad' and 'worse' seemed to be the only ones he got to make any more, and this was no different. *Kamehameha* was easily his most potent mech in a subterranean setting, with its railguns capable of direct-fire unlike the artillery that required significantly raised fire angles to reach ranges greater than two kilometers, angles which low cavern ceilings precluded.

"All right..." Jenkins nodded, his decision made. "Send *Centipede* and *Kamehameha* to the cavern's center at maximum speed. *Kamehameha*'s crew is to initiate the overload on a time-delay, set the mech on autopilot to the center of the cavern, and then they're to transfer to *Centipede*. *Centipede*'s systems are the oldest in the battalion, so the only thing the EMP will fry is her comm gear and automated fire control systems."

Styles seemed reluctant to relay the orders. "This is just a theory, sir."

"I'm in command, Styles," Jenkins said firmly. "This is my call. Relay my orders."

Styles nodded and did as commanded, and soon the two mechs were moving toward the center of the cavern at best possible speed, as a surging tide of Arh'Kel soldiers advanced ahead of the emerging railgun platforms.

"New fire orders," Jenkins barked. "Clear a hole for *Kamehameha*. I don't want those rock-biters tearing it down before it delivers its surprise."

Roy took a direct hit as an enemy railgun sniped it from across the cavern. Chaps was unable to return fire with non-HE shells, but the closer *Babycake* returned fire and scratched the offending vehicle from the field.

Arh'Kel infantry crossed the cavern's mid-line, cartwheeling at fantastic speeds. The aliens' railgun mounts moved into the cavern behind them, with each spewing a bolt of tungsten as soon as it emerged from its tunnel. *Monsoon* was struck by a pair of bolts, each a relatively glancing hit, but those hits still cost the humanoid mech two of its six arms. The track-mounted *Jammer* took a hit as well, and like *Rammer* before it, survived the initial hit. Unlike *Rammer*, *Jammer* was fortunate enough to avoid a second hit when the railgun was knocked off-target by *Babycake*'s counterfire.

Kamehameha continued its charge to the center of the cavern, where its EMP would have the greatest effect. The approaching tide of enemy soldiers adjusted until nearly half of the charging enemy were moving to intercept it. Like self-setting bowling pins, they converged into dense lines as they sought to prevent *Kamehameha* from reaching its objective.

Jenkins loved a target-rich environment.

Kamehameha slowed its charge for a few seconds as its crew abandoned it. *Centipede*, the long-bodied and aptly-named APC—armored personnel carrier—powered by honest-to-God diesel engines with design components dating back to World War II, moved to collect the crew as the auto-piloted mech resumed its charge toward the swarm of rock-biters.

The heavily-armored *Centipede*, made of five segments with four tracks apiece, turned and red-lined its engines as it attempted to return to the eastern edge of the cavern. A pair of railgun impacts destroyed the fifth segment of the black-hulled mech, but the other four continued pulling away at maximum speed.

Kamehameha took a pair of railgun strikes to its upper torso, with a brilliant flare of blue-white energy accompanying the destruction of the humanoid mech's left arm and shoulder. The mech stumbled, but it regained its balance as its footsteps brought it ever-nearer to the horde of advancing rock-biters.

"2nd Company," Jenkins barked after approving a fire pattern and forwarding it to Styles, "clear a path for *Kamehameha*. Fire all HE rockets at the transmitted coordinates on my command… fire, fire, fire!"

2nd Company's launchers cleared one hundred and ninety rockets on his command with terrifying effect. The first launch preceded the last by three-point-two-seconds as HE missiles tore loose from their tubes, furiously streaking toward the converging Arh'Kel infantry.

And when they struck, it was like the maw of Hell opened to consume the Arh'Kel horde within a raging inferno.

A thousand Arh'Kel died in those three-point-two seconds, as even their rock-hard skins were unable to save them from the devastating barrage. Before the still-charging *Kamehameha*, a V-shaped wedge of the Arh'Kel horde was reduced to rubble and silicon slime. The one-armed mech continued its charge, and was struck in the torso by an enemy railgun as a trio of streaking tungsten bolts converged on it.

Kamehameha's status telemetry, displayed on a nearby monitor, began to flicker with a series of alarms, one of which was for the mech's power plant.

"All units, brace for EMP," Jenkins commanded over the company channel. He watched as another railgun struck the humanoid mech's torso. "Blow it, Styles," Jenkins urged.

"Six more seconds, sir," Styles replied tensely.

"Blow it!" Jenkins snapped as *Kamehameha*'s fusion reactor containment began to fail.

"Three...two...one...now!" Styles declared, and a blinding flash filled the cavern as Kamehameha's plant overloaded with a deafening peal.

Roy's onboard virtual systems reflexively shut down, but quickly cycled back online and began feeding data to the various displays in Jenkins' command center.

And that data confirmed Styles' hypothesis: the Arh'Kel appeared to have been stunned by the EMP. Even the HWPs were dormant, though how long they would remain that way was anyone's guess.

"New order to the column," Jenkins snapped. "Advance on the enemy at full speed with weapons hot. Hit anything that moves with secondary weapon systems—let's clear this cavern before they wake up!"

The column advanced as one in a crescent, sweeping from east-to-west. The northern and southern tips of the formation engaged fallen rock-biters first, sweeping across the stunned Arh'Kel with machine guns, coilguns, and flamers as they methodically purged the cavern of enemy soldiers.

After the atrocities committed by Arh'Kel infantry on New Australia decades earlier, where over ninety percent of the colony had been brutally slaughtered in a surprise attack, the Terran Republic had declared the rock-biters a clear and present danger to humanity. Orders were simple: shoot on sight and without hesitation.

Which was precisely what Jenkins' people did.

When the last of the Arh'Kel HWPs was scrapped, Jenkins growled, "Now in the name of all that's holy, would somebody clear that fucking tunnel?!"

BREAKING THROUGH

"That's it," Podsy declared triumphantly. "The last of the components have been transferred. *Devil Crab* is now fully online, sans the missile launcher which is bingo ammo anyway after *Elvira*'s remaining supply was bricked by the EMP."

"Missiles? Where we're going, we won't need...missiles." Xi smirked tightly as she directed *Devil Crab* down Bravo Tunnel in hope of rejoining the column. Working the manual controls was tricky, but Xi Bao had always enjoyed a challenge that required her full attention, and manually directing the movements of a six-legged mech weighing eighty-six tons definitely fit that bill. She switched to Lieutenant Koch's dedicated channel. "Good work, Lieutenant. We'll rejoin the column and see you on the other side."

"Copy that, *Devil Crab*," Koch acknowledged. "We'll take *Elvira* back to the barn and see what else we can salvage. Bust some rocks, Lieutenant."

"We're a regular chain gang, we are," Xi snickered before cutting the channel and realizing she hadn't signed off correctly. Comm discipline, like so many other forms of discipline, had never come easily to her.

"You know, she didn't look that bad," Podsy mused as Xi tramped *Devil Crab* down the tunnel.

"I find that hard to believe if *you* bagged her," Xi quipped. "Oh wait, I thought you didn't swing our way?"

"You're a riot and a half, Bao," Podsy drawled. "I was talking about *Elvira*."

"I figured as much," she said as the tunnel grew darker with each of *Devil Crab*'s steps. "Honestly, I doubt it matters. We're marching to meet up with an armor column that's got to be several kilometers below ground now. Whose bright idea was it to send armor underground, anyway?"

"It's a test program, LT," Podsednik repeated, and Bao could almost see the eye-roll in spite of their in-cabin vid system being offline. "And since it was a bunch of rust-buckets like this one manned by convicts and bust-outs, Fleet brass didn't see any downside in sending us in here to soften the landing for the main Fleet when they arrive in two days"

"As if those guys like *anything* soft," Xi snorted.

"Commander Jenkins is good people." Podsy shrugged. "He gave most of us a chance to slash our prison sentences by two-thirds or more, along with an honorable public service discharge to offset whatever felonies we might be dragging with us. Frankly, I doubt I'd have survived my full sentence. New Australia isn't exactly known for having a posh penal system."

"Especially not for necrophiliacs," Xi observed dryly.

"Jesus, you're never gonna let that one go, are you?" Podsy sighed.

"I'll die first," she chuckled.

"Usually, I'd try to hurry that kind of thing along," Podsednik deadpanned, "but in this case, it would mean cutting my own meager existence short."

"Classic Catch-22," Xi declared triumphantly. "Caught in a crossfire between the need to survive and the desire not to be known as the most infamous sexual deviant in Republic history."

"No press is bad press," Podsy muttered weakly as a warning light came on for leg number three's motivators. "Dammit...the coils are out of alignment. We're going to burn through our lubricant in thirty minutes at this rate. Can you ease up on the forward motion by about eight degrees in Three's walk cycle?"

Xi adjusted her controls as he suggested, and after completing a dozen walk cycles, asked, "Is that better?"

"Looks like it," he agreed. "The recoil dampeners aren't going to be much good on Three until we can rebuild the main joint. Until then, try to limit range of motion like this."

"It won't slow us down much," Xi said as she focused on improving her control of the mech's drive system. Before long, she was moving *Devil Crab* down the tunnel at forty kilometers per hour, fully five times the speed the column would have traveled during its sojourn into the bowels of this God-forsaken planet. What took Commander Jenkins an hour should only take *Devil Crab* eleven minutes and change.

A few minutes into the journey through the dark, *Devil Crab*'s comm system buzzed and a friendly icon appeared on the tactical plotter.

"It's one of our Owl drones. It's en route to the surface requesting reinforcements," Podsy said as the drone's icon streaked past *Devil Crab* on its way back up the tunnel. "It looks like the column's been separated. 1st Company is stuck behind a tunnel collapse while 2nd Company is cut off in a major transit nexus. Looks like Commander Jenkins is using HE shells down there," he reported grimly.

"Which means we need to hurry the hell up," Xi snapped, throwing caution to the wind and maxing out *Devil Crab*'s walk cycle. "Keep an eye on Three's main joint, but we can fight on five legs if we have to."

"You're the boss, LT," Podsy acknowledged tersely.

"Damn right," she agreed, though she felt like a fraud for doing so. She was barely nineteen years old while Podsy was already in his thirties. "Try to let me know before it goes kaput. I'll back off if I need to, but every second counts."

"Agreed," Podsednik replied. "I'll pressurize Three's main joint lube to stave off damage. It'll shred the pumps, but we should get enough use out of them to make it back to the surface."

"If we survive that long," Xi observed pointedly as she miscalculated one of her mech's steps on a tight corner. *Devil Crab*'s front-right leg struck the tunnel wall, jarring her against her seat's restraints as she adjusted course without losing speed.

"Women drivers," Podsy sighed in mock exasperation.

"This bucket needed a new paint job anyway," Xi retorted, flushing with embarrassment at the rookie error.

"The Owl's data packet showed 2nd Company is half a kilometer ahead," Podsy reported. "Better slow down."

"Copy that," she acknowledged, and soon the IFF—identification friend or foe—blips of 2nd Company appeared on her tactical display.

Blue Lotus, Priscilla, Forktail, Creeper's Daughter, and *Dynamite* were the first to appear on the screen, arranged in a dispersed file. They were soon joined by *Mad Dog, Preacher, Spin Doctor, Dog Meat, Bad Joke, Wolverine,* and *Stuttering Steve. Devil Crab*'s headlamps eventually illuminated the rear-most, humanoid *Creeper's Daughter* in the hot, humid tunnel. As that light mech came into view, the final mech icon in 2nd Company, the bridge-laying *Racetrack,* appeared at the head of the company.

"*Devil Crab,* this is *Forktail,*" came the nasal voice of *Forktail*'s Jock, Ensign Ford. "Take up position at the rear of the column and await further orders."

Xi bristled at Ford's tone, haughty and hardly befitting the address of an officer in command. "What's the situation, *Forktail?*" Xi demanded after biting back the flood of retorts that sprang to mind.

"1st Company is cut off from 2nd Company by a cave-in," Ford replied. "With Captain Murdoch engaged on the other side of the collapse, I am in command of 2nd Company. Stand by and await further orders, *Devil Crab*."

Xi had no idea how to respond to that. She knew that Ford was making some sort of power play at her expense, and she also knew that even as a lieutenant junior grade, Xi was Ford's superior, even though Ford was a professional officer, straight from school, and Xi was merely the recipient of a battlefield commission. But precisely how she was supposed to respond to such insubordination escaped her.

Thankfully, Podsy was quicker on his feet in this particular situation and cut in, "The *lieutenant* gave you an order, *Ensign*. Status report."

"Who is this?" Ford demanded.

"This is *Lieutenant* Xi Bao," Xi interrupted, fed up with the posturing in the middle of a combat operation. A garrison officer versus a combat officer—the difference was stark. She almost felt sorry for the pogue. "Let's hear that status report, Ensign Ford."

A brief delay. "The tunnel collapsed during the insertion to the cavern, *Lieutenant*. We've tried clearing the rubble with explosives twice, and 1st Company has done the same from the other side, but the enemy has prepared counter-collapses. No matter how hard we try to…"

The link went dead as *Devil Crab*'s systems briefly shut down. "What the hell?" Xi demanded before realizing what had happened: an EMP had just struck her mech. But this one was considerably less potent than the one she and Podsy had used on the surface, so *Devil Crab*'s systems were able to recover with a quick reboot. "I thought we had the only pulse warhead in the battalion," she snapped as she manually restarted several of *Devil Crab*'s systems.

"That wasn't a pulse warhead. Too weak," Podsy explained before it came to him. "It must have been a fusion plant overload."

"Only *Kamehameha*'s got a fusion plant." Xi furrowed her brow as the last of the systems came back online.

"Reports were after we spiked the rock-biters top-side, they went into a stupor," Podsy mused.

Xi nodded in understanding as she stomped *Devil Crab* past the motionless 2nd Company mechs, which were only now beginning to stir. "Which means Commander Jenkins knowingly popped *Kamehameha*'s core, and that we've got a window to breach the cavern before the enemy can counter our efforts. We've got to move. Load AP into the fifteens," she ordered, smirking triumphantly as she added, "let's blow this hole."

"Seriously?" Podsy drawled as he directed the auto-loading system of *Devil Crab*'s twin fifteen-kilo guns. "Your one-liners could use some work. AP shells up."

She brought *Devil Crab* to a stop fifty meters from the pile of rubble blocking their path, a pile which was significantly smaller than she had expected it to be. At the very top, she could see muzzle flashes lighting the cavern beyond, which meant that with a few shots, she could probably clear a hold large enough to squeeze some of the smaller mechs through.

A few dozen FGF Pounders were clinging to the tunnel's walls, prompting her to pipe her voice through the mech's external speakers. "This is *Devil Crab*. We're going to clear the tunnel. All personnel are ordered to take cover."

The Pounders scrambled to safety behind the various mechs lining the tunnel, and when the last of them had reached safety, she commanded, "Fire One."

"Roger," Podsy confirmed. *Devil Crab* bucked violently as her left gun thundered, sending its slug into the upper part of the rubble pile.

"Fire Two."

"On the way," Podsy acknowledged, and again the Scorpion-class mech rocked. When the dust had settled, she could see far more light streaming through the gap at the top of the rubble pile.

Before she could call for the guns to be reloaded, the radio crackled to life with Ford's pinched, nasal voice, "Cease fire! Cease fire, *Devil Crab*. Cease fire!"

"Report, Ensign," Xi demanded, more surprised than anything at Ford's histrionics.

"Are you insane?!" Ford screeched as his mech, *Forktail*, turned toward *Devil Crab*. "We're half a kilometer underground! You'll collapse the whole system on top of our heads!"

"Stand down, Ensign," Xi growled, noting that *Forktail*'s rocket launchers were cycling through their target-acquisition sequence. "We've got comrades fighting on the other side of that rock pile and we're going to reinforce them."

"In Captain Murdoch's absence, *I* am in command of 2nd Company," Ford shrilled, clearly shaken by some combination of recent events. "Cease fire immediately and power down your mech. The last thing we need right now is a hothead blowing off ordnance like it's a Founding Festival Fire-show!"

Xi was stunned into silence. Again, she knew what she was supposed to do, but for some reason, she faltered in the very moment she knew she needed to do it.

Perhaps uncouthly, Podsy took that moment to declare, over the open line, no less, "AP up. On the way!"

Devil Crab bucked as her left gun sent an AP round into the top of the rubble pile with devastating effect. As the dust settled and Xi took a closer look at the scattered boulders, she saw that they were fairly uniform in their rectangular cuboid shapes. The stone had been quarried with some sort of saw, probably a wire, into blocks several meters on a side, and while some of those blocks had shattered, many more were in good enough shape that they stacked well atop each other.

Clearing this boulder pile was going to be less work than she had expected, but the only way she could have seen that was by clearing enough of the loose upper rubble away.

"Stand down, *Devil Crab!*" Ford snapped over the line, and Xi could almost hear the frothing saliva landing on his mic. "Do not fire! I say again, do not fire!"

To Xi's eye, it looked like one more shot would be needed to clear the most dangerous loose rubble from the top of the pile. She took Podsy's lead and felt a great deal of satisfaction as she did so, by raising her voice and declaring over the line, "AP up. On the way!"

Another thunderous blast tore several tons of loose rubble from the top of the boulder pile, exposing even more of the larger, rectangular pieces beneath.

"*Bad Joke, Wolverine,* and *Creeper's Daughter,*" Xi called out over the open line, overriding Ford's hysterical objections by raising *Devil Crab's* transceiver output to overpower the shrieking ensign, "get in there and clear those larger boulders. Watch out for the loose rocks up top."

There was a brief delay, followed by a chorus of, "Copy that, Lieutenant."

"This is insubordination, Xi," Ford finally managed to transmit over Xi's subtle attempts to prevent communication with the hysterical officer. "You'll be court-martialed for this!"

"Let's get our people out of that hole before we start with administrative procedures, En-swine," Xi retorted. "Now shut your suck and fall in behind as we breach this fall."

"You've got a lot to learn, little girl," Ford growled as he guided his mech through the entry to the cavern.

"I'd gladly take a lesson once we see daylight. Now keep this channel clear," she said easily, and she could hear a short chorus of snickers over the open channel from the other mechs' crews.

They'd seen what happened to those who tussled with her, but Ford was just stupid enough that he might actually take her up on it.

"Until then," she continued blithely, "I think it's best if you reported to your superior, after you've located him, of course."

Silence was her only reply as the three humanoid mechs moved forward to excavate the passage. In less than ten minutes, they had cleared enough rubble to permit most of the column to pass into the cavern beyond. The smaller mechs went through while the three humanoid units continued excavating the boulders, but *Devil Crab*'s girth meant she would be the last vehicle capable of passing through the portal.

Thick, black smoke clung to the tunnel's roof as it billowed steadily up Bravo Tunnel en route to the surface.

"Glad to see you could join us, Lieutenant Xi," Commander Jenkins said over the battalion channel.

"Sorry we weren't in there sooner, sir," she said as a sudden wave of nausea swept over her. "What are your orders?"

"We're gathering a few of the more intact rock-biter corpses for study," he replied, "along with some of their railgun tech components. Your danger-close pulse missile strike topside is the only reason we're still alive down here."

Her brow scrunched up in confusion, "I don't understand, sir."

"The battalion will be briefed after we get back to HQ," he assured her, "but for now, we need to clear the rest of this rubble and get out of this hole. There are a whole lot more of these sandy bastards down here than we thought. We have to fall back, regroup, and await the main body of Fleet Ground."

Her lips twisted sourly. "I thought *we* were the cavalry, sir."

"One step at a time, Lieutenant," Jenkins chuckled. "As far as first deployments go, this one was more successful than anyone outside this hole gave us credit for. It's time to head for the barn and relay what we've learned to Fleet."

"You're the commander, sir," she said with as much deference as she could force into her voice. She *hated* waiting for help from others, even when that help happened to be delivered by the most devastating armed forces branch in the Terran Republic.

"Stand by to assist recovering whatever salvage we can drag out of here," Jenkins commanded. "We roll in fifteen, well before the rock-biters have a chance to regroup."

"Copy that," Xi acknowledged, but less than two minutes later, that plan was out the window.

The rock-biters had returned.

ELVIRA REBORN

"I've got over a thousand inbound rock-biters on the screen, Commander," Styles reported.

"You're using their comm-linkage to locate them?" Jenkins asked.

"Yes, sir," Styles acknowledged. "I can't listen in on the chatter yet, but I can identify individual infantry from HWPs. They'll breach the perimeter in forty seconds."

Jenkins switched his mic to the battalion-wide channel, "*Devil Crab, Flaming Rose,* and *Babycake* will advance with *Roy* at flank speed..." He paused, silently cursing himself for using fleet terminology instead of land. "We take the center while all units not assigned to salvage are to assume guandao formation along the eastern edge of the cavern, ordered by the numbers."

The acknowledgments came as the battalion sprang into action. The majority of the enemy was approaching from the south, which meant he might be able to keep them from entering the cavern. And even if the Arh'Kel breached, sustained fire from the fresher 1st Company mechs would provide ample cover for the rest of the battered battalion to withdraw.

No sooner had the four heaviest mechs reached the cavern's

center than the first Arh'Kel soldiers emerged from the southern tunnels.

And when they did, they were *pissed*.

"RPGs inbound!" Styles called out before *Roy*'s armor was struck by a barrage of grenades.

"Kill-box that tunnel," Jenkins commanded the fourteen mechs ready to engage the enemy. "Fire, fire, fire!"

Arranged like the eponymous *guandao* halberd, the four heavy mechs near the cavern's center sent artillery and rockets toward the southern tunnel's mouth. The 'shaft' of the formation was comprised of the ten lighter mechs, each of which lent whatever long-range fire support they could while spraying anti-personnel rounds into the emerging Arh'Kel. Accuracy at the median range of just over a kilometer left much to be desired, but the volume of fire was nothing short of terrifying.

Thousands of rounds per second slammed into the cavern's south wall during the fierce barrage, while only dozens struck enemy targets. Tracer rounds, sent from some of the older track-style mechs, lit up the cavern as the deafening roar of machine guns rattled dust loose from the cavern's ceiling.

And the Arh'Kel kept coming.

Devil Crab sent a pair of AP shells into the middle southern tunnel, scrubbing a railgun platform before it could fire a single shot. *Flaming Rose* added a pair of HE rockets to the onslaught, killing fifty Arh'Kel and partially collapsing one of the smaller tunnels. Hundreds of Arh'Kel died in the first seconds of the engagement, their corpses barely distinguishable from the granite debris which fell over them.

And still, the rock-biters kept coming.

Babycake spat a rocket-assisted explosive round into the main southern tunnel and received railgun fire in reply. Jenkins felt his breath catch at the initial damage reports: *Babycake*'s drive system had been compromised and its main gun was offline. Fire raged inside the mech's cabin, and Jenkins felt himself silently willing *Babycake*'s crew to abandon the mech and save themselves.

But, like the horde of oncoming rock-biters, his people stood tall and mercilessly returned fire. A pair of rockets tore loose from their mounts on *Babycake*'s undercarriage, with one taking the offending HWP off the board and the other causing a partial collapse of the cavern's southern edge.

A collapse which soon began to spread throughout the cavern, dropping jagged boulders from the ceiling, some of which were larger than *Roy*.

The humanoid mech, *Creeper's Daughter*, which stood nine-point-five meters tall, was crushed by one of the larger boulders. Skewering its main compartment from above, *Creeper's Daughter* was nearly bifurcated by the falling wedge-shaped slab of rock.

Blue Lotus, a five-legged Crab-class artillery mech, lost two legs when a trio of boulders struck it from above. Amazingly, the mech somehow managed to use its remaining three legs to maintain an upright posture and keep anti-personnel fire pouring into the southern tunnels. But without all five of its legs, its artillery was no longer functional.

The primitive side of Jenkins' brain told him to cease heavy weapons fire to prevent similar cave-ins. Friendly fire had just killed two of his crew aboard *Creeper's Daughter* and cost him one mech and badly damaged a second.

But Jenkins' higher brain told him that if those Arh'Kel made it into the cavern, with less than a kilometer separating their tunnels and his people, no one in the battalion would survive.

So he did the exact opposite of ordering his people to cease fire.

"All units, fire HE rockets," he commanded, sensing hesitation among his crews. "Pour it on. Remember New Melbourne!"

At invoking the site of the worst massacre in the conflict's history, one which saw three million people slaughtered in under six hours when the Arh'Kel attacked New Australia's most populous settlement, Jenkins saw his people renew their efforts.

A wave of HE rockets tore from their tubes, obliterating most of the Arh'Kel's ranks before they could emerge from the tunnels. Machine gun barrels glowed bright orange from sustained fire, and the few Arh'Kel who survived the kill-zone were quickly cut down by precise fire delivered by the FGF Pounders.

And still the Arh'Kel continued their charge.

A wave of HE rockets finally collapsed the largest of the southern tunnels, breaking loose another deadly shower of boulders from the cavern's ceiling. The quadrupedal *Priscilla* was struck by a six-ton boulder falling from fifty meters above. *Priscilla* crumpled and quickly exploded with a roar as its liquid fuel supply was ignited by her overheated machine gun barrels.

It was clear that something would need to change, fast, or Jenkins' fire was going to cause a massive cave-in. There were at least four more railgun platforms en route from the southern tunnels, and if they decided to collapse Bravo Tunnel instead of attacking his mechs directly, the entire column would be trapped and at the enemy's mercy. But he couldn't stand his ground and pour fire into the rock-biters at this rate for more than another thirty seconds before many of his mechs' ammo was exhausted.

Something had to give, and Lee Jenkins grudgingly accepted that it would have to be his battle line.

Just as he was about to give an order for his people to begin retreating through Bravo Tunnel, he noticed that one of his mechs had already broken formation.

And when he saw whose mech it was, he was filled with a warring mixture of respect and outrage for that particular Jock having taken the initiative.

She aimed to provide them cover while the rest of the battalion retreated, which was exactly what Jenkins ordered them to do.

"All units, retreat through Bravo Tunnel," he barked as *Roy's* tactical display showed they had already dropped over a thousand Arh'Kel while at least that many continued shuffling through the southern tunnels and into the cavern. "Retreat," he reiterated through gritted teeth, even as the units closest to Bravo Tunnel had already begun to do so. "I say again: retreat."

"This is stupid, Bao." Podsy grimaced as he fought to balance *Devil Crab*'s increasingly fragile motive systems. "If the enemy doesn't kill us, Commander Jenkins will."

"Quit bitching and load some HE rounds," Bao snapped. Despite his irritation, Podsy was in awe of Bao's ability to manually drive a Scorpion-class mech at top-rated speed, a hundred kilometers per hour, across the cavern floor. "I'm taking us into the heart of these ugly bastards, and we'll only get one good shot to close that tunnel before we're swarmed."

Podsy couldn't argue with the tactical merits of her decision. *Devil Crab* was the second-fastest heavy mech in the battalion, behind the assault mech *Roy*, which meant that only Bao and Jenkins were able to contemplate an attack like the one she and Podsednik were executing.

The left fifteen's loading system jammed, causing Podsy to scramble as he ran a re-cycle but found that there was some sort of mechanical failure in the breach-closing mechanism. The shell was in the pipe, but firing it without the breach locked would be suicidal for *Devil Crab*'s crew.

Devil Crab stomped toward the wave of rock-biters, which turned as one to intercept her instead of pursuing the smartly-fleeing battalion at her back. Her machine guns roared, rapidly depleting their ammo stores as she tore into the advancing Arh'Kel.

Podsy worked frantically to close the left gun's breach, trying every trick in the book as he fought desperately to locate the true source of the problem. It looked like the mechanism's hydraulics were properly functioning, and the sensors throughout the system checked out, but the damned thing still wouldn't load!

Gripping the heaviest thing he could find, an angled spanner weighing five kilos, he unstrapped from his chair and made his way to the left gun's control module. It was old school, comprised of a rat's nest of interconnected electrical switches housed in a half-meter-square junction box, and Podsy threw the cover back to quickly inspect the elements within. There didn't look to be any obstructions or burn marks, but a thorough inspection would take at least twenty minutes—time they obviously did not have.

So he employed the oldest trick in any grease-monkey's book: percussion therapy.

Gripping the spanner in both hands, Podsy gently tapped the side of the control box while keeping an eye on the breach.

Nothing happened.

He tapped it again, this time hard enough to dent the control box's housing.

Again, nothing.

"You ugly bangle snatch," he growled, striking the box once more from the other side.

Still nothing.

"Smug bitch," he barked, striking the housing from above with the spanner. This time, he was legitimately concerned he might have broken something with his love-taps.

Nothing.

"I'm gonna shove my fist so far up your..." he yelled, kicking the lower part of the box with his steel-toed boot.

The breach closed with an audible clank, and the electrical switches inside the battered box clicked open and closed in rapid succession as the system finally recycled back to zero.

"Careful, Podsy," Bao quipped. "Talk like that better be backed up. You don't want to juice a girl up with dirty talk and then leave her hangin'."

"Fucking bullshit," Podsy growled, causing Bao to laugh as he resumed his seat. "HE up," he finally acknowledged as *Devil Crab* waded into the thick of the enemy horde.

"Almost there," Bao called out as small arms fire plinked into *Devil Crab's* armor with steadily increasing frequency. "I've got a warning light on Three and Four legs," she said tightly just as Podsednik noticed them on his own panel.

Three was about to overheat its main joint after a catastrophic lubrication system failure. There was nothing he could do about that now. But Four looked to be suffering from some sort of power failure, which probably meant a stuck valve in the main hydraulic system.

There was nothing he could do about either until they came to a complete stop for at least three seconds, so he shut down the sensors feeding both alarms and said, "Fixed 'em."

"You're a terrible liar, Podsy," Bao laughed, her infectious, and some might say suicidal, energy filling *Devil Crab's* every nook and cranny just before the mech was rocked by an inbound strike.

"Railgun impact," Podsy called out as system reports flooded his screens. One of their machine guns was offline and Leg One had lost its lubrication feeds, but other than that no serious system damage had occurred. "Minor damage," he called out.

"Kill it," Bao ordered.

"On the way," Podsy acknowledged, sending the HE round loaded into their left gun down-range at the offending HWP. Predictably, the enemy platform exploded on impact, with shrapnel knocking fifteen nearby rock-biters to the rocky floor.

Podsy felt like crossing his fingers as he initiated a reload cycle of the left gun, and he was pleasantly surprised when the cycle completed without delay.

"HE up," he reported as another railgun impact struck their

forward hull, snapping Podsy's head from left to right so violently he felt something give in his neck. Ignoring the pain, he focused on the screens as more serious damage reports came in through *Devil Crab*'s automated sensors.

"Kill it," Bao urged, and this time, Podsy fired the right main.

The fifteen-kilo thundered, sending its ordnance into the railgun platform and scrubbing it from the board.

But now it was the right gun's turn to fail during the reload cycle.

"We collapse the tunnel in five seconds," Bao called out, though Podsy knew that to successfully blow the tunnel, or even to have a realistic chance to do so, they would need both guns to fire at least twice.

Arh'Kel infantry continued swarming toward *Devil Crab*, with the mech's machine guns flashing overheating alarms while ammo stores fell to dangerously low levels. They were less than five hundred meters from the target tunnel, which meant they could shoot more-or-less straight down its throat and hit the bend a hundred and fifty meters from the cavern.

"Five," she declared while Podsy worked to reinitialize the right gun's reload mechanism.

"Four."

He completed a quick diagnostic of the system, finding the problem to be with the same hydraulic feed that had been acting up on the drive assembly.

"Three."

Podsy barely managed to shunt enough pressure from the left gun's hydraulic feeders over to the right gun without compromising the system.

"Two."

The reload cycle initiated, with the spent casing ejecting and a fresh one moving up into the breach.

"One."

The breach snapped shut with a clang, and the gun's sensors showed green across the board.

"Fire!"

Podsy gave the tunnel both barrels. *Devil's Crab* bounced from the recoil.

The muffled explosions down the tunnel were far from climactic, but he saw that he had scrubbed at least one railgun platform while damaging the tunnel itself.

The guns' loading mechanisms cycled in three seconds, during which time two of *Devil Crab's* three remaining machine guns shut down due to critical overheating. They were nearly out of ammo anyway, but their sudden silence left open lines of attack, lines which the Arh'Kel flooded into with murderous ferocity.

Rock-biter infantry slammed into the hull, carving deep gouges into *Devil Crab's* armor with their plasma torch sidearms. In the three seconds it took for the mech's fifteen-kilo guns to reload, twenty rock-biters began slicing into every sensitive point on the mech's hull.

"Fire!" Bao commanded, her voice filled with every bit as much desperation as Podsy felt.

Devil Crab's guns cleared again, with both rounds striking home. A low rumble shook the entire cavern. The mech was tossed and the rock-biters were thrown off. The tunnel moaned in its death throes as the walls caved in, cutting off the Arh'Kel reinforcements.

Bao swept *Devil Crab* left and right, while Podsy tried, and failed, to reinitialize their offline machine guns.

There were at least three hundred rock-biters returning to swarm the hull, with a few dozen standing atop its broad, heavy chassis where they began to cut into the big guns themselves.

Bao bucked, pitched, yawed, and did everything in her power to dislodge them, but she had little effect on their progress. The torches cut deep rents into *Devil Crab*, but the mech defiantly continued to struggle against them, even managing to dislodge and crush a handful with expert stomps of the six-legged mech's limbs.

Then small arms fire slammed against her hull in rapid-succession, far too rapid to be rock-biter sidearms.

"It's *Roy!*" Podsy declared, seeing the command vehicle's icon appear on his screen. Not only was Commander Jenkins' mech moving to support them by scraping Arh'Kel from *Devil Crab's* hull, but nearly a hundred FGF Pounders were doing likewise, while their nested fellows sent a barrage into the rock-biter horde.

Finally, and for the first time since Terran forces had engaged the Arh'Kel on this hellhole of a planet, the rock-biters made a human decision.

They turned as one and retreated.

"Fall back to Bravo Tunnel, *Elvira,*" Commander Jenkins' voice came over the line. "We're headed back to the barn."

"Copy that," Bao acknowledged. "*Devil Crab* withdrawing."

"Negative. *Devil Crab* isn't on this battalion's active rolls," Jenkins said, his voice filled with mixed approval and consternation, "but as of this moment, *Elvira* is, and she's going to stay that way…at least until I figure out how to discipline her for the most bone-headed stunt I've ever seen."

"Understood," Bao said, though some of the nuance was lost on Podsy as he worked the restore the mech's drive systems. It looked like they would be able to limp out of there, but full-speed charges were out of the question until they'd had at least a few days' wrench time to patch her back up again.

Ten minutes later, the FGF spent the rest of their demo charges on sealing Bravo Tunnel. An hour after that, the battered column emerged from the hole in the ground and squinted from the daylight.

BARN & ITS BEASTS

Two hours after reaching the surface, the last of the battalion's mechs fell into their mobile HQ. Situated atop a granite outcropping forty meters tall and six hundred meters long, the plateau was the only spot within a hundred clicks which provided safety from a subterranean ambush. Seismic sensors lined the perimeter, and mobile weapon emplacements skirted the edge of the plateau.

A half-dozen APCs formed the HQ's essential facilities. Two served as hospitals, which were soon filled with wounded FGF and mech crews, while the rest housed the battalion's ammunition perishables.

The first thing Bao did after parking *Elvira* in its assigned slot and powering it down was look for Ensign Ford.

Serendipity put their mechs in adjacent parking slots.

She saw the olive-skinned Ford clamber down *Forktail's* ladder, and she clenched her fists in eager anticipation of the beatdown she was about to administer to the insubordinate ensign.

Judging by the set of Ford's jaw, he was every bit as ready for a fistfight as she was. Bao barely noticed Podsy at her flank, but she silently appreciated him having her back in case *Forktail*'s crew decided to intervene.

"What the fuck do you think you're doing..." Ford began furiously before, seemingly out of nowhere, Podsy cracked a right hand across the ensign's face.

Ford's eyes rolled back into his head as he staggered, never quite hitting the deck thanks to his Wrench's steadying hands.

"You're up on charges, Podsednik!" Ford's Wrench, a woman named Vasquez, seethed. "Striking a superior officer in a combat zone is..."

"Is exactly what that fuck-stain deserves," Podsy retorted hotly as Ford's eyes focused on him. "And I'll take whatever punishment the commander sees fit, up to and including summary execution! But I wonder—" He raised his voice as a small crowd began to gather around the affair. "—what's the punishment for cycling your rockets on a superior officer in the middle of an active engagement?"

"You'll hang for this, Podsednik," Ford growled, gripping his profusely-bleeding nose to slow the flow. "I'll tie the rope myself..."

"Can it, *Ensign*," Bao barked, the primal fire suddenly gone from her after Podsy had gotten in an admittedly good shot in on the haughty ensign. "I'm willing to leave what happened down there out of my report if you man up and admit, right here and right now, that you threatened to open fire on my mech when I assumed command of 1st Company as the superior officer. Otherwise, I'm taking this straight to Commander Jenkins and we'll see whose side he comes down on!"

The truth was that Bao had no idea how Jenkins would react. She had only spent the last year and a half in the military, so most of the finer points of the system were still opaque to her. But Podsy had been in for over a decade, so she decided to trust his judgment on the matter.

Ford's eyes smoldered with rage. "I never threatened to open fire on you..."

"Stuff that mealy-mouth horseshit up your ass where it squirted from," Podsy snarled. "Everyone on the high-side of Bravo saw *exactly* what you did, and their sensor logs will confirm it." At that, Ford's face twisted into the very definition of bitter impotence, which only served to bolster Podsy as he lifted his voice again. "If you won't admit it, you don't belong anywhere but the stockade beside me. Say it—" he set his jaw, balling his badly-burned hands into fists at his sides, "—and let's all move on to more important things, like patching up these rigs and reloading our mags for when those sand-fuckers counterattack!"

By now, Captain Murdoch had made his way out of *Flaming Rose* on the opposite side of the parking lot and was within earshot of the exchange. He raised his booming voice to demand, "What in the name of Barack Hussein Obama the Fourth is going on here?!"

All eyes snapped back and forth between Ensign Ford and Lieutenant Xi, and when silence was the captain's only reply, he stomped to the center of the gathering and glared at the assemblage.

"Do I need to ask again?" Murdoch growled in a low, dangerous voice.

"It's an engineering dispute, sir," Vasquez replied sourly.

Murdoch turned his fiery gaze on the stocky Wrench. "A *what?*" he asked deliberately.

"An engineering dispute, sir," Podsy confirmed. "The ensign experienced a weapon system malfunction down in Bravo Tunnel and I offered a solution to the problem. We were just in the process of finalizing repair plans when he fell, nose-first, onto the deck."

Murdoch gave Podsy a withering gaze, "Do I look stupid to you, Podsednik?"

Podsy recoiled for the briefest instant, a delay and gesture that gave lie to the next words to pass his lips. "No, sir, definitely not."

Murdoch set his jaw and turned to Ensign Ford. "Well, Ensign? I'm waiting for the truth."

Ford glanced nervously around before nodding grudgingly. "It is, sir. I had a weapon system malfunction down in Bravo and the chief warrant was making suggestions how to avoid future recurrences."

Murdoch sneered at the ensign. "And how did you find his 'suggestions'?"

Ford shot a resentful look at Podsednik, then at Xi, before relenting. "They were…appropriate, sir."

Murdoch was no fool. He knew exactly what had happened, but somewhat surprisingly, he nodded. "Very well. Then I suggest you all report to the hydro-can to drop off your H2O for recycle and then get your asses back to work fixing your gear."

For a moment, nobody moved. They were either too exhausted from the fight or too stunned by Murdoch's uncharacteristic decision to ignore the breakdown in discipline, but whatever the reason, nobody moved.

"That was an order!" Murdoch barked.

At that, the various crews scrambled away, but before Murdoch did likewise. He met and held Xi's gaze for a long while before shaking his head and walking off.

After he had gone, Xi rounded on Podsy. "You asshole, I was going to break his nose!"

"And a finer job you'd have done of it," Podsy said, wincing as he cradled his burnt hands in front of his chest. "But I couldn't let you do it, LT."

"Why the hell not?!" she demanded, her anger rising at being denied the chance to put Ford on his ass, where he belonged.

"Because I know the score." Podsy shrugged. "After Murdoch, Jenkins doesn't have anyone with the brains, guts, and tactical know-how to assume command of anything more than an individual mech. You're young, and you lack confidence in dealing with subordinates, but you're the clear-cut choice for platoon command."

Xi wrinkled her nose in disgust, "What is this? You're trying to white knight for me so that I'll let you into my pants?"

Podsy chuckled. "You're not my type, remember? Too warm and animated. I like my lays like I like my sushi: cold and smelly."

"I'm serious, Chief," she snapped. "Why the sudden concern for my career? Have I ever once done anything to make you think I care about that at all?"

"Nope," Podsy allowed, "but unlike you, I do care about getting off this rock alive. Which means the battalion needs someone like you, not that festering pustule." Podsy pointed at the ensign. "Which means its best officers need to be in command. You're not perfect, but you're obviously better than a nepotistic shit-stain like Ford who got into Fleet Academy by having the right last name. So rather than have us come under his command, or even staying under Murdoch's," he added pointedly, "our best chance to survive is by pushing you up the ladder. And once you're there, you'll need to command the respect of your subordinates. That means no fisticuffs with anyone lower-ranked than you."

"You think they won't respect me even if I rearrange their dental work?"

"I think they'll fear and despise you, and that won't be good for *anyone*," Podsy said, meeting and holding her gaze before finishing. "I know a thing or two about this, LT, remember?"

Xi wanted to argue, but the unusual severity of his expression and tone deflated her. "Fine," she allowed, "but next time, expect friendly fire if you step between me and someone who deserves a beatdown."

"Will do." He nodded, wincing again as he cradled his hands.

"Let's get you to medical," she urged.

"Agreed." They had already emptied their moisture-retention

suits during their brief stop at HQ a few hours earlier, and since nobody liked visiting the so-called 'hydro-can,' they made their way to the hospital so that Podsy could get his hands looked at.

"What's the damage, Koch?" Jenkins asked after exiting *Roy* and making his way to the repair crew chief.

"Of the mechs you dragged back here—" Koch gestured to the five vehicles so badly damaged they couldn't move under their own power. "—none of them can be repaired down here. And of the rest—" He gestured to the parking lot. "—at least two need to be taken off the line immediately."

"I need better than that," Jenkins said, but the truth was he knew Koch was probably right.

"It's all we've got." Koch shrugged. "As it is, I'm pressing three of those damaged units back up against my better judgment, including *Devil Crab*..."

"*Elvira*," Jenkins interrupted with a lopsided grin. "Xi's earned her 'sign on this rock twice over."

"She's feisty," Koch allowed. "Maybe too feisty."

"Maybe," Jenkins admitted. "She saved all our lives down there, twice. I'm pinning the biggest and baddest medal on her even though she doesn't want it. And besides, she's all we've got."

"Touché," Koch snorted. "But seriously, we've barely got a full-strength company left here, even after we put everything we can back onto the line. A couple mechs can be used as stationary platforms to defend HQ, but they won't roll or walk again until they've been to a proper repair yard."

It wasn't what Jenkins wanted to hear, but it was what he had expected.

"How long to get everything else back online?" Jenkins pressed.

"Three days," Koch replied firmly. When Jenkins went to open his mouth, the repair chief added, "And not one minute less. I can't do much for most of the battered armor plates, but we can get the rest of the primary systems back online before them."

"Then I'd better let you get to work," Jenkins said with a nod, turning to leave but pausing to add, "Oh, and good work transplanting *Elvira*'s neural interface systems on short notice."

"Xi didn't have an NI in *Devil Crab*, Commander," Koch said with a knowing look.

"Really?" Jenkins' brow rose in surprise. "You transplanted the auto-pilot system? I thought the onboard computers were incompatible between *Elvira* and *Devil Crab*."

"They are," Koch said matter-of-factly.

Jenkins cocked his head in confusion, and his eyes bulged slightly as the gravity of Koch's suggestion sank in. "Wait... You're saying she *manually* walked a hexapedal mech down there at top speed, *fought* it without an NI, and made it back here without a single trip-up?"

"She's got skills, you said as much when you gave her first pick of the rigs," Koch said dryly. "Now, if you'll excuse me, I've got work to do."

Jenkins was stunned. He knew Xi was good, it was why he'd pushed for her field commission to lieutenant JG prior to deployment, but it was becoming painfully clear just how good she really was.

He shook his head to clear it as he made his way to the water reclamation facility, aka the 'hydro-can.'

The hydro-can was a heavily modified APC, which had been equipped with the best water-reclamation systems the Terran Republic could cram into its eight-meter-long chassis. Storage tanks sat on the ground beside the foul-smelling vehicle, which was unfortunately situated in the center of the camp. FGF Pounders and mech crews queued before these tanks, into which they emptied their environmentally-contained suits' combined urine and sweat stores into the first set of tanks.

Pumps cycled those first tanks' contents, not-so-affectionately referred to as 'clear water' by the men and women stationed here, through the filters inside the hydro-can APC until they were potable. The potable water tanks were situated on the opposite side of the hydro-can, and after emptying their 'clear water' bags into the tanks, the soldiers filled their reservoirs from the potable tanks.

This part of the system was fast, capable of processing two thousand gallons per hour with minimal power consumption. Jenkins had difficulty telling the difference between the hydro-can's product and the stuff they drank while aboard the Fleet carrier which had borne them here.

Unfortunately, sweat and piss weren't the only fluids the hydro-can extracted from the men and women of Jenkins' battalion.

The so-called 'dark water' tanks, situated fifty meters from the hydro-can, were where the battalion's bodily waste was deposited. Nobody liked the dark water tanks. Nobody liked what they represented, and nobody liked the possibility that they might come into play during this deployment. So people were understandably frugal with their water usage, even while rinsing their backsides after making routine deposits to the dark water supply.

Even Jenkins shuddered at the thought of drinking the stuff. No amount of technobabble or gobbledygook could ever convince a thinking human that drinking the water extracted from his own ass-faucet was a good idea. It wasn't. It was a bad idea, a *stupid* idea, but the dark water tanks' very existence suggested that someone was stupid for daring to *think* that the whole concept of drinking butt-water was anything but stupid.

Those tanks were a monument to many things that had gone wrong with humanity, in Jenkins' humble opinion, but after spending a few weeks on this blasted hellhole of a world, he was silently grateful that they existed.

Not much was worse than dying of thirst. And however unpalatable the idea of drinking rectal juice seemed to him, it was immeasurably preferable to being slowly mummified inside one's own skin by the inexorable process of dehydration.

So after making his deposits and withdrawals from the hydro-can, he made his way to a small quarantine zone that had been prepared prior to their arrival.

Arranged within that cordoned off area were parts of two dozen Arh'Kel infantry. They were hideous creatures for which there were no real comparisons outside of themselves. Silica-based lifeforms had been theorized for centuries, and given the chemical reactivity of silica being so similar to that of carbon, it had long been deemed inevitable that such lifeforms would exist.

But even after being taught about them in school, and after slaughtering *thousands* of them in the last few hours, the sight of their massive, six-limbed bodies sent an uncontrollable shiver down his spine.

Styles knelt beside one of the less-preserved specimens. It featured only two limbs connected to roughly half of its central 'torso' region, but Styles was digging around in its gore like a dog looking for a bone it had buried in the backyard.

"What have you got, Styles?" Jenkins asked, crouching down beside the battalion's de facto intelligence officer.

"I've found a few device fragments, but nothing intact," Styles said, gritting his teeth as he carefully rooted around inside the thing's guts. He withdrew his hand, which was covered in purple-blue gore, and plucked a small piece of metal from it. It was silvery and smooth, like a spoon sans handle, but its jagged edge made clear that it had been broken off from a larger device. "They're all like this," he said in disgust as he handed the piece to Jenkins.

"Pure platinum," Jenkins concluded.

"That'd be my guess, sir." Styles nodded. "It's an abundant

noble metal, so it's ideal for internal implants since it won't break down in body fluids."

"Do you think the devices self-destructed?" Jenkins mused.

"That'd also be my guess, Commander," Styles agreed as he moved to another corpse and broke out a small, diamond-edged circular saw that he used to cut into the relatively intact rock-biter. "All of these ones died from weapons fire or concussions." He gestured toward the arranged corpses before tilting his chin to the other side of the quarantine zone. "Those three over there didn't have any visible wounds. Two came from the tunnel where *Elvira* fired the pulse missile. The other came from near *Kamehameha*'s wreck in the cavern. My hope?" he offered before Jenkins could press the point, prompting Jenkins to nod encouragingly. "These devices weren't designed to deal with high-powered EMPs, and whatever self-destruct mechanisms they've got built into them weren't tripped when they overloaded their bearers' nervous systems. Rock-biter neurology's different from ours; their brains were probably scrambled by the EMP at the same time as the devices were shut off. Those three are my best bet to find intact linkages, but before I go cutting into them, I want to brush up on my Arh'Kel biology."

"Do you need any help?" Jenkins asked.

"Better I do it myself, sir." Styles shook his head confidently. "These things look pretty fragile. I should be through the pile in the hour, and an hour after that, I'll be cracking open the first of those three." He jerked a thumb toward the three fully intact Arh'Kel bodies.

"Are you sure they're dead?" Jenkins asked warily, noting with approval the eight-man fire team which had them under constant watch.

"They're dead, sir," Styles said with certainty. "Ran a few tests just to be sure," he added with a smirk, patting his sidearm emphatically.

"All the same," Jenkins allowed, "I want these things out of my camp as soon as you're finished with them. Clear?"

"As a Solarian's conscience," Styles acknowledged with a smirk, drawing a forced look of disapproval from Jenkins.

"Eye on the ball, Chief," he mildly rebuked. He had no more love for the Sol-bound humans than any other warm-blooded Terran, but at the end of the day, they were still human. Living in the past was a sure way to darken the future, and at this moment in time, the human race, whether they lived in the Solar System or on a Terran colony, needed to come together more than it needed to be cast apart. And that reunion, the oft-cited goal of many political minorities in the Terran Republic, was one of the most important projects before the Republic. And Jenkins, somewhat unusually for a career military man, happened to agree with the importance of reuniting the far-flung tribes of humanity.

Even if the damn Solarians *had* left the Terran Republic colonies to the proverbial wolves while hiding out in the safety of Sol.

"LT," Podsy called out after returning from the hydro-can, "Commander wants to see us pronto."

Xi sighed in frustration. She was working to restore lube flow to Three Leg on *Elvira* but had made zero progress in the last twenty minutes. Everything was seized or blocked to the point that it would take a proper machine shop to put it to rights.

"Fine, fine," she grunted, slipping out from beneath the exposed assembly and brushing herself off. "Let's go face the music."

Podsy nodded, gesturing for her to take the lead as they made their way across the plateau toward Jenkins' command vehicle.

The system primary was barely visible on the horizon, with less than an eighth of its orb peeking over the edge of the world at them. It still filled the sky with an angry, orange glow, just as it had done since they'd set down on this miserable lump of rock.

The planet they were on, named Durgan's Folly after its first attempted colonization efforts, led by Chairman Durgan who controlled one of the most powerful corporations this side of the wormholes, was tidally-locked to its parent star. As a result, half of the planet saw constant, burning daylight while the other half saw perpetual night.

The thin band between these two wildly opposite halves was where the Arh'Kel had concentrated their previous efforts, and it was there that they had appeared during this particular attack. It had been decades since the Arh'Kel had been seen on this world, and the Terran government had thought the planet to be free of their influence. With no Arh'Kel ships breaching the Terran wormhole gates since the Second Terran-Arh'Kel Conflict, it had been assumed that the rock-biters had been effectively cast out of human-controlled territory.

But after the engagement in the tunnels that *Elvira* had breached, it was now abundantly clear that the rock-biters were playing a longer game than the Terrans, and that they intended to take control of this mineral-rich world.

Solar harvest arrays served as dual-purpose energy producers and heat shields atop the rocky plateau, with most of the soldiers opting to sleep near the four-hundred-meter-long line of three-meter-tall film since it was the most comfortable spot under the sun.

Xi and Podsy walked past the line of cots, a quarter of which were occupied by recovering wounded, eventually making their way to *Roy*.

Just looking at that battlefield behemoth sent a thrill up Xi's spine. It was a rare combination-drive mech, with both rolling and walking capabilities due to its advanced limb design, and its armaments outstripped any two mechs in the battalion. With armor that could soak up multiple direct railgun hits to any given segment, it was only fitting that Commander Lee 'Roy' Jenkins ride it into battle.

Roy was a prototype designed by none other than Edgar Durgan, the great grandson of the same Richard Durgan for whom this blasted rock was named. The Durgans were military collectors, operating two dozen military-themed museums across the Terran Republic, with two facilities recently opening on Mars and Earth, respectively, much to the general surprise and chagrin of Terrans.

Edgar Durgan had been one of Commander Jenkins' key contacts and allies in trying to get the new Fleet Armor Corps approved for use against the rock-biters. No sane Terran doubted the supremacy of the Fleet Marine Corps in dealing death to the enemies of humanity, with its hyper-advanced power armor and rigorously-trained warriors, but the Arh'Kel had destroyed the armor production facilities and crippled key infrastructure points that permitted the Terran Republic to replenish material losses.

Stopgap plans had been called for, to bridge the gap while new power-armor-production facilities were brought online, and one of those plans had been Commander Jenkins' idea that old-style mechs could be of use against the rock-biters.

And after the subterranean engagement they had just returned from, it was clear that the commander's plan had proven its merits beyond a shadow of a doubt.

Xi stepped up the ramp leading to *Roy's* interior and soon made eye contact with the commander, who beckoned, "Lieutenant, come in. Chief." He nodded as Podsednik reached the top of the ramp. "First off..." Jenkins set aside a data slate he had been perusing. "Are the two of you fit for duty?"

"Yes, sir," Xi and Podsy replied in unison.

"Doctor Fellows tells me to order you both onto forty-eight-hour medical leave," the commander continued, glancing back and forth between the two of them. "What do you think about that?"

"Candidly, sir?" Xi arched a brow.

"Of course." Jenkins gestured invitingly.

"My mech's down, I've got a headache that just won't quit, an enemy that wants to rip my throat out, and to be perfectly blunt, it's nearing that time of the month," she said, stone-faced and serious, "the last thing this unit needs is for Doctor Strange Bed to pull my team off the line. Sir," she added belatedly.

"You won't do this battalion any good if you develop meningitis, Lieutenant," Jenkins warned before turning to Podsy. "Be straight with me, Chief: is she good to go?"

Without missing a beat, Podsednik nodded. "She is, sir. And I won't hesitate to send her to the nurse's office if she starts looking delicate."

Xi's eyes widened in outrage as she flashed an angry look Podsy's way. Meanwhile, Jenkins' composed mask of professionalism broke into a broad grin as he chuckled. "Not much chance of that happening though, eh, Chief?"

"Not if history's any kind of predictor, no, sir," Podsy said with a lopsided grin of his own.

"All right." Jenkins nodded as footfalls came up the ramp behind them. "Oh, good, Captain Murdoch," the commander greeted, causing Xi's hackles to rise as 2nd Company's captain arrived, "you're just in time. I was just assigning Lieutenant Xi command of 5th Platoon."

Murdoch stiffened and Xi felt herself go numb from the neck down as her company captain said, "Sir?"

"We're down to fifteen combat-ready mechs, Captain," Jenkins explained, "it's time we built up the command structure a bit. We'll go with 1st, 2nd, 4th, and 5th Platoons to be filled out as follows." He handed slates to both Murdoch and Xi. "I'll take 1st, Lieutenant Koch will take 2nd, you'll take 4th, and Xi will take 5th.

Understood?" he asked, his eyes never wavering from Captain Murdoch.

Murdoch scowled, making clear his disapproval while replying, "Yes, sir."

"Good." Jenkins' gaze lingered on Murdoch for a few seconds before shifting to Xi. "You'll be assigned *Elvira II*, *Spin Doctor*, *Wolverine*, and *Forktail*. You won't have a dedicated recon mech, and your unit will be one of the slower ones in the battalion, so I'm reassigning our last Owl drone directly to 5th Platoon to mitigate those shortcomings. Any questions?" he asked, and the brief glimmer in his eye told her that he had assigned her *Forktail* specifically because of the spat back in the parking lot.

"No, s..." She shook her head firmly, her voice breaking at the end of the second word. She cleared her throat and reiterated, "No, sir, Commander Jenkins."

"Before I dismiss you, let me give you this." Jenkins held out his hand. In it, a crumpled ribbon was attached to a shiny bronze medallion. "Bronze Star. It's the highest I can give on the spot, but I'm putting you in for the button, the Medal of Honor."

"Why?" the lieutenant asked, confusion seizing her features.

"For actions above and beyond. There's no way you thought you were coming out of there alive, Bao. Just like throwing yourself on a grenade so others could live. This medal is just a thing. It doesn't matter, but what you did does. It's my responsibility to recognize you for that." The commander dug into his pocket and fished out a second medal. "You, too, Chief."

"She made me do it, sir," Podsy replied, keeping his hands at his side.

"Take it, you goddamn ingrate. A pay raise goes with those, but not if you don't take it. Spend your extra money on booze, hookers, or the church. I don't care which."

Podsy shook his head and smiled. "Thank you, sir. For what it's worth, it was all my idea."

Xi punched Podsy in the arm hard enough to make him stumble.

"Or not," he added.

"Now you're dismissed." Jenkins waved them away, and Xi saluted before returning down the ramp they had just climbed.

After they were a few dozen paces from *Roy*, she hissed, "I hope you're pleased with yourself, Chief."

"Just looking out for Number One, LT," he replied smugly.

She slugged him in the shoulder, hard, before resigning herself to her new circumstances.

She was now the commanding officer of her own armored platoon. *Her*, Xi Bao, a former political dissident and potentially life-long prisoner of Terra Han, the most populous world in the Terran Republic. She had always been a trouble-maker, a rebel, and sometimes, an out-and-out criminal.

What the hell is Commander Jenkins thinking? First a medal and then he puts me in command of a platoon? She seethed as she worked to come to terms with these latest prison shackles, shackles which would require her to actually *lead* people, be responsible for their lives, lest they, and she, die for her failure to do so effectively. *God help anyone who makes this job any harder than it has to be, like that flaming jagoff Ensign Asswipe.*

TRADING, DEGENERACY, & BELONGING

"Oh, come on, Lieutenant," Podsy pleaded with the repair crew's, and 2nd Platoon's, commanding officer. "*Elvira* needs those lube systems online or she'll be limited to a five-legged crawl."

"I can fix two other mechs in the time it would take my people to clear your Scorpion's lube system," Koch reiterated. "I'm sorry, Chief, I can't help you until I've gotten *Racetrack* and *Flaming Rose* back up to snuff."

"Murdoch's mech?!" Podsednik feigned incredulity. "He barely took any fire, and all of his key systems are operating, unlike 5th Platoon's command mech, *Elvira*, which is already the slowest command mech in the battalion."

"You're not moving the needle, Chief," Koch cut in. "My hands are tied. I've got direct orders from Captain Murdoch to prioritize *Flaming Rose* in my queue. Now, if you can get the commander to override that order, I'd be happy to look into *Elvira*'s problems. But as it stands right now, all you're doing is pissing me off, and one Wrench to another, you know that's not a smart thing to do. *Elvira*'s fourth in the queue, barring new orders from Commander Jenkins or Captain Murdoch. Is there anything else?"

Podsy hadn't expected to get anywhere with Koch, but it had been worth a try. "Fine," he grunted. "Can you at least have *Kochtopussy* come over and detach *Elvira* II's third leg, main joint and all?"

Koch seemed to consider that as his eyes flicked across the parking lot, and for a moment, Podsy thought he would deny the request. "I can do that," Koch agreed.

"Thank you," Podsy gushed, but Koch held up a hand haltingly.

"I need something in return, though," the repair chief said knowingly.

Podsy scowled. "If you're going to ask for some 'private time' with Xi, let me do my best to warn..."

"No," Koch snorted, "I may be as horny as every other swinging dick on this rock, but I'm not suicidal. No..." He leaned conspiratorially toward Podsednik, who reluctantly obliged by mirroring the gesture as the lieutenant whispered, "I want Captain Murdoch's enviro-suit."

Podsy recoiled in alarm. "Why, Lieutenant," he recovered hastily, "I didn't know you have a thing for the captain."

"Will you cut that crap out." Koch rolled his eyes. "Everyone in this battalion received two fully-functional enviro-suits—one primary, one back-up. Now, unlike most of these degenerate slobs..." He scowled at a nearby group of his grease-monkeys. "I know how to maintain my suit, which is why, unlike just about everyone else, my backup was still in its original packaging when it disappeared three days ago."

"You think Murdoch stole it?" Podsy asked in confusion.

"Maybe, maybe not." Koch shrugged. "But I do know that he's been belligerent in 'requisitioning' supplies for himself and his crews at the expense of everyone else. I can see why he got clinked as a field quartermaster. Bastard's fingers are stickier than yours are after a long night with a fresh corpse."

"Hey now," Podsy drawled, "this isn't about me, and that was different. Get caught in a completely innocent yet suggestive position with a dead body and it becomes everyone's favorite gossip."

"Fine, fine," Koch chuckled, "but I happen to know that Murdoch and I share nearly-identical physical measurements, and he's got at least two unopened enviro-suits, and this is after he's gone through at least *three* of them already."

"If you know how to maintain your suit," Podsy mused, "why do you need a backup badly enough to risk Captain Murdoch's wrath?"

Koch gave him a withering look. "This one's starting to chafe, bad, and I'm not about to give Doc Strange Bed access to my high-security sectors. So either you get me one of Murdoch's enviro-suits, or you'll have to wait until my queue clears before I can see to *Elvira's* repairs."

Podsy nodded. "Fine. How long have I got?"

"*Kochtopussy* will be available in three hours," Koch replied. "After that, she'll be indisposed for about two days. If I don't have my suit by then..." He left the remainder unspoken.

"Yeah, yeah." Podsy waved him off as he turned to leave. "I'll get it done."

"You're good people, Podsednik," Koch said before amending, "actually, you're the most degenerate knuckle-dragger in this battalion."

"Yeah," Podsy called over his shoulder, "but I'm *your* kind of degenerate, Cock."

"It's *Koch*, you numbskull," the lieutenant snapped.

"That's what I said." Podsy turned mid-stride, splaying his arms innocently to either side. "Cock."

Koch's back was already turned, which meant that the male-bonding banter was at an end.

It was time for Podsy to get serious about finding that enviro-suit.

"Which leaves us with two options," Podsy explained after breaking down the situation for Xi.

"We aren't waiting," Xi said adamantly, "so there's only one option."

"Of course we're not waiting," Podsy said dismissively. "But there *are* two options. First, we cut a deal with Murdoch's Wrench, Chippy, since she's the only one who gets round-the-clock access to his bunk aboard *Flaming Rose*. Odds are the old paper-pusher won't even notice in the three days it takes for Fleet to drop reinforcements in and begin evacuating us off this rock."

"Are Murdoch and Chippy sleeping together?" Xi asked.

"What?" Podsy made a distasteful expression before shaking it off. "Not to my knowledge. Why would that matter?"

"If they're sleeping together then she's not going to betray him, even over a suit, for any of the crap we could offer her," Xi explained with an emphatic eye-roll.

"I think you might overestimate the emotional entanglements formed by sometimes bunkmates," Podsy snickered.

"And I think *you* might overestimate your understanding of women," Xi retorted.

He paused, then shrugged, "Yeah, you're probably right about that, but that just makes me a regular guy, right?"

Xi laughed mercilessly. "You're many things, Podsy, but 'regular' isn't one of them."

"True enough," he agreed with a mischievous grin.

"So what's the other option?" she asked.

"What?"

"The other option—" Xi rolled her eyes again. "What is it?"

"Oh, that? Yeah, you were right. There isn't another option," he snickered.

"Then what the hell?"

"I mean to say that there isn't a second option *yet*," Podsy explained. "See, the reason I doubt Murdoch and Chippy are doing the horizontal mambo is because, well...he's not her type."

"I can't imagine Captain Murdoch is *any* woman's type," Xi scoffed.

"You misunderstand," Podsy sighed. "I'm sayin' that *you're* more her type than Murdoch is."

Xi glared at him. "If you're suggesting I..."

"Of course not," he interrupted hastily, "but I do happen to know there's a few Pounders that might be to her liking. But Chippy... Well, see, Chippy's not personable. She'll need someone to help break the ice for her."

"Fine, go ahead and be her ice-breaker." Xi shrugged.

"I ain't exactly their type, remember?" Podsy said dryly, causing her to clench her fists in anticipation of what he might say next. "Besides, attractive as you are, you're not likely to get their motors revving."

"What?" she asked in confusion. First she had felt insulted that he suggest she use her body in order to get Lieutenant Koch a fresh enviro-suit, and now she felt insulted by the intimation that she was somehow not attractive enough to succeed even if she tried! Then she had a thought. "If this is some kind of sick, reverse psychology, I swear to God, I'll..."

"No, no, no, nothing like that," he assured her. "See, these people are mostly xenophiles with more than a few misandrists sprinkled in for good measure. And rumor has it that Chief Styles has the most..." Podsy hesitated, becoming visibly uncomfortable as he spoke, "*robust* collection of 'exotic imagery' in the battalion. And I'm talking hundred percent, all-natural recordings, none of that computer-generated garbage, starring every permutation you can think of. Arh'Kel, Vorr, Jemmin, you name it, he's got it."

"I don't want to know how you know any of this, Podsy," Xi scowled before sighing. "Fine, so we've got to give Chippy some of Styles' sicko alien porn so that she can get in for a few rounds of fun with the Pounders. What's Styles going to want?"

"Oh, that?" Podsy chuckled. "That part's easy, he just wants you."

"Podsy," she snapped, standing with a fist cocked in preparation for her first attempt at rhinoplasty.

"He assures me it's not like that." Podsy held up his hands in mock surrender, though from the smile tugging at the corners of his mouth, it was clear he was enjoying this far more than he should. "I mean, he also assures me that nothing would make him happier." She fired a left hand at his face, but her blow was blocked by his crossed arms. He laughed as she slammed a few more half-hearted punches into his defensive shell, before he finally turned serious. "He says he thinks you two knew each other from before you were arrested."

She stopped mid-punch and drew back in alarm. "That's impossible. We're from totally different worlds," she said in flat denial.

"I know, I know," Podsy assured her, "but he said that if I could get you to come see him, he'd owe me one. It's the only way I know how to get Koch to help us replace *Elvira*'s leg."

Xi was surprised, but more than that, she was curious. She considered the situation for a few minutes before finally relenting. "Fine, I'll go see him. But if this is a trick…" she warned.

"If it's a trick, I'll deal with him myself," Podsy assured her with chilling severity.

No one knew exactly why Podsednik had been in prison when Jenkins' recruiting drive had come through. On Podsy's native Terra Australiana, sometimes called 'New Australia' by Terrans, the local government did not make public a prisoner's crime, only the severity of it and the sentence terms. It was deemed to be a protection of privacy that was often lauded by one side of the political spectrum and lambasted by the other.

As a result, a guessing game had come into being with people betting on the nature of Podsednik's actual crime. Long story short, Podsednik had denied every single theory until, strangely, someone half-heartedly accused him of multiple counts of necrophilia.

Even stranger than the accusation itself was Podsednik's uncharacteristic hesitation to refute it.

So the battalion had quickly decided he was a necrophiliac, and wave after wave of low-brow jokes at his expense began making the rounds. Podsy seemed to encourage these theories, but Xi was completely unconvinced.

Xi had been with him every single day for six months prior to deployment on Durgan's Folly, and the more time she spent with him, the more she came to suspect he had been convicted of murdering a superior officer. Podsy brushed her off whenever she attempted to broach the subject, which did nothing to dissuade her from this line of thinking.

"Fine," Xi grimaced. "I'll go talk with this alien-porn-collecting jackass."

"Good." Podsy nodded. "I'll go see about a few other loose ends in the meantime. If I'm lucky, I might be able to get the missile launcher on *Devil Crab*, make that *Elvira II*," he corrected with a grin, "back up and running. Let me know as soon as you've gotten the stuff from Styles."

Xi moved to the quarantine area where Styles was still rooting around in the Arh'Kel corpses. At first, she had thought the task would be universally considered a gruesome and distasteful one, but after learning of Styles' porn collection, she was beginning to doubt whether he was displeased with the assignment.

She came to a perimeter established by a detail of Pounders, who interdicted her passage. "Authorized personnel only, Lieutenant," said one of the lightly-armored troopers.

"I'm here to see Chief Styles," she explained.

"He ordered us to prevent disturbances," the trooper denied with a firm shake of his head.

Xi hesitated. She very much disliked the notion of being in such close proximity to a weirdo like Styles. As the only teenage woman in the unit, she had become the instant target of all kinds of lewd commentary. The fact that she could hold her own in hand-to-hand combat, owing to lifelong training and her impressive, athletic physique, seemed to do little to dissuade the mostly good-natured displays of camaraderie disguised as sexual harassment.

But Podsy had gone through a lot for her, including donating his own cerebrospinal fluid in order to get her back on her feet. She owed him. And the entire Ponzi trading scheme was to get *Elvira* back to full combat readiness, and that was the effort she could throw her full weight behind.

She sighed. "He's wanted to see me since we set down on this rock. I haven't had the time before, but now I do. Let him know this might be the only chance he gets."

The Pounder hesitated before making his way to Styles' side. The chief warrant, stooped over a seemingly undamaged Arh'Kel corpse, tore his attention from the work at hand after the Pounder relayed Xi's message. Styles waved her over, and the Pounders at the perimeter gestured for her to proceed.

The Arh'Kel, somewhat surprisingly, didn't stink nearly as badly as she thought they would. They had a distinctive odor, like a faint trace of rotten eggs buried beneath something metallic, like fresh blood. But considering the several tons of carnage they had brought back for study, the smell was far from overpowering.

"Lieutenant Xi," Styles greeted, wiping his hands on a nearby cloth as he stood from his gruesome autopsy, "what brings you here?"

"Podsednik said you were interested in speaking with me," she replied, looking down at the carefully-dissected Arh'Kel corpse. "And he said you've got something I need, so this seemed like a good opportunity for mutual satisfaction."

At saying that last bit, she gritted her teeth in annoyance with herself. *If he makes some off-color comment, I'll knee him in the groin.*

Styles cocked his head in confusion before realization dawned and he laughed. "That makes sense, I guess," he chuckled.

"Why?" she demanded defensively. "Why does that make sense?"

He held up his hands in mock surrender. "I didn't mean anything by it. No." He shook his head, wiping his forehead with the back of his sleeve. "I don't think you're into that kind of thing. It's too degenerate."

She cocked her head in guarded confusion. "I'm starting to think this was a mistake."

Before she could turn and leave, he said, "I think you and I frequented the same virtual communities. Never at the same time, of course," he added hastily, "since instant communication between the Terran colonies is still impossible, but I've seen your work. I know why you were imprisoned. It took me awhile to figure it out, but after I did, I thought it would be a good idea to introduce myself," he explained, offering a mostly-clean hand as he said, "I'm not baroque or gothic enough."

She furrowed her brow in confusion. "What the hell is that supposed to mean?"

He laughed. "Okay, you probably knew me better as N609E."

She gasped and took a step back.

"Perfect." He grinned triumphantly. "See, that's what N609E stands for: 'Not Baroque Or Gothic Enough.' You were one of the only people on Terra Han that actually fed back into our little community of virtual miscreants and rebels."

She eyed him warily, considering whether or not she should incriminate herself by acknowledging that she was, in fact, extensively familiar with N609E's work. During her criminal trial, prosecutors had tried to make her flip on the underground virtual academy that N609E and his allies had established. She'd inadvertently given up some information about them, but the fact was that she had been too peripheral to know much of import.

"How do I know this isn't some kind of trap?" she asked warily.

Styles looked around and chuckled. "Lieutenant, look around you. We're stuck on an inhospitable world, surrounded by rock-biters and running low on supplies. Not to mention that we're both convicts. The systems chewed both of us up and spat us out."

She nodded slowly as she wrapped her brain around the situation. "Why tell me this? Why reveal yourself to be one of the most wanted data criminals in the Republic? They still think you're at large."

"They do," he agreed, "since I, and everyone else in the network, had contingencies set up that would keep my work from being compromised should something minor, like incarceration or death, befall me. Freedom of information is the only battle truly worth waging, as far as I'm concerned. Well..." He smirked, casting a wayward look at the rock-biter corpses surrounding them. "Maybe not the *only* one."

Xi was still dumbfounded by what Styles had just told her. N609E was a legend in the underground information community. He had singlehandedly cracked government databases considered uncrackable, and used data gleaned from them to expose hundreds of high-level officials for political corruption, and even mass murder on one particularly memorable instance.

Frankly, it defied belief.

"I'm skeptical," she said after thinking long and hard about it.

"I never had direct interactions with N609E. I only ever accessed some of the files he uploaded."

"Files which you then strategically spread across your home world's public data nets." He nodded approvingly. "You knew where to put it so it would have maximum impact, like the upload to the weather broadcast servers," he added matter-of-factly, a crime which the government had never formally brought against her. "And it *did* have maximum impact, which led to your prison sentence. I'm not going to apologize for that, either." He shrugged. "You did what you thought you should with that data, and it saved lives, *thousands* of them. You made me, all of us, really proud, especially the way you stood tall under fire."

She shrugged. "I never fit into the big, wide world. Prison didn't seem like it would be a bad thing."

"Was it?"

"It was…different than I expected," she said hesitantly. "Being cut off from the feeds was the hardest part, but I was never a coder or architect, so it wasn't about not expressing myself. It didn't bother me to be denied access to the information, but not being able to send that information to others who could use it… that hurt more than I thought it would."

He nodded solemnly. "I understand…*completely*. It's why you and I jumped at the chance to have our sentences commuted through public service. Both of us care about the big, wide world, even though it doesn't care about us." He looked around the plateau, his eyes skipping over the Pounders and snagging on the various mech crews working to restore their platforms to fighting strength. "I think that's about the only thing that unites the people in this battalion, or at least those of us who weren't military before the commander started recruiting," he added sourly as his gaze lingered on *Flaming Rose*, where Captain Murdoch stood directing a full repair team.

"What a jackass," she muttered.

"You said it," Styles agreed. "He got nabbed for diverting

supplies, and not even for money or career advancement, those motives I could understand," he said with a derisive snort. "No, he was diverting supplies so that he could get a cushier assignment. Too bad for him that his benefactor fell under investigation and had to flip on his many co-conspirators in order to walk out with his pension, let alone his freedom. He put the lives of servicemen in jeopardy so that he could get a more comfortable chair to sit in while he rides out his service contract," he said through gritted teeth. "He's what's wrong with the bureaucracy."

Xi suddenly took Styles' meaning, "You exposed him?"

"Yep." Styles smirked. "One of the last things I did before they nabbed me. I tried to dissuade the commander from bringing him aboard, but there weren't any other command-level officers available. It was probably the right call bringing him aboard," he allowed, "but that doesn't mean I have to like it."

He shook his head and looked out at the perpetually-setting sun, causing Bao to do likewise. After a few seconds, he reached into his breast pocket and handed her a small data storage chip. "Here. I think this is what you came for, right?"

Snapping her focus back to the here and now, Xi recalled why she had come to see Styles in the first place and nodded. She scrunched her face up in disgust as she plucked it from his fingers. She deposited it into her hip pocket and nodded. "Thank you, Chief."

"Any time, Lieutenant," he chuckled. "Just see that it's returned to me after Podsy's gotten what he needs from it."

She hesitated before asking, "Why do you have this...filth?"

He shrugged indifferently. "They need their fix just like the rest of us. And since nobody was harmed in producing that 'filth' and it's likely to come in handy scratching someone's itch out here on the front-lines, I'm not going to be a power-mad prude and deny them a back-scratcher just because I can. These people need reasons to fight and, if necessary, to die. The way I see it, they've earned the right to be weird just by lacing up those boots and doing their bit for their fellow Terrans. Still, I don't like hanging onto that crap any more than you do. It makes my skin crawl..." He rolled his eyes exaggeratedly. "Fucking degenerates."

Xi laughed in spite of herself. "All right...thank you, Chief."

"Any time, Lieutenant," he replied with a nod before returning to his grisly duties. "Oh," he called out as she turned to leave, "and if you're up for some trolling..."

She saw a mischievous grin on his lips, which she couldn't help but return as she said, "Always."

"I made it pretty clear to Podsy that my interest in you was purely sexual," he explained. "I'd consider it both top-form trolling *and* a personal favor to me if you could reinforce that suggestion. I don't want anyone putting two-and-two together here about our prior relationship. Your world has a statute of limitations on this kind of thing, but mine doesn't. I'm taking a big risk telling you about myself, so anything you can do to watch my back would be appreciated. And I'm not going to lie: the social credit around here would do wonders for my image."

She rolled her eyes, but ultimately knew he was right. Styles was one of the most hunted criminals in the Republic, but from her perspective, he had never done anything destructive. His only goal had been to disseminate otherwise suppressed information, and if he was indeed who he claimed, which seemed likely at this point, then he truly had placed his fate in her hands.

"I'll think of something," she agreed as a plan began to form in her mind.

"Perfect." He nodded, his grin suggesting he knew she was up to something that would probably come around to bite him. "Good luck, Lieutenant."

Podsy had just successfully concluded a round of negotiations with a group of off-duty Pounders and returned to *Elvira* when Xi stepped into the mech's cabin.

Her expression was twisted into one of extreme distaste as she reached for a nearby water bottle. Dumping more than half of it onto her suit as she rinsed something apparently foul out of her mouth, Podsy was just about to ask what happened when she shot him a fiery look.

"Not *one* word about this to *anyone*, Podsy," she snapped.

He furrowed his brow in confusion. "What happened?"

"Oh please," she sneered, "you knew all he wanted was a piece of me. Well, he got it, and you got your sicko porn collection." She flung a data chip onto his lap. She visibly gagged, doubling over for a moment before once again straightening herself and fixing him with an angry glare. "Not one word to anyone. I get fetishized enough *without* rumors spreading through the battalion like a case of the clap."

"If he hurt you..." Podsy growled, the threat hanging heavily in the air.

"Oh, please." She rolled her eyes. "He had his price and I paid it. Just because I think something's gross and degenerate doesn't mean it was violent or forced on me. I'm a big girl. I don't need a white knight rushing to defend me at every turn. Besides," she said, her moue of distaste softening fractionally as a glimmer flickered across her eyes, "it's not like it was *all* bad. But having to watch *that* crap the whole time...and the audio..." She glanced bitterly down at the data chip in his lap. Her hand went to her mouth and she burped. "I think I'm going to throw up..."

Podsy was thoroughly confused, and unsure if he should go privately address the matter with Styles. Yes, he had known that Styles had a sexual interest in Xi, but that was true for at least three-quarters of the battalion, including the women! She had curves in all the right places, striking facial features, and a fiery, playful personality that was every bit as alluring as her physique.

As far as he was concerned, she was the perfect woman. But she was also barely more than half his age, and despite her attractiveness, he had never really thought of her romantically.

"Well…" he finally hazarded, looking down at the data chip. "I mean…fine. If you say it's all good, I'll drop it…for now."

"He's a pencil-neck, Podsy," she said dismissively, after sitting down and apparently getting her guts under control. "You could drop him with a stiff jab, but there's no need. Still…" she said awkwardly, "thanks for…you know…caring."

"Of course, LT." He nodded, picking the data chip up and declaring, "It's getting late. I'd better go make this handoff so we can get Koch's people to push us up the line."

"Go." She waved a hand, which soon went to her lips as her cheeks turned a tortured shade of green.

After Podsy was out of earshot, Xi closed *Elvira*'s hatch and erupted into full-throated laughter.

"Men," she snickered, taking a deep, steadying breath as she refocused on the repair work awaiting her at the pilot's console. "Sometimes it's so easy, you almost feel sorry for them…*almost*."

TALL WAGONS & INITIATIVE

Commander Jenkins was struggling. The battle in the cavern had been greater than he had expected it to be. The enemy were at least ten times more numerous than Fleet Intelligence had suggested they would be. Durgan's Folly continued to live down to its name.

The Arh'Kel had almost destroyed his battalion and killed everyone under his command, and in the full day since they had returned to the plateau, that thought had dominated his consciousness.

He looked up at the full bottle on his shelf. Whisky. Old and dry. Imported from Earth under a centuries-old label, it was easily one of the most sought-after bottles in the Terran Republic and there it sat, staring at him.

Describing the urge to crack that bottle open and guzzle it was impossible. Even after years of waging, and often losing, his personal war with the stuff's impact on his life, Jenkins could offer no verbal description of its allure that made sense.

Hunger. Gravity. Lust. Yearning. Incompletion. Familiarity. Companionship. None of those things described the urge that rose within him like the tide rising and falling, slowly eroding the shore with its rhythmic caress. And yet, in a way, all of those words did describe it.

Telling a drunk like Jenkins not to drink was like telling a politician not to lie, or a doctor not to heal, or a teacher not to teach, or a parent not to love their children. Drinking wasn't something he did, or even *wanted* to do. It was more like *not* doing it somehow denied him access to a part of himself, a part he was ashamed of, certainly, but a part that he had come to accept was inextricable from his core being.

And there that bottle sat, daring him to give in and love that wicked part of himself. Telling him that it wasn't weakness to seek comfort in a lifelong companion, one he could never, and *would* never, truly be rid of.

The problem was that Jenkins was giving serious consideration to doing just that.

Standing up, he reached out with hesitant fingers, like a teenager's first brush with sex, and touched the outside of the bottle. The thrill that went through him was tantalizing, and he decided this was it. He only had the one bottle, after all, and once it was gone, so too would be the temptation to drink it. Fleet reinforcements would arrive in two days' time, and the plateau was well-defended. They could get along without him for a few hours.

He grabbed the bottle and turned it over, reading the label as he had done a hundred times before. The seal on the cap was intact, and he could almost hear the snapping and crinkling of the plastic wrap seal. The metal-on-glass of the lid twisting off. The deep aroma wafting through his nose. He could feel all of it as acutely as anything without even opening the bottle.

Jenkins paused briefly before reaching up to twist the top off. No more hesitation. No more delays. It was time.

Just as his fingers closed on the lid, the chime at his door rang, freezing him mid-motion.

He looked down at the bottle in his hands, and it was as if a spell had been broken. He stood in horrified silence for a long moment while the back of his mind was filled with a devious cackle. *It's okay*, that silent voice mocked, *I'll be back later.*

Jenkins gave serious thought to smashing the bottle on the floor, but he knew that it served him better intact than it ever would in pieces, or worse, lying empty on the floor beside his passed-out body.

The chime rang again, and he carefully replaced the bottle in its place on the shelf before acknowledging, "Enter."

The hatch popped open and Styles stepped through. "Sir, I've got Captain Murdoch outside for you."

Jenkins resisted the urge to roll his eyes. "I'll be right there."

Straightening his uniform, Jenkins followed Styles out of his cramped cabin inside *Roy's* rear compartment. Outside, at the base of the ramp, Murdoch waited with that insufferably entitled expression, the same one he had worn when Jenkins had broken the news of Xi being promoted to platoon leader.

"Captain," Jenkins acknowledged, "what can I do for you?"

"I'm lodging a formal complaint against Lieutenant Xi, Lieutenant Koch, and Chief Warrant Podsednik," Murdoch declared.

Jenkins quirked a brow. "On what grounds?"

"The details are here, sir," Murdoch said, handing Jenkins a data chip.

"Answer the question, Captain," Jenkins said flatly.

Murdoch purpled with anger. "Lieutenant Koch, in defiance of direct orders issued by a superior officer, diverted vital personnel from repairs on 4th Platoon's command vehicle to inexplicably work on one of the down-checked mechs."

"Which one?" Jenkins asked in confusion.

"It's in the report, sir," Murdoch reiterated, causing Jenkins' jaw to set.

"I'm not in the habit of repeating myself to a subordinate, *Captain*," he growled. "Which down-check were Koch's people working on?"

Murdoch's ears turned red as he jutted his chin defiantly. "*Elvira*, Commander."

"I see." Jenkins nodded as he began to understand the nature of the situation. "What was the impact of these personnel diversions?"

"Sir?" Murdoch asked, blank-faced like a particularly dim student, or like someone pretending to be such.

"You're testing my patience, Captain," Jenkins growled.

"Sorry, Commander, it's just, I…" Murdoch stammered before stiffening his spine, at least as much as he seemed capable of. "Vital personnel were diverted from a mission-critical assignment without prior authorization from a superior officer. It's impossible to know exactly what the impact was, sir, though I would hope we agree that rank insubordination is dangerous in any command structure, doubly so during combat conditions."

"I see." Jenkins grimaced. "So what you're saying is that there was no impact, at least none that you could detail in this report." He waved the data chip pointedly. "Is that correct, Captain Murdoch?"

"I…" Murdoch's blank-faced stare returned as he stood there, apparently dumbfounded before finally replying, "I did not detail the observable impacts in my report, Commander, no, sir."

"Did you observe any practical impact?" Jenkins pressed, deciding it was high time to snap Murdoch's leash, hard. "If so, I'll accept your verbal report here and spare you the trouble of transcribing it. After all, as you correctly pointed out, we are in combat conditions."

Murdoch's brow lowered thunderously. "Commander, if you do not intend to…"

"What I intend, Captain Murdoch," Jenkins snapped, raising his voice without consciously thinking to do so, "is to receive your verbal report on the observable impact of these personnel transfers. Is that understood?" he barked.

Murdoch's visage hardened. "It is, sir."

"Then you would do well to give me that report, now!"

The captain straightened, squaring his shoulders and snapping to attention before replying, "Sir, yes, sir. Sir, I am unable at this time to report any such impact."

"Thank you, Captain," Jenkins said, his voice still louder than he would have liked. He locked eyes with the other man, who was fifteen years his elder, and held his gaze for an uncomfortable length of time before continuing, in a more controlled tone, "So Lieutenant Koch diverted personnel without prior authorization. I'll discuss this with him at the earliest convenience. What is the nature of your complaint against Lieutenant Xi and Chief Podsednik?"

Murdoch remained at strict attention as he spoke. "They conspired to steal mission-critical gear from company storage, sir."

"Where is the stolen gear now?" Jenkins pressed, mildly dismayed at hearing of such hijinks less than a day after Xi had been promoted to platoon leader.

"I..." Murdoch trailed off before rallying. "I do not know, sir."

"Then how, exactly, can you be certain they stole it?"

"I have received multiple, independent, and voluntarily-given corroborative testimonies which confirm they are the thieves, sir," Murdoch replied. "And since the article in question is indeed missing from company storage, I demand a formal investigation so that the lost article might be reclaimed."

"What is the article in question?" Jenkins asked, suspecting anything from ordnance salvaged from the wrecked mechs to onboard computer components needed to get *Elvira II* up to fighting trim. He couldn't just ignore the unlawful transfer of such items, but in the end, he was just as impressed by Xi and Podsy's initiative as he was perturbed by their bold antagonism of Murdoch. He knew that Murdoch was far from beloved by his subordinates, but now it seemed clear that the problem was deeper than Jenkins had initially surmised.

"It is mission-critical equipment, Commander. I don't see the relevance of the article's..."

"Luckily for both of us," Jenkins interrupted hotly, "whether or not you recognize its relevance is, itself, completely irrelevant, and you are dangerously close to earning an official mark in *your* file, Captain Murdoch. This is the last time I'm going to repeat myself: what is the article in question?!"

Murdoch purpled once again, though this time he seemed genuinely embarrassed as he replied, "A spare, unopened enviro-suit, sir."

Jenkins was stunned into silence, unable to believe what he had just heard. "Tell me this is a joke," he finally said in a low, dangerous voice. "Tell me that you, Xi, Koch, and Podsy sat down and whipped this little story up just to get a rise out of me. That I could forgive, even support," he said as he stepped forward, bringing his face mere centimeters from Murdoch's. "So please, Captain, tell me this is all an ill-timed game of grab-ass that spiraled out of control. Tell me that, contrary to my quickly-eroding faith in your ability to command your people's respect, you hatched this scheme to build fraternity and camaraderie with your men by putting one over on the battalion commander." He paused, taking deep, measured breaths as he glared down at the older man. "Go on, Captain. Reassure me that this wasn't really an instance of one of my sticky-fingered officers seeking petty, vindictive revenge after getting his hand caught in the cookie jar, again."

Murdoch visibly bristled. "Sir, I never..."

"Everyone in the Fleet knows, Murdoch!" Jenkins snapped. "For Christ's sake, I'd be surprised if the fucking *rock-biters* don't know about your hoarding! But instead of dealing with the matter in a productive fashion, specifically, since you *clearly* can't see how that might have been accomplished, by one-upping this little game of capture-the-suit with an off-the-books retaliation in the same spirit, you came to me?! WE ARE AT WAR,

CAPTAIN MURDOCH!" Jenkins roared, thrusting a finger toward the perpetually-setting sun. "Any minute now, the enemy might breach that glass-field and do their level best to kill every man and woman on this lump of rock, but you thought it prudent to come to *me* to address a deficiency of discipline within what I thought was *your* company? Was I mistaken to place you in command of 2nd Company, Captain?"

"No, sir," Murdoch said through gritted teeth.

Jenkins held the data chip up between his fingers, his disgust with the man having finally reached a boiling point. "Are there any changes you'd like to make to this report before I file it in the battalion records?"

The captain looked fit to explode, with veins across his forehead and neck bulging so badly they looked ready to spontaneously rupture. "Yes, sir, there are," he finally said.

"Very well." Jenkins flipped the chip back to him. "Dismissed, Captain."

Murdoch snapped a picture-perfect salute, turned on his heel, and walked off with a decided air of discontent.

It wasn't until he had been gone for a few minutes that Jenkins was able to crack a smile about the whole thing.

Xi was shaping up to be everything he had hoped for, and pairing her with Podsednik had been the best roster move of his command to date.

THE ISLAND

"Let's hear it, Styles," Jenkins urged after the chief warrant officer had sat down for the mid-morning briefing.

"I managed to extract one completely intact device, Commander," Styles explained, gently presenting a tray containing the bizarre device, which looked like five spoons of various sizes ranging from a one centimeter in diameter to seven centimeters across. The spoon-shaped 'paddles' were connected via a delicate frame of wires and rods, each of which was covered in some sort of insulation sheath. "And after monkeying with the broken pieces, I think I'm starting to get a handle on how it works. Basically, these smaller paddles create cognitive feedback loops in the mid and high-brain functions which I think mask regular brain activity, or possibly even feeds false stimuli directly into the brain. Meanwhile, these two larger paddles," he continued, gesturing to the largest spoon-shaped sections, "look like they directly stimulate certain muscles."

"These things turn Arh'Kel soldiers into super-soldiers?" Jenkins asked, slightly confused by the purpose of such an elaborate device.

"I don't think so," Styles said hesitantly. "I've talked with Doc

Fellows and we think these are too small to produce a total body control system. Arh'Kel neurophysiology is still something of a mystery to Terran experts, but we're fairly confident that this system isn't directly controlling the body's voluntary movements. It seems more likely that the muscles being controlled are in their internal organ systems, like their cardiopulmonary networks, which has quite a few similarities with our own for obvious reasons."

"Obvious?" Jenkins repeated skeptically.

"Arh'Kel and human physiologies only differ on the basic building blocks: carbon vs. silica," Styles explained. "Beyond that, most everything deeper than the skin is structurally similar. Sure, they directly incorporate iron into their skeletons, but they breathe oxygen just like we do. They've got the ability to store and extract that oxygen from the air or from mineral forms, permitting them to hibernate for long periods of time in the presence of oxidized iron, but beyond that, our cardiopulmonary systems are generally the same. Special muscles circulate oxygen-rich blood cells based on iron, they've got a fairly narrow range of internal pH they can tolerate, and they digest nutrients by breaking materials down with acid stored in their digestive tracts. Life is pretty varied, but the fundamentals are remarkably similar no matter where a given life tree took root."

"Fine," Jenkins said, hoping to get to the substance of the briefing before enduring too much more technobabble. "Why is there nothing in the archives about this device being found on Arh'Kel corpses?"

"I think this is something new, sir," Styles explained. "The Arh'Kel are extremely unified in social purpose, but they're also just as extremely solitary and individualistic. The almost mind-less waves of soldiers that we've encountered here are totally unlike anything previously reported during the Arh'Kel wars, and this almost hive-mind is far from normal for Arh'Kel psychology. When they attack, they do so with single-minded purpose, but until our engagements here on Durgan's Folly, they have never stood their ground while getting slaughtered. Guerilla tactics are much more their style. Displace, disperse, fortify, and counter-raid is what we've come to expect from rock-biters once they're on their heels."

"Is it possible we stumbled onto something critical down there?" Jenkins offered. "Maybe their backs were to the wall and they felt they didn't have a choice?"

"It's possible, but unlikely," Styles said dubiously. "They reproduce in a process somewhere between egg-laying and spore-casting, leaving fertilized zygotes in prepared caverns and then leaving them behind to develop on their own. They indirectly supervise conditions in the hatcheries, but there isn't much in the way of familial bonding in their society, so the way they think about protecting sensitive locations is alien to us. What we do know is that they're unusually unified in their purpose, which is predominantly to spread their influence, and that means increasing the species' numbers. Also, I should point out that Fleet Intel says that anything they have down here was built here. None of this gear was built elsewhere and dropped in from orbit, which means they've got factories and mining operations well-established all across the twilight band."

"And they've been operating here, potentially, for thirty years," Jenkins mused.

"It's a long time for rock-biters."

"How many are we looking at down here, worst-case scenario?" Jenkins finally asked.

"Under ideal conditions, an Arh'Kel takes about eight years to develop to maturity and can live for centuries, possibly even millennia. They're asexual, so there's no reproductive bottleneck except for the presence of the rare minerals needed to form their nervous systems. So with an ideal diet and environmental conditions, a dedicated spawning Arh'Kel can make about two zygotes per Earth day. It takes them about a month to get into spawning mode, but once they're there, they can continue making offspring indefinitely. Between a quarter and three-quarters of these zygotes reach maturity, again, depending on the environment and dietary conditions."

Jenkins nodded, having familiarized himself with their reproductive systems and growth potential prior to deployment. "How ideal are these conditions, Chief?"

"Honestly," Styles replied grimly, "it looks like they've got everything they need to extract the rare minerals faster than our ninetieth percentile projections. But even if we only project half of their zygotes surviving to maturity..."

"In thirty standard years, that's over ten thousand Arh'Kel per spawner," Jenkins finished for him.

"With about three-fourths of those reaching maturity by now," Styles agreed. "I'd probably run the number down to five thousand combat-ready Arh'Kel per dedicated spawner, and using primitive tools, it takes about ten Arh'Kel to feed one spawner. Using more advanced extraction methods, it gets closer to one-to-one, so even if there were only a hundred Arh'Kel here when Fleet withdrew three decades ago, and even if they've been operating with primitive extraction systems for the bulk of that time..."

Jenkins sank back in his chair. "A low-end estimate is still around fifty thousand Arh'Kel just from those initial breeders."

"With a high-end estimate, based on the number of HWPs and orbital guns we've encountered, well over ten million," Styles finished ominously.

"Critical mass on an Arh'Kel foothold is three hundred thousand." Jenkins set his jaw.

"That's the point at which they start building orbital infrastructure, including warships," Styles confirmed. "Their population growth and behavioral patterns work like a clock. Even the databases we managed to steal from the interstellar Illumination League, an 'august' multi-species organization to which our oh-so-beloved Solarian cousins belong, confirm that there doesn't appear to be much deviation in Arh'Kel behavior. Once they reach a given population point, they invariably do certain things."

"But with these devices directly influencing their thoughts..." Jenkins mused, turning one of the broken implant fragments over in his hand.

"We have no idea what their behavior patterns will be," Styles finished.

Jenkins closed his eyes and considered the possibility that this rock might harbor ten million Arh'Kel soldiers.

Then, like puzzle pieces falling together, he understood what all of this meant, and that realization chilled him to the bone.

"All they need are troop transports," he whispered.

"And they'll be able to send Arh'Kel soldiers through the wormhole gates fast enough to wipe out every human colony in the Terran Republic before our enlightened Solar cousins, or any other member species of the Illumination League, for that matter, can intercede on our behalf," Styles declared flatly.

"Arh'Kel have been popping up all over the Republic in the last six months," Jenkins mused. "They can't *all* have these devices, can they?"

"No." Styles shook his head firmly. "To my knowledge, this is the only encounter the Terran Fleet has had with this technology."

"Are you confident about that?" Jenkins pressed.

"*Extremely*, Commander," Styles confirmed, and Jenkins believed him. He didn't know how Styles got his intel, moreover, he knew that he very much did *not want* to know, but Styles' confidence had not yet been misplaced.

"Did they steal the technology from Sol?" Jenkins wondered aloud.

"It's possible, and given the available information, it's probably our best current guess," Styles said with a shrug, "but I wouldn't venture that far. All I know is that there are significant structural and functional similarities between these things and the uplinks the Solarians use to connect to their One Mind network. The architecture and tech base are a hundred percent Arh'Kel, let me be absolutely clear about that," he said pointedly. "From the base-six coding to the flexible ceramic insulators, these were without a doubt manufactured by Arh'Kel for Arh'Kel. But the way the devices go about the process of interconnecting individuals…it was similar enough to make me see a potential link with the Solarians."

Jenkins opened his mouth to continue the dialogue, but he was interrupted by a priority chime from the comm panel built into his tiny desk.

The chime signaled a P2P link-up with Fleet, a link he wasn't expecting for another two days.

"This is Commander Lee Jenkins," he greeted after accepting the incoming link.

"Commander," came the friendly voice of Sergeant Major Tim Trapper. "It's good to hear your voice, Leeroy."

"Sergeant Major." Jenkins cocked his head in alarm. "I didn't expect to hear from an old Pounder like you. What's our status?"

"I'm inbound with two hundred and fifty Pounders from the 203rd," Trapper replied. "Heard you kids could use a couple cans of supplies and decided to deliver 'em personally." Jenkins and Styles made brief eye contact, but they both knew what Trapper's arrival meant.

Fleet wasn't going to arrive in two days as scheduled, and the old dog had probably bucked the chain of command in order to deliver supplies and badly-needed reinforcements, however meager, to the soon-to-be cut-off battalion.

Putting up a false front, Jenkins laughed. "I guess it's true what they say: life's one big circle. You start delivering pizza in your teens, take a break for a few decades, then pick right back up a year or two before they put you out to pasture."

"Fuck you very much, Commander," Trapper retorted.

Jenkins chuckled hollowly. "I'll have my boys spit a steer and tap a keg."

"Sounds good. I'm relaying my target zone coordinates, but the bus driver was in a rush to drop us off so we might need a little help finding the front door," Trapper explained.

"I'll dispatch a platoon to rendezvous with you and escort you to HQ," Jenkins assured him as the coordinates hit his screen. The drop zone was fifteen clicks from the plateau, so escorting these reinforcements back to the barn seemed like the perfect job for the newly-promoted leader of 5th Platoon.

"ETA twelve minutes," Trapper said.

"I'll have my people there in twenty," he said while Styles, without being urged, had already summoned Xi to the command center. "Stay frosty, Sergeant Major. The natives are restless and if you don't watch your six, they'll kill all of you and take my supplies."

"Will do. I wouldn't want you to miss out on hot chow and mail," the sergeant major acknowledged. "See you in twenty. Trapper out."

The line went dead, and Styles gave voice to their mutual concern. "The Arh'Kel fleet must have already arrived."

"Which means that, aside from a couple hundred more Pounders and some fresh ordnance..." Jenkins nodded heavily. "We're not getting reinforced any time soon, because Fleet is fighting the bad guys at the outer edge of this system."

The situation had been 'bad' a few minutes earlier, but it had just rocketed past 'worse' on its way to 'apocalyptic.'

"Signal the battalion," Jenkins said grimly. "It's time we hunkered down. I don't want our names added to those lost on Durgan's Folly. From here until Fleet shows up, our mission is to survive."

THE HOOK-UP

"I've got 'em, LT," Podsy declared after finally maneuvering the Owl-class drone into position over the quartet of drop-cans —massive cargo pods used to drop personnel and material from low orbit. "Forwarding the coordinates now."

"They missed their DZ by twenty clicks," Xi said in surprise. "How the hell do you miss that bad?"

"They must've been taking fire," Podsy suggested.

"Either that or the pilot was stoned," Xi quipped.

"Could be. Not everyone is the cream of the crop like us."

"All right," Xi piped into the 5th Platoon's dedicated comm channel, "we've sighted the supply drop. I'm forwarding a new itinerary now; follow my lead and keep up the pace. The rock-biters have better seismic scanners than we do so they know our people are out there, which means every second brings them closer to those cans."

"Why did Fleet drop these cans way out here?" Ford asked. Xi didn't know the answer to that question. All Commander Jenkins had told her was to rendezvous with over two hundred Pounders and collect the supply crates they came with. "Why not wait until Fleet Ground touches down to resupply us?"

"I heard there's a VIP from Fleet Command coming to personally inspect your tailpipe, *Forktail*," quipped Nakamura, *Wolverine*'s Jock.

"Haha, *Wolverine*," Ford deadpanned. "I'm sure you make your mama proud with that mouth."

"Proud?" Nakamura feigned incredulity. "I make my mama *scream* with this mouth."

"Jesus..." Ford said in clear disgust.

"I heard it's Tim Trapper and the 203rd with what's left of your pet octopus, *Wolverine*," interjected Nazair, *Spin Doctor*'s Jock. "He said the thing's filthier than the inside of your envirosuit and he wants a full refund since there was nothing pleasurable about it."

"Fuck you, Nazi," Nakamura weakly retorted. "The octopus joke was old when your mom still had teeth, and we all know that's been awhile."

"Hit a little close to home, did it?" Nazair chuckled. "You can't run from who you are, *Wolverine*, and you, my friend, are the end product of a long line of sexually twisted people. I mean seriously, octopuses? How desperate do you have to be to stick one of those things up..."

"Cut the chatter," Xi interrupted halfheartedly. She enjoyed the exchange far more than she probably should have and had no intention of being a mere bystander to such banter. "I want everyone in 5th Platoon to know that you're all sick and I'm ordering each and every one of you report to Doc Fellows for a full physical examination as soon we get back to the barn."

"Oh, Mommy, do I have to?" Nazair whined.

"*Spin Doctor*, if I ever had the misfortune to expel something as pathetic as you from my body, I'd have the good sense to lock myself away and beg the universe's forgiveness for my transgression for the rest of my days," she retorted.

"But to expel me, you'd first have to let me in," Nazair chuckled.

"Eww." Xi wrinkled her nose in disgust. "I'd rather close my eyes and give *Wolverine*'s octopus a go."

"Dammit," Nakamura groaned, "are you people ever going to let that joke die?"

"Why, so Podsy can finally get some action?" Nazair asked with mock sincerity, causing even Podsednik to laugh.

"All right," Ford grunted, "that's enough chatter."

Xi scowled, knowing it wasn't Ford's place to make the correction but deciding that he was probably right. She refused to think of him as her XO—executive officer—even though he was the second-highest ranking officer in the platoon. Which meant if she was ganked, he'd take over. *Don't get killed,* she reminded herself.

"Heads up," she said as soon as the first glint of a drop-can appeared on her visual pick-up. "I've got eyes on the cans."

"Copy that," Ford acknowledged.

"*Forktail* and *Spin Doctor*, prepare to load up," Xi ordered. "*Wolverine*, help reposition the canisters if they're dug in too deep to unload."

Soon the mechs came to a stop in front of the four identical drop-cans. Their parachutes and braking thrusters had clearly been deployed, and only one of the cans had suffered any kind of real damage upon impact with the relatively soft volcanic glass.

Positioned around the canisters was a well-organized defensive line of FGF Pounders, the 203rd, just as Nazair had suggested.

And standing at the center of the formation was a man whose demeanor and physique made it clear he was someone to be reckoned with.

The long, gray-white handlebar mustache and clean-shaven head were distinctive enough for the *Elvira's* facial-recognition software to easily identify the man as Sergeant Major Tim Trapper, Jr. He was a legend in the FGF, known as much for being a hard-ass as for his utter devotion to the people under his command.

Even before *Elvira* came to a stop, he strode purposefully toward the mech and timed his approach so that he set foot on the bottom step of *Elvira*'s boarding ramp as it touched the ground without breaking stride.

He entered the compartment and Xi stood from her chair to meet him.

"Don't break your neural link..." he began before realizing Xi had no such connection. "You walked this thing out here double-time on manual?" he asked, his eyebrows rising minutely in apparent surprise. "What is that, eight inputs per second just for the full-speed walk cycle?"

"Between seven and eleven," Xi agreed, impressed at his knowledge of her mech's control interface, "depending on the terrain. In this shit, it averages about nine and a half at full speed."

He whistled appreciatively. "I'd like to see that sometime, if you don't mind."

"It would be my pleasure, Sergeant Major," she agreed.

"All right," he said, handing her a data chip. "This is an upload for Commander Jenkins that he needs to receive ASAP. It's encrypted, so you can send it in the open if you have to, but a P2P link would be better if you've got one available."

"We've got a relay-capable drone assigned to the platoon." She nodded, handing the chip to Podsy. "The commander will receive the packet as soon as the drone reaches relay altitude."

"Good." Trapper nodded. "I've got twenty-three casualties and six fatalities from the landing. I'll need to transfer the wounded to these walker mechs since some have spinal damage and the ride will be smoother on a walker than a roller."

"Understood," she said. "*Wolverine*, our humanoid mech, isn't well-suited to carrying supply pods so have your people rig up some slings and they can ride in those."

"Will do." Trapper cocked his head to rattle off a series of commands using Pounder shorthand. "As for the supplies, I'm afraid I couldn't get my hands on very much. Mostly chain gun rounds, a few rockets, some fifteen shells, and a few odds and ends that I didn't think Fleet would notice were gone until after we'd touched down."

"Everything makes a difference, Sergeant Major," she said. "We're glad to have you."

"I'd like to say I'm glad to be here, but I'm not. Still, someone needs to keep today's youth off the streets and out of trouble," he quipped, a challenging twinkle in his eye as the first of the crates were loaded onto *Elvira*'s broad, flat topside.

She hesitated before flashing a lopsided grin. "That would be a fair characterization."

"Indeed." He nodded approvingly. "Let's get these supplies loaded and make our way back to the barn."

"Sergeant Major," Podsy called out. "Commander Jenkins confirms receipt of your data packet. He says, 'The steer's on the spit.'"

"Thank you, Chief," Trapper acknowledged. "We'll be ready to roll in eight minutes," he said, turning back toward Xi. "Mind if I ride along?"

"Not at all," she said, feeling an unaccustomed thrill at the request.

Just as he said, eight minutes later, the last of the crates was loaded and the column, now flanked by a quartet of APCs bearing Trapper's people and some of the more delicate supplies, headed back to the plateau.

"Sergeant Major," Jenkins greeted as soon as Trapper stepped out of *Elvira*. "It's good to have you."

"Good to be back," Trapper drawled, projecting the very

image of a lifelong warrior and leader of men. He cast a dark, brooding look out at the horizon and snorted. "Never thought I'd set foot here again."

"You were part of the last engagement here on Durgan's Folly." Jenkins nodded, having reviewed Trapper's file in-depth over the previous half-hour.

"Back then, we were waiting around on the Marines to come in and show us how it was done," Trapper chuckled. "Truth be told, Pounders ain't got no business going up against rock-biters line-to-line. But we gave 'em hell and held our ground long enough for the Marines to come in and do their thing. I was stationed on this very rock, in fact."

"Really?" Jenkins cocked his head in surprise while gesturing for them to proceed to *Roy*, where they could have a more meaningful dialog than these unexpected pleasantries.

Trapper fell in beside him, pointing to the southern ridge. "Sandy bastards crested right over there so many times, we started shooting the cliff's edge with artillery just to give us a better line-of-fire during their approach." He nodded approvingly as his eyes flicked from one Pounder nest to another. "You put yours a meter or so closer than we did. Good work, it'll save lives when they come."

Jenkins disliked the suggestion that the enemy would attack them there, but if they had done it before, there was good reason to expect them to do it again. "Do you have any other recommendations?" Jenkins asked as they approached *Roy*.

"I might. Who's in command of your Pounders?"

"Major Piper is the ranking FGF field officer," Jenkins replied.

"Pete Piper?" Trapper clarified. "Good leader but not much of a thinker, tends to trip over himself. I'll sit down with him and see what we can hash out."

"That would be greatly appreciated," Jenkins agreed as they stepped up *Roy*'s boarding ramp. Soon they were in Jenkins' cramped cabin, and after closing the hatch, he asked, "How bad is it up there?"

"Like nothing we've ever seen," Trapper said grimly. "We lost five dreadnoughts in the first hour."

"What?!" Jenkins felt his whole body go numb. "Fleet's never lost a *single* dreadnought before."

"The rock-biters loaded fireships with limpets and self-propelled kinetic warheads that fired as soon as they were through the gate," Trapper explained, sitting down in the chair opposite Jenkins. "Three dreadnoughts, the *Marcus Aurelius*, *John Locke*, and *Thomas Jefferson*, went down in the first three minutes. The other two, the *Descartes* and *Zhuge Liang*, were badly-damaged but managed to hang on long enough to clean up the first wave. They kept firing until Terra Han sent their SDF to bolster the line, and those boys managed to fight a draw long enough for Sixth Fleet to arrive in force. But you should've seen it, Lee…a hundred thousand of our boys, gone like that." He snapped his fingers emphatically.

"Fireships attacking our dreadnoughts so close to the gates…" Jenkins shook his head in disbelief. "What does the League say?"

Trapper scoffed. "The League? They've never cared about the Terran colonies before. Why would you expect them to start now? They'll probably wait until the dust's settled and then come riding in with another round of sanctions to threaten us with if we don't back our ships off the gates even farther than we already have. Hell, I'd be surprised if Sol hasn't already denounced us for successfully defending ourselves."

"Sol isn't that bad," Jenkins chided.

"If you ask me, they're *worse*. We would never abandon Sol like they abandoned us. You know that," Trapper said passionately.

"I like to think that's true," Jenkins allowed, but in recent years, he had seen a more parochial mindset spread throughout the Terran Republic. Anti-Sol sentiment in some colonies, especially those worst-hit by the Arh'Kel wars, like New Australia, had reached dangerous levels. The rhetoric was so bad that some of the minority political parties had adopted the position that Solarian humans were no longer human at all.

Given a few decades of unchecked growth, such rhetoric could well and truly divide the far-flung tribes of humanity on a potentially permanent basis, and as far as Jenkins was concerned, that would only serve hostile alien races like the Arh'Kel.

"You *know* it's true," Trapper said dismissively. "You and I would be the first boots on the ground if Sol ever needed help, to hell with what the politicians or brass said."

Jenkins sat back in thought. "Do we have any idea how long it might take for Fleet to reinforce us?"

"Honestly? I loaded those cans and hopped a slow-rider over here as soon as it became clear they weren't going to make good on their commitments to your battalion. The Fleet is trapped at the edge of this system fighting for their lives. Dropping you off here and then turning their backs like that..." He shook his head adamantly. "I couldn't have lived with myself if I hadn't done something about it. I'm just sorry I couldn't bring a few squads of Marines with me. But with the extra ordnance and a few fresh Pounders, we should be able to hold this rock for a few weeks if needed."

"A couple of days ago, I would have agreed with you," Jenkins said heavily, sliding a data slate over for Trapper to review. It contained mission logs of the underground engagement, along with portions of what Styles had reported in his latest debriefing regarding potential enemy strength on Durgan's Folly.

Like the seasoned professional he was, Sergeant Major Tim Trapper scanned the reports with calm stoicism, offering the odd nod of approval while reading through the engagement details. But when he came to the final analysis put forth by Chief Styles, an analysis which suggested there were millions of Arh'Kel on

Durgan's Folly instead of mere tens of thousands, he did a rare double-take.

"Your man's not crazy, is he?" he asked without tearing his eyes from the slate.

"He's the best I've ever worked with."

Trapper whistled appreciatively before cracking a wry grin. "Well, that's what I get for being an upright son-of-a-bitch more concerned with loyalty than covering his own ass. This here—" He tossed the slate onto the desk in disgust. "—is FUBAR."

"Ordinarily, I'd argue with you." Jenkins smirked.

Trapper looked up to the shelf where the purple-label whisky bottle sat. "How long has it been?"

"Two thousand, three hundred, and thirty-five days," Jenkins replied without a second thought.

"Days?" Trapper chuckled. "Son, that word doesn't mean spit on this hunk of rock." He suddenly turned serious. "But good for you. I just might have to keep you on that wagon while the rest of us celebrate."

"And I just might take you up on that," he replied with a tight smile.

"Well then…" Trapper stood from the chair. "Looks like we've got some work to do."

LONG LIVE ROCK & ROLL

Six hours later, HQ's seismic alarms went off. The rock-biters were breaching the surface in force.

They had completely surrounded the plateau.

"All crews, report to your mechs," Jenkins ordered over the battalion-wide priority channel. "I say again, all crews, report to your mechs. This is not a drill. We have enemy inbound." He switched to the Pounder command channel. "Major Piper, Sergeant Major Trapper, are your people prepared to receive the enemy?"

"Yes, sir," Piper acknowledged promptly.

"Sar," Trapper replied, as was his wont. Jenkins had served with Trapper once before, back when Jenkins had been a wide-eyed ensign and Trapper, oddly enough, had been the same rank he was today.

It was comforting having familiar faces on the line with him.

They had drilled this scenario forty-one times since arriving on Durgan's Folly, and Jenkins had every confidence that his people would successfully repel the enemy.

The only question was how bad the butcher's bill would be.

He switched back to battalion command. "2nd Platoon,"

Jenkins barked, referring to the unit of fast-moving, light-duty scout vehicles that had no hope of surviving direct railgun strikes, "assume reserve posture in support of the ridge-line."

"Assuming reserve posture, Commander," acknowledged Koch, commander of that unit.

"4th Platoon," Jenkins continued, "cover the southern quadrant with artillery fire at established perimeter."

"Southern quadrant, yes, sir," replied Captain Murdoch.

"5th Platoon," he snapped, "cover the northern quadrant."

"Northern quadrant, aye, sir," Xi replied promptly and calmly, her tone and composure suggesting she was an officer much older than nineteen.

"3rd Platoon," Jenkins continued, referring to the down-checked and immobile mechs which still had the ability to engage at long range via artillery, "cover the western quadrant and stand ready to deploy our Vultures. But keep them grounded until we need them. Rock-biter railguns are deadly accurate above ground."

"3rd Platoon stands ready," replied Ensign 'George' Roden-baugh, commanding the *Generally*. He had demonstrated his superior artillery skill in support of Xi when they repelled the flanking attack at the collapsed tunnel, and he'd had been given fire control of the crippled vehicles as a result. If Jenkins had his way, he'd put George in charge of training every gun crew in the battalion.

"1st Platoon," Jenkins continued as *Roy*'s systems sprang to life under Chaps' expert control, "the eastern quadrant is ours."

Acknowledgments streamed across his screen, and when they had done so, he noted with satisfaction that the Pounders had already manned every gun nest on the plateau's ridge-line.

As a fortress used in previous campaigns, the ridge of the HQ plateau was piled high with multi-ton boulders, atop which sat precisely-positioned gun nests. The north, west, and southern faces of the granite plateau were nearly vertical, making them difficult, but far from impossible, for Arh'Kel infantry to scale. The faces were lined with a contiguous wall that stood an average of five meters high and was four times as thick at the base.

The eastern face, on the other hand, was gently sloped and presented every bit as tempting a target as slowly swimming fish snapping at bugs.

It was there where the boulder wall was segmented, forming inward-flexing V-shaped fortifications which featured three times as many nests-per-kilometer as the other faces of the plateau. It was there that the Arh'Kel had made their assaults during previous campaigns, and just as Sergeant Major Trapper had noted, Jenkins' people had done their level best to refine the already-deadly kill-boxes.

Jenkins settled into his command chair and noted no fewer than fifteen separate breach points in the glass-field surrounding the plateau. The enemy had tunneled beneath the surface for days, possibly even weeks, carving new passages to serve the same purpose as the dozens of similar tunnels FGF forces had collapsed decades earlier. In spite of the consistent winds buffeting the glassy plain, those collapsed tunnels stretched forth in all directions from the plateau. To Jenkins, they had served as reminders of battles long-since concluded and warnings of those yet to come.

Battles like the one his people were about to fight.

"Twelve thousand Arh'Kel infantry identified, sir," Styles reported, but Jenkins knew the number would be at least ten times that many before the dust settled. "Fifteen HWPs have already breached the surface and are converging on our position."

Jenkins' tactical plotter showed the encroaching enemy, led by their terrifying infantry which cartwheeled at speeds unattainable by humans. They had surrounded the plateau, but everyone knew that the northern, western, and southern offenses were diversions, feints designed to keep his attention from being entirely focused on the breach-point to the east.

As the enemy drew steadily nearer, they crossed the effective artillery range of fifteen kilometers. But at that range, only three mechs in the battalion—*Roy*, *Elvira*, and *Generally*—were capable of accurately engaging.

So the engagement perimeter had been set at eight kilometers, with fire authorized to a danger-close level of two hundred meters from the plateau's ridgeline.

Thankfully, 1st Platoon had one long-range-missile mech, *Preacher*, whose crew had been itching to engage the enemy on their terms.

"*Preacher*, you are authorized to engage Alpha Package: HWPs designated 6, 7, 9, and 10," Jenkins ordered.

"Copy that. Engaging 6, 7, 9, and 10," Falwell, *Preacher*'s Jock, acknowledged with relish.

Preacher's left missile mount, containing four cruise missiles capable of engaging vehicle-sized targets at up to a hundred kilometers, rotated toward its first target with an audible whine. The first missile tore loose of its tube, streaking toward the enemy heavy weapons platform as the LRM—the long-range missile—mount rotated toward the second target. Another missile was loosed, and another, and another until the four-missile launcher was empty.

Seconds later, all four missiles struck their targets in near-perfect unison, scrapping all four HWPs and leaving deep craters in the glass-field, each of which was littered with hundreds of rock-biter corpses.

Preacher's crew worked with professional precision to reload the launcher with fresh ordnance as Falwell reported, "Targets down, sir."

"Good work." Jenkins nodded as the tide of rock-biters closed in. "Prepare to engage Bravo Package: HWPs 8, 11, 12, and 13 on my command."

"Targets verified," Falwell acknowledged, and thirty seconds later, *Preacher*'s crew had reloaded the left mount with four fresh missiles.

"Engage," Jenkins said, and again *Preacher*'s crew unleashed four perfectly-timed cruise missiles, which left more corpse-strewn gashes in the glassy rock-field.

"Bravo Package down," Falwell reported as his crews worked to reload *Preacher*'s right mount.

Railgun fire spat into the rock wall lining the southern ridge. Rubble was blasted loose, spraying deadly shrapnel inward. A dozen Pounders died when their nests were sniped by enemy fire.

"Requesting permission to engage, sir," Captain Murdoch said over the command line.

"Negative, *Flaming Rose*," Jenkins replied tersely. "Hold until the enemy reaches the perimeter."

A pause, as was usual when dealing with the insufferable Murdoch. "Order received and acknowledged, Commander."

No one liked holding their fire, but the truth was they simply didn't have enough artillery shells or short-range missiles to fire at anything less than peak accuracy. If there were as many rock-biters on Durgan's Folly as now seemed likely, they would need to make every shot count.

At this point, much as he hated to admit it, ammunition was worth more than the men and women who would fire it.

"*Preacher*," he said, his resolve firming as he identified a fresh package of targets, "engage Charlie Package: HWPs 1, 3, and 5."

"Charlie Package: 1, 3, and 5," Falwell acknowledged with gusto. "Engaging."

Four missiles tore loose in rapid-succession, and this time instead of four kills, *Preacher* managed to take out five, killing HWP 4 with the same strike that flattened 5.

"Charlie plus one down," Falwell reported smugly.

Another wave of railgun strikes, this one to the north,

slammed into the boulder-pile protecting that part of the ridge-line. Normally, Jenkins would have ordered *Elvira II* to engage with her LRMs, but the fire control systems in the down-checked *Elvira* had been destroyed by the danger-close EMP, so she was down to fifteens for long-range engagement.

But with only forty-six remaining LRMs in his arsenal, Jenkins suspected he would have no real trouble finding suitable targets for them as the engagement went on.

On the eastern front, the enemy finally crossed the eight-kilometer line, causing Jenkins to call out, "Hold…hold…hold…"

The enemy were trickling across the line, growing steadily in number as the onrushing horde's main body surged into the engagement zone. Once the environment was target-rich enough for him, Jenkins gave the eagerly-anticipated order.

"1st Platoon, engage."

Artillery thundered as eight and fifteen-kilo guns dropped HE rounds on the advancing enemy. The first strike was delivered by *Roy*, and it sent up a plume of glassy dust with the HE shell shredding thirty Arh'Kel and wounding twice as many more.

Roy's long guns cycled as fast as they could, sending shell after shell down-range while the rest of 1st Platoon's did the same. Short-range rockets whooshed from 1st Platoon's mounts in perfect coordination, with fifty strikes rippling across the advancing line in a span of two seconds. No fewer than two thousand rock-biters were laid low as the short-range rockets cleared a gap nearly two kilometers long in the densely-packed enemy line.

A gap which the rock-biters quickly filled.

A flashing icon to the north drew Jenkins' attention to that quadrant, where the enemy line was also beginning to encroach. Another handful of railgun strikes pulverized the northern wall, killing three nests full of Pounders and spraying jagged stones across other positions. Some of those stones struck *Elvira*'s hull, but as the second-most-heavily-armored vehicle in the battalion, she was barely even scratched.

He watched as the northern line encroached further and further across the engagement line, and just as he was ready to order Xi's people to open fire, he heard her voice on the command channel, "5th Platoon, engage."

Elvira's dual fifteen-kilo guns roared in rapid succession, with *Wolverine* and *Forktail* adding to the deadly barrage. Every six seconds, *Elvira* sent a pair of HE shells toward the enemy, while *Wolverine* and *Forktail* cycled at nine and ten seconds, respectively.

Shell after shell rained down on the charging rock-biters as Xi's platoon tore into the thinner northern line. Eighteen rockets flew from *Wolverine's* shoulder-mounted launchers, tearing a nearly perfect, circular hole into the heart of the charging wave. A thousand rock-biters died under 5th Platoon's guns in the first thirty seconds, with two railgun mounts being expertly sniped with rocket-fire for good measure.

And still the Arh'Kel advanced at breathtaking speed, with thousands more pouring out of the breaches at their backs.

Roy's artillery thermal alarms began to chime, signaling that their thermal sinks were red-lined. If nothing changed, they could continue firing uninterrupted for another eight minutes before needing to be taken off-line for a three-minute cooldown.

Soon the western and southern quadrants had been encroached by the horde. Unlike Lieutenant Xi to the north, Captain Murdoch's people opened fire the instant a single rock-biter crossed the engagement line. Rodenbaugh had better sense to the west, waiting until his zone was heavy with enemy targets before unleashing *Generally's* artillery along with the rest of the down-checked vehicles' arsenals.

The first of the rock-biters crossed the two-kilometer line, and the Pounders greeted them with a barrage of mortar rounds. Staccato mortar strikes tore into the approaching rock-biters, with each mortar round clearing a handful of Arh'Kel, and soon the mortars were joined by crew-served RPG launchers as the Pounders worked their nests with ruthless efficiency.

Standing atop the eastern fortifications was Major Pete Piper, who directed his people with combined radio commands and flag communication. He was old school, just like Sergeant Major Trapper, whose people were moving to reinforce the southern line where the rock-biters were more heavily-concentrated than on the northern or western fronts.

At the one-kilometer line, the Pounder nests opened fire with machine guns and coilguns, spraying hot death into the stone-skinned Arh'Kel. The closer they came to the battalion's head-quarters, the more intense the Terrans' counter-fire became, and soon every face of the fortified plateau was awash with outbound fire tearing into the enemy with anti-personnel and light-anti-material rounds.

A line of nine Arh'Kel railguns had formed along the south-eastern edge of the engagement zone, and they soon made their presence known. Coordinating fire into the southern rock-wall with a concerted volley, they blew a ten-meter-wide hole into the fortifications. Forty Pounders were killed as half a dozen nests were sniped by enemy railguns, and Jenkins was pleased to see 2nd Platoon immediately move to reinforce the sudden gap in their defenses.

Sergeant Major Trapper, possessing uncanny foresight, had already brought half of his reserve company to the southern ridge-line. Standing tall and barking orders, even as railgun strikes tore into the wall at his back, he directed his people to set up new gun nests to replace the ones taken out by the rock-biter artillery.

"*Preacher*," Jenkins snapped, "engage Delta Package: HWPs 18 through 25."

"Delta, 18 through 25," Falwell acknowledged, his missiles

tearing from their mounts as both launchers cleared in rapid succession. "Engaged."

One by one, seven of the southeastern railguns were neutralized by *Preacher*'s LRMs.

"Stand by, Commander," Falwell reported. "We've got a launch failure on tube three."

"Lieutenant Koch—" Jenkins switched to the dedicated repair channel. "—send a team to *Preacher*. They've got a jammed tube."

"On it, Commander," Koch acknowledged as fire continued to pour from the ridge-line in all directions. Artillery thundered, coilguns sprayed, and mortar rounds erupted among the enemy line as the seemingly endless tide of rock-biters converged on the plateau.

"*Preacher*, are you hot on your second launcher?" Jenkins asked. He knew that without the LRMs, they would be at the mercy of the enemy railguns.

"Affirmative, Commander," came the prompt reply. "Mount Two is green."

"Echo Package," Jenkins called out after identifying a second quickly-forming line of railguns, "targets 28, 29, 31, and 2."

"Echo Package, 28, 29, 31, and 2," acknowledged Falwell, "engaging."

The launcher sent its missiles toward the enemy formation, which only managed a single shot from one HWP before all four were scrapped by the inbound missiles.

"Neutralized," Falwell reported.

Along the eastern front, the enemy had reached the base of the plateau's slope. Gun nests built atop the ramparts lining the kill-zone erupted, catching the Arh'Kel in a vicious crossfire as every gun capable of spitting projectiles was turned on the approaching horde.

The rock-biters fell in droves, with dozens dying each second as their fellows charged past their corpses. The kill-zone was soon a field of carnage, with hardly a square meter barren of Arh'Kel gore.

And still, the rock-biters charged on.

A warning icon appeared on 4th Platoon's dedicated display, and what Jenkins saw there made him set his jaw.

"Fifteens are off-line," Murdoch reported. "Initiating emergency cooldown in accordance with protocol."

Flaming Rose's guns were no hotter than *Roy*'s or *Elvira*'s, but Captain Murdoch had just proven Jenkins' worst fears about the man:

His nerves simply weren't up to this kind of engagement.

When given a choice between the risk of cooking off your own ammo while pouring fire into the enemy or hoping someone else comes along to save your ass while you cower behind safety protocols, Jenkins had always believed that the only defense was an overwhelming offense. Better to die from friendly fire than to let someone else die because you were too afraid to peek above your foxhole.

Thankfully, Sergeant Major Trapper had already reestablished several gun nests in optimal secondary locations. Along with 2nd Platoon, which had arrived and was pouring antipersonnel fire down the near-vertical slope as Arh'Kel began to clamber up it, the men and women on the southern ridge were holding the enemy at bay.

For now.

Koch's people quickly completed field repairs on *Preacher*'s missile launcher, and soon Jenkins was once again feeding targets to the invaluable mech's Jock.

With ammo running low and Arh'Kel continuing to belch from the ground, Jenkins knew that if he was going to hold this rock, something would have to give.

Soon.

With the first notes of Ronnie James Dio's *Long Live Rock & Roll* blaring inside *Elvira*'s cabin, Xi and Podsy worked with ruthless efficiency to clear the northern front of approaching Arh'Kel.

A pair of enemy railguns had set up fourteen kilometers from the ridge-line and spat roaring bolts of tungsten into the rubble wall directly in front of *Elvira II*. Xi's fingertips were raw from working the manual inputs, with trickles of blood running down her hands as she repositioned her mech for optimal firing position on the enemy railguns.

While she moved, a railgun bolt killed five Pounders inside one of the gun nests atop the wall. Snarling in anger, she decided it was time for a little insubordination.

"Let's kill those fuckers, Podsy," she growled. "Load up extended-range AP rounds."

"ERAPs up," he replied, his tone making clear that he agreed with her decision to fire beyond the engagement zone.

"Make 'em count," she snarled.

"On the way!" he declared, and *Elvira*'s whole chassis bucked upward twice in rapid-succession as he sent two shells at the offending enemy weapons.

The first strike was a bulls-eye, scrapping the enemy railgun and sending up a tiny plume of glassy dust.

The second was a near-miss, but it collapsed the ground near the enemy HWP such that the vehicle was forced to move to more stable ground before resuming fire.

"Finish it off," she growled.

"ERAPs up," Podsy acknowledged. "On the way!"

Elvira's guns thundered as Podsednik sent two more shells the enemy's way. This time, both were direct hits and the enemy mount was neutralized, clearing the northern quadrant of HWPs.

"Resume HE fire on the field," she ordered, repositioning *Elvira* with increasingly painful fingers as the southern edge of the plateau erupted into chaos. "What the fuck is Murdoch doing down there?!" she snapped in disbelief after seeing that *Flaming Rose* hadn't fired its long guns in nearly two minutes.

"Looks like he's leaning on the reserves," Podsy said in open disgust.

Xi hesitated for a split-second before deciding to act, again in defiance of orders.

"Clear those HEs," she commanded, "then load standard APs."

"LT…" Podsy trailed off warningly.

"Just do it, Podsy," she snapped. "People are dying down there because of that desk-jockey's incompetence. If the commander puts one between my eyes because I cleared my board and decided to help Murdoch clear his, I'm fine with that." Podsy sent the two loaded HE shells down-range, killing dozens of Arh'Kel at the two-kilometer mark before she pivoted *Elvira* away from the northern zone and aimed her fifteens to the south. "APs up," she commanded.

"Lieutenant," Ensign Ford's predictable objection came over the line, "what are you doing?"

"Engaging the enemy," Xi replied. "You know, that thing we came down here to do? Continue clearing the northern quadrant, 5th Platoon, that's a direct order."

"You can't do this, Lieutenant Xi," Ford's whiny, nasally voice cried. "You have orders to engage the northern quadrant. Return to the line…"

"Back on target, *Forktail*," she snapped, "or I'll relieve you of command, as I, the platoon leader, am authorized to do at my discretion, *Ensign*."

Silence was her only reply, but *Forktail*'s eight-kilo gun continued dropping shells on the enemy in the northern quadrant.

The opening riff of *Man on the Silver Mountain* replaced the last notes of *Long Live Rock & Roll* just as Xi finished positioning *Elvira*. She was stunned to see that Arh'Kel had already reached the top of the southern ridge-line and were cartwheeling through the now-fifteen-meter gap in the rock-wall.

She knew that what she was about to do could kill the Pounders stationed nearby. But as four Arh'Kel infantry broke through the line, tearing into the lightly-armored reserve mechs and totally scrapping one, *Silent Fox*, in a matter of seconds, she knew there was no real choice in the matter.

"Fire on the breach, Podsy," she commanded. "Tight groupings. We just want to keep them from coming through."

"Targeting the breach," he acknowledged. "Firing."

Elvira's guns took aim and fired, one after the other, three seconds apart. Rubble in the breach flew, spraying deadly shrapnel toward the incoming enemy.

She winced as she saw a pair of exposed Pounders brought down by her fire, but she breathed a sigh of relief when one scrambled to his feet and dragged the other away from the blast zone.

Rhythmically pumping shell after shell into the breach, she cut the enemy completely off from the obvious weak point in their defenses.

She caught sight of a lone figure standing on the open plain of the plateau, directing Pounders here and there as they quickly set up machine guns and RPG launchers. That figure was Sergeant Major Tim Trapper, who was nothing short of a heroic figure as he stood tall, seemingly ignorant of the hellfire raining down around him as he pointed with one hand and occasionally fired his sidearm at a rock-biter with the other.

Xi had never been so impressed by a human being in her entire life. Not even fictional figures from myth and popular holo-vids had made such an impression.

"Good work, *Elvira*," Commander Jenkins' voice came across the line just as Trapper's Pounders established a defensible inner line and began working their new nests. "Concentrate your fire on the eastern field," he continued as *Flaming Rose* finally, after four minutes of silence, a full minute longer than the emergency cooldown required, resumed firing on the encroaching rock-biters in his quadrant. "North and south are under control."

"Copy that," she said, feeling a wave of relief wash over her at receiving her commanding officer's approval. She knew he might still punish her later, but for now, she was able to re-focus and cast aside doubts about her decision. Soon she and Podsy were helping to clear the eastern fields, but the number of rock-biters there was well over ten thousand, with more pouring steadily up from the tunnel mouths surrounding the plateau.

Xi doubted they had enough ammo to cut all of them down.

"Commander," Styles called out anxiously from the far side of *Roy*'s command center, "I need all of our drones in the air and transferred to my command, now."

"Do it," Jenkins agreed, and soon all three of the battalion's remaining drones, two Vultures and one Owl, were in the air. He made his way to Styles' side, where the technician worked with furious intensity as he called up files and programs that were completely unfamiliar to Jenkins. He waited a few seconds before prompting, "Talk to me."

"I think I can sleep them," Styles said tersely without tearing his eyes from the screen. "I need to position these drones...just like that..." he said, his fingers flying across his console as his words came sporadically, "and send a command...telling them...there!"

Suddenly, something bizarre happened.

Rippling outward from points centered directly beneath the airborne drones, rock-biters began to stop, fall, or slump over mid-stride.

"How did you..." Jenkins began, only to be interrupted.

"I have no idea how long it will last, sir," Styles said shortly.

Jenkins nodded before issuing orders. "All mechs: target railgun mounts in your assigned quadrants and fire at will. Ground forces: dust this rock off."

"Sar," acknowledged Sergeant Trapper with gusto, while Jenkins' mechs began scrapping every railgun mount in sight with rockets and artillery. One shot, one kill.

The Arh'Kel began to scatter, no longer united in their mindless assault on the plateau. Streaming back into their tunnels, they fled as fast as they could while Jenkins' people cleared out everything within three kilometers of their plateau fortress and scrubbed every HWP farther out than that.

Two minutes after they had been thrown into confusion, the last rock-biter had left the three-kilometer perimeter and Jenkins gave the engagement's final order. "Cease fire, cease fire, cease fire. Let 'em go, people. All crews, see to your wounded. Ground forces, triage casualties to medical. Platoon commanders, deliver personnel and ammo reports to Chief Styles."

He breathed a short sigh of relief before finishing, "This round's to us."

THE PLAN

"Okay, Styles," Jenkins said, sitting down with the technician two hours after the last Arh'Kel had disappeared back underground, where they belonged, as far as Jenkins was concerned. "Bring me up to speed."

"I was playing around with some virtual models," Styles explained, "and found that the Arh'Kel cybernetic implants have got some problems, like, *major* design flaws. They're so huge, and so glaring, if you know what you're looking for," he allowed, "that frankly I'm stunned they were used in a combat zone."

Jenkins' brow furrowed. "What do you mean?"

Styles hesitated, trying to summon the right words. "Imagine... Okay, it's like this." He took out a data slate and began tapping dozens of little dots into a rudimentary image-generation program. "Most control systems have a centralized control system, right? Even the Solarians' One Mind network has sub-nodes and central checkpoints that monitor all peer-to-peer data that gets disseminated to the rest of the network." As he spoke, he tapped out a handful of triangles in the midst of the scattered dots. "The dots are the individual Arh'Kel and, if I was designing the system, the triangles would represent sub-nodes and checkpoints installed onto either individual Arh'Kel or, even better, onto their HWPs. These nodes would provide protection against the mass-introduction of commands like the one I sent to the horde, and would be relatively easy to design and install, certainly they'd be easier to come up with than the individual links."

Jenkins nodded along as he slowly took Styles' meaning, "So you assumed that's what the Arh'Kel had done."

"Right!" Styles nodded enthusiastically. "It seemed so natural, so absurdly obvious, that such a decentralized system would require checks and balances, that I just assumed they'd done that. But I thought it was worth a test when the southern ridge-line was breached, especially when Xi started firing on the breach, so I used *Roy's* high-wattage transceiver to send a few test commands. At first, nothing worked, but eventually I hit on a command line that worked, written in their base six virtual coding language, of course," he added, as though it was nothing, but while Jenkins knew little about coding, he did know that coding in base six was beyond even most lifelong coders. That kind of job was always relegated to virtual bots because the human mind had too much difficulty working in base six.

"What was the command intended to do?" Jenkins asked.

"Create a feedback loop," Styles replied. "My hope was that it would short the implants out, or trigger some sort of built-in safeguards, and it looks like that's exactly what happened. They were in a stupor for about twenty seconds before they regained voluntary muscle control..."

"But when they did—" Jenkins nodded in comprehension. "—their implants were offline."

"And they lost the will to fight on," Styles confirmed, "which means that there might be more direct control being exerted through these implants than I initially thought. It could also simply be that, absent the implants' ongoing signals, they were thrown into confusion and decided to withdraw as a tactical decision in the face of an enemy capable of breaking their P2P linkage."

"Do you think you can do this again?" Jenkins pressed.

"Probably," Styles allowed, "but the rock-biters aren't stupid. Their extreme xenophobic mindset and bizarre sense of individualism made them overlook the possibility that we might do something like this through their network, but honestly?" He drew a deep breath before shaking his head resolutely. "Now that we've exposed the weakness, there's no way they don't shore this hole up, soon. If we want to take full advantage of this discovery, we need to mount an offensive."

Jenkins didn't like what he was hearing, holding his head in one hand and gesturing invitingly with the other. "Let's hear your plan."

Styles leaned forward intently, "I think I can do better than simply shutting these things down for a few seconds, Commander. I think I *might* be able to assume control of the whole system before they wise up."

Jenkins skeptically narrowed his eyes. "Talk me through it."

"Well…remember those 'friends' I mentioned earlier, the ones who once planned to break into the One Mind network?" Styles began.

"It's not the kind of thing I'd soon forget."

"Right…" Styles hesitated. "Well, 'their' plan hinged on insinuating a virus into every single sub-node simultaneously in order to prevent the system from seeing what 'they' were doing before it was too late. The problem with a distributed system is that it's self-descriptive. The virus 'my friends' worked to build was one which, in theory, would have overwritten enough segments of the system that it would have been inextricable from the system itself."

"I thought distributed systems built on blockchains or similar frameworks made that impossible?" Jenkins asked with a furrowed brow.

"There's a lot of technobabble here," Styles said dismissively, "but the central governments leave backdoors into all distributed systems so that they can go monkey with things later if they want. The trick is finding the backdoor and using it before the fuzz catches onto what you're doing. My initial hunch was right, Commander." Styles leaned in and lowered his voice. "These implants are uncannily similar to the One Mind systems."

"Are you suggesting that *Sol* gave the Arh'Kel this technology?" Jenkins asked in flat disbelief. He could accept that the Sol-bound humans looked down their noses at the Terran colonies. He could even understand and agree with some of their reasoning! But to suggest that Sol would actively work against the Republic with the Arh'Kel, a species which had quit the interstellar alliance known as the 'Illumination League' specifically so they could wage war against the Terran Republic...it was too much for Jenkins to believe.

"I have no idea if they bought it or stole it." Styles sank back into his chair and shrugged. "What I do know is that there's absolutely *no way*—" He emphatically thumped his finger down on the desk. "—that I could have done what I did if there hadn't been enough similarities between the One Mind system and this one, similarities which, practically speaking, could not have *possibly* been coincidental. The Solarians turned their backs on the colonies of the Terran Republic as soon as we told them we were happy just like we were." He leaned forward again, his eyes blazing with the same passion that had filled anti-Sol sentiment throughout the Republic in recent decades. "I think they were offended when we said we didn't need to be folded back into their hive-minded society after seventy-six years of fending for ourselves while the wormholes were offline. I think the Solarians don't consider Terrans as equals and view us as a bunch of low-browed frontiersmen clinging to an outdated concept of humanity. I also think most Terrans fear that the One Mind network has turned the Solarians into something that isn't really human any more. This cultural divide is only growing, Commander, and I think it's not impossible that the Solarians, who, since the last World War on Earth, haven't been too keen on individualism or non-conformity, saw a chance to get rid of us without dirtying their hands."

Jenkins had difficulty finding fault in Styles' logic, but he was keen to nip this type of talk in the bud. "The official stance of the Terran Republic is one which seeks reunification with Sol," he said firmly, holding up a halting hand when Styles made to object. "Both of us know that support for reunification is waning, but as long as we wear these uniforms—" He looked pointedly at Styles' collar, where his rank insignia was pinned. "—we need to keep talk like this to ourselves. Am I clear, Chief?" he asked knowingly.

Styles was easily the most intelligent member of the battalion, and he thankfully caught Jenkins' meaning despite his obviously strong feelings on the subject. "As a Solarian's conscience, sir," the chief warrant replied with a wry grin.

"Good." Jenkins nodded, leaning forward on his elbows. "Now tell me how long until we can execute this plan of yours."

"I'm going to need at least two days running tests," he replied promptly, "and I'll need the help of a few key personnel, chief among them Lieutenant Xi."

"Why Xi?" Jenkins asked in surprise.

"She…" Styles hesitated before wincing. "It would be better if I didn't have to explain, sir, at least not until I've talked with her. Suffice to say, she's got knowledge which could be useful."

Jenkins nodded. "Done. This project is top priority, so you can make any personnel or material transfers you deem necessary without prior approval from me. Is there anything else?"

"No, sir," Styles said confidently.

"Then hop to it, Chief."

"It's been years since I did anything like this," Xi said angrily after encountering another error in the short code she had just written. *Roy*'s command center was several times the size of *Elvira's* interior cabin, but the longer she worked within, the more claustrophobic she felt. "And I've *never* worked in base six," she snapped.

"It's okay, *Elvira*," Styles assured her. "Just keep working through it. I'll need you to run those checks against my main program as soon as it's written."

"My name's Xi Bao," she responded irritably, "or you can refer to me by my rank, Chief."

"Oh, please," he snickered, "everyone knows you're about as committed to military discipline as a whore is to a John."

"Did you just call me a whore?" she demanded only half-seriously.

"We're all whores, *Elvira*," he chuckled. "But some people are stuck with the boring names our parents gave us, while others go out into the world and earn callsigns that belong to our souls!"

"You mean like N609E?" she muttered under her breath.

Styles laughed. "Yeah, kind of like that, but yours has the benefit of being earned while N609E was something I came up with myself."

She completed the code fragment and ran it through a check program, and this time, it came back clean. She sighed in relief. "There. That one's finished."

"Good work." He nodded approvingly as he continued building the larger program to which her small collection of fragments would eventually be attached. "Get started on the next one, and remember to look out for..."

"Yeah, yeah," she sighed, "no recursives in the individual code fragments. They need to be recombinant. I *was* listening two hours ago when you laid this out."

Silence hung between them for a long while as they went

about their respective tasks, but eventually, Styles broke it. "Thanks for painting a target on my back, by the way."

"Excuse me?" she asked in momentary confusion.

"Oh, come on," he laughed. "You sic'd Podsednik on me. He's been giving me the hairy eyeball ever since you agreed to lie about us sleeping together."

She couldn't help herself from giggling gleefully. "You wanted the social credit, and now you're going to get the whole nine meters."

"Oh, it was well-played." He grinned. "I can't say I'm looking forward to losing a tooth or two when he finally boils over about it, but it'll be worth it to see the look on his face when you break it to him afterward."

"Podsy's good people," she said dismissively. "He'll probably just slap you around a few times."

"Are you kidding?" Styles blurted. "You seriously don't see the way he looks at you?"

She snorted derisively. "He doesn't think of me like that."

"Oh, I know that," he assured her. "He doesn't want to sleep with you, he sees you like a kid sister. Didn't you have any brothers?"

"No," she admitted, "I was an only child."

"Well, the memes and axioms don't do it justice," Styles said knowingly. "I've got a sister who's two years older than me, and one time after a boyfriend knocked her around a little, I fucked him up good."

"You?" Xi laughed incredulously. "You don't weigh a buck twenty and your neck's barely thicker than my bicep. Don't try telling me you beat him up."

"I never said I hit him with my fists," he said dismissively.

"Okay, I'll bite." She rolled her eyes. "What did you do?"

His grin turned mischievous, and a savage twinkle entered his eye as he lowered his voice. "I edited some amateur porn to make it look like he was doing some extreme BDSM stuff with a woman whose husband was unaware of her voyeuristic tendencies. Then I made sure the husband ran across it in his data feeds, along with the asshole's personal info." Styles straightened with pride. "Two months in traction can have a transformative impact on a man."

"What about the woman?" Xi asked in alarm, though she was mostly impressed by the story.

"I made sure she had ample warning beforehand." He shrugged. "She ended up smoothing things over with him and they discovered that he, too, was plenty comfortable in front of the camera. At last check, their voyeur channels had become pretty popular, and both of them quit their jobs to make porn full-time. *Together*," he added triumphantly.

"Look at you," Xi snickered. "Redefining revenge porn as a marriage counselor."

"And career counseling," he noted with insufferable, but seemingly well-earned, smugness. "They make more now doing what they love than they would have ever made working their dead-ends."

"True or not," Xi admitted, "that's a hell of a story."

"Isn't it?" He grinned.

She needed a break. "I've got to get some chow and check on Podsy."

"Sure thing," he agreed. "Be back in thirty minutes."

"Will do." She nodded, standing and stretching luxuriously before exiting *Roy*.

Once outside, she heard a familiar voice barking orders nearby. She turned toward the source and saw the sergeant major. He was dressing down two Pounders for some reason or another, and Xi could not help but watch as he stood there, tall and imposing but measured and under absolute control.

He soon dismissed the Pounders before turning on his heel and making his way for *Roy*. Xi turned in a mix of embarrassment and trepidation. She had sent uncalled-for danger-close artillery strikes right behind him, after all, and she doubted anyone would be inclined to view such an act favorably.

"Lieutenant Xi," he snapped, his deep voice easily carrying over the sounds of pounding hammers, screeching drills, and hissing plasma torches as mech crews worked to patch up their vehicles.

She pretended not to hear him, blushing from the collar up as she moved in the opposite direction, which, it happened, was the wrong way from where *Elvira II* was parked.

"*Elvira*," Trapper called out in an even louder voice, and by now, a handful of nearby heads had swiveled to investigate the scene.

Deciding it was time to face the music, she stopped and turned toward him. "Yes, Sergeant Major Trapper?"

He clomped toward her, his heavy all-terrain boots loudly grinding bits of glassy dust with each step. He came to within arm's reach without slowing, and for a moment, she was afraid he would actually punch her.

She knew she deserved it, so she planted her feet and set her jaw in preparation for what was soon to come.

But instead of hitting her, he stopped a third of a meter from where she stood and fixed her with a hard, unreadable look as he barked, "Who ordered you to fire danger-close artillery on my position?"

She squared her shoulders. "No one, Sergeant Major. That was my call, and it went against my commander's orders. I accept full responsibility."

He held her with his steel-gray eyes for a long moment before, inexplicably, thrusting his hand between them and declaring, "Your quick thinking saved a lot of my people's lives, Lieutenant. Thank you for making a tough call when your supposed superiors—" He cast a dark glance toward *Flaming Rose*. "—wouldn't do the same."

She hesitated before gripping his hand with her own. His skin was leathery and cool, and he had a grip like a vice. Thankfully, he was gentle enough to avoid hurting her still-raw fingers.

"I'm sorry about the two Pounders that took shrapnel," she said with feeling as she withdrew her hand. "How are they?"

"Davis and Michaelson." Trapper nodded knowingly. "Davis will be fine, thanks to you, though he'll be deaf as a post until he gets home and finds a new set of ears. Michaelson was pronounced an hour ago," he added matter-of-factly.

She winced at hearing that both had been badly injured, and one had died as a result of those injuries. "I'm sorry to hear about that."

"Don't be," he said, doffing his helmet and running a hand across his immaculately smooth, perfectly-shaped head. "I'd fight with you anywhere, Lieutenant." With that, he turned and made his way to a nearby group of Pounders who were repairing a damaged machine gun. "Oh, come on, Velasquez, if you're using that much lube, it means you didn't do a good enough job of prepping her."

Xi stifled a giggle at the obvious sexual innuendo and made for *Elvira*, where Podsy was hard at work replacing some of her missile rack's components.

Her eyes briefly met Trapper's, and when they did, she felt a wholly unexpected, and totally undeniable, thrill which she did her best to ignore before turning her attention back to her distant mech.

"It looks like that's the limit," Xi said after running simulations with Styles for six straight hours. "We can't squeeze it down below five hundred, and there's no way we can use multiple broadcast points. The signal simply won't propagate if it doesn't originate from the same source."

Styles rubbed the bridge of his nose wearily while Xi rolled her neck to relieve pent-up tension. They had been working on this problem for a full day and had made consistent progress in decreasing the number of simultaneous 'flips' they needed to achieve. But the number had stalled out at five hundred, which was concerning given the necessary proximity to the transceiver.

"Fifty meters," he grunted sourly. "I'm just… I'm not sure any vehicle, even *Roy*, can survive long enough to get into five hundred rock-biter infantry. They scrapped *Silent Fox* in under ten seconds and would have torn into *Elvira* in no more than thirty seconds if you two hadn't brought that pulse missile down on yourselves."

Xi nodded slowly. "I might have an idea on that."

"Oh?" he asked in mixed annoyance and amusement. "You think you can work this number down, or the range of the transceiver up?"

"Neither," she said as she considered the matter. "It's something Podsy and I have been working up, but it's still in the 'drawing board' stage."

"You and Podsednik have been thinking about how to overtake a decentralized neural net via mass takeover?" Styles deadpanned. "Well, forgive me for standing on your capes, please, enlighten me."

The stress of the project was starting to wear thin on them both, but Xi did her best to ignore the barb as she explained, "We can't survive very long at knife-range with the rock-biters because of those plasma torches, right?"

"Right," Styles drawled irritably.

"Well…we've been thinking about how to keep them off the hull," she explained, and Styles' eyebrows rose in guarded surprise.

"What were you thinking, high-voltage?" he asked.

She shook her head. "Only *Roy*'s got non-conductive contacts with the ground, so we haven't been thinking along those lines." She tapped up a series of images from *Roy's* main database, some of which were clearly stylized, but which she hoped would get the message across well enough. "We've got enough spare motors and other components lying around," she explained as he leaned forward to examine the images in detail. "And it's not like anyone's asking these things to last more than a minute or two, right?"

He nodded slowly. "You know...this isn't a stupid idea."

She snorted in annoyance. "Gee, thanks."

Styles gave her a withering look which soon morphed to one of apology. "You know what I meant."

"Yeah," she quipped, "you were surprised I didn't have a stupid idea."

"Piss off," he said dismissively as he flipped through the images and nodded with increasing frequency. "Yeah...yeah, okay, let's be clear—this *looks* as fucking dumb as a box of rocks, but it might actually buy us a little more time."

"Enough to get the job done, though?" she asked skeptically.

"Every little bit helps," he said confidently. "All right." He nodded decisively. "Let's go see the commander. I don't think this is enough on its own, but we need to get started on these retrofits immediately while we try to figure out how to extend this clock."

They stood from their stations and went to Jenkins' hovel at the rear of *Roy's* cabin. The hatch was shut, and Styles chimed the comm-panel beside it. A few seconds later, the hatch opened and a half-dressed, bleary-eyed Commander Jenkins greeted them.

"Chief..." He blinked hard before seemingly noticing Xi. "Lieutenant. You're still working?"

"No rest for the wicked." Styles smirked before handing the commander a slate with a rough outline of Xi's idea. "We're still not done improving the takeover program, but it looks like we're going to need at least five hundred Arh'Kel within fifty meters of *Roy's* transceiver, and only *Roy's* transceiver," he added sourly, "before it can work."

"Five hundred within fifty meters?" Jenkins blinked again, and at seeing the dark semicircles beneath his eyes, Xi felt the irresistible urge to yawn. "They'll carve into us with plasma torches before..." He trailed off before his eyes settled on some of the images Xi had shown Styles. As he flipped through the images, his expression went from disbelieving, to skeptical, to sour, to grudging acceptance before he finally muttered, "This has got to be the stupidest-looking mod proposal I've ever seen." He handed the slate back to Styles and deadpanned, "This is the best you two can come up with?"

Xi was surprised that the commander, who had always been sagacious and flexible in his thinking as far as she could tell, was so quick to dismiss the plan. She opened her mouth to plead their case, but Styles beat her to the punch.

"It is, sir," Styles said confidently.

Jenkins looked back and forth between them several times before sighing. "Well...by any objective measure, you're the two smartest people in this battalion." He then affixed his signature to the slate. "I asked you for a solution and you've given me one. Good work. Now go tell Koch to start modifying *Roy*, *Elvira*, and *Flaming Rose* per these..." His lips twisted into a smirk. "...designs, and then hit your racks for at least four hours. That's an order."

He closed the hatch, leaving Xi thoroughly confused.

"Good work, *Elvira*," Styles said with a grin.

"Don't call me that," she grunted, but she suspected that there was no escaping the moniker.

After relaying the commander's orders to Lieutenant Koch, she found her bunk aboard *Elvira II* and was out before she remembered to take her boots off.

COMMAND & CONTROL

Work on *Elvira*'s modifications was proceeding well, with the job over half done. Xi had enlisted the aid of every mech crewman in her platoon, including Ensign Ford, who was fraying every last nerve she had.

"Ford," she said through gritted teeth, "I told you already that the angle needs to be greater than that."

"You go with a steep angle and these things are going to come right off the hull," he retorted. "If you want these things to last more than a few seconds, we have to bolt the motors flush to the plate."

"If they're flush to the plate, they'll only be half as effective," she fired back. "Which is clearly good enough for you but is not good enough for me."

The heat was bad and the tension unhealthy, but the bigger problem was the fact that the entire battalion had been forced to start drinking recycled dark water due to the supply of clear water having been exhausted when shrapnel had punctured the tanks during the fight.

"Everything you do," Ford sneered, stopping the work and throwing his arc welder onto the ground, "is against convention.

You don't follow orders, you don't listen to advice, and you don't give a rat's ass about whether or not you're doing the right thing. All you care about is being in charge. You're a danger to the unit, *Lieutenant*," he spat, turning to leave his assigned duty as he started walking toward the command center, "and I think it's time I spoke with the commander about that."

"Get back on task, Ensign Ford," she growled, dropping her own tools and jumping down from *Elvira's* stern, sticking the three-meter-drop's landing before stomping toward him. "That's an order!"

"What are you going to do about it?" Ford turned defiantly. "I outweigh you by fifteen kilos, and my mama raised me better than to hit a woman."

"I may be a woman—" Xi stomped up to him, looking up into his eyes while he wore a condescending smirk. "—but judging by the smell of you, those fifteen kilos you're so proud of are pure cat piss, and from that pathetic 'bulge' in your pants, it's clear I'm more man than you'll ever be!"

A chorus of jeers and hoots erupted from nearby crews as all eyes fell on the pair of them, but Xi wasn't about to back down. Ford was bigger than her, that was certain, and in spite of her training, she gave herself no better than a one-in-three chance of beating him in a bare-knuckle fight.

But she was through dealing with his bullshit. One way or another, it ended right there.

Ford smirked down at her. "Your corpse-fucker's not here to protect you this time."

"Careful." She balled her hands into fists at her sides, causing her raw fingertips to scream in pain. "That's my Wrench you're talking about."

"How do you two do it, anyway?" Ford's lip curled venomously. "Do you strip and turn the AC down real low so you're cold as a corpse before he f..."

Xi delivered a knee to Ford's groin, cutting him off mid-sentence. He bore the blow well, but it still bought her enough time to launch an uppercut into his jaw and slip free of his clumsy grappling attempt.

"You bitch," he growled, quickly recovering from the near-miss nut-shot. She crouched low, prepared for the counterattack he soon launched. She easily avoided the first two punches, both wild haymakers, but was caught by the crisp jab that followed.

Snapping a low leg kick, she buried her shin into his knee, buckling it just as he swung a brutal overhand right. He missed with the punch and staggered over his briefly-buckling leg, giving Xi time to once again slip away.

"What's the matter, Ford?" She smirked. "Your mama teach you how to fight, too?"

"Don't talk about my mom," he snarled, raising his fists and firing a series of quick, accurate jabs that she slipped and blocked until he sent a surprise left kick into her side. She trapped the kick and, acting purely on long-trained reflex, executed a flying kneebar. Leaving her feet and wrapping both of her legs around his left one, she locked his ankle into the crook of her elbow and torqued her hips over, dragging him to the ground while a growing chorus hoots and cheers surrounded the combatants.

She didn't want to break his knee, but she was acutely aware that his mech's neural interface still worked perfectly fine. He didn't *need* his leg to operate his mech, and in the heat of the moment, she decided to go for the joint lock with everything she had.

Unfortunately, as they fell to the ground, he managed to pop his ankle loose just enough to prevent her from getting the necessary leverage.

Now she was in trouble.

Ford's superior length and his superior strength proved decisive as a brief scramble saw him emerge in top position. Once there, he rained down a flurry of punches, most of which missed as she twisted and fought to a full-guard position with her legs wrapped around his torso.

"Yeah," he leered, reaching and gripping her left wrist in his sweaty hand. "That's more like it..."

She bucked her hips hard enough to create some distance, then 'shrimped' onto her left side and kicked down with her right foot against his thigh. She bought just enough space with the move to use his own grip against him, pivoting and spinning on her back while isolating the arm he had gripped her wrist with.

He quickly let go of her wrist, but it was too late. She'd reversed the position, and now had his arm between her legs in a classic *omoplata* position. From there, it would be little trouble for her to rip his rotator cuff apart, but she knew that would be imprudent. A torn knee was a smaller problem than a wrecked arm, and no matter how much she wanted to do it, she decided not to down-check one of her platoon's Jocks.

Snarling in irritation, she released the grip and drove a pair of hard knees into his right side. He grunted in pain when the second landed right over his kidney, and once again, he used his superior size and strength to grapple and put her on her back.

"Big mistake," he growled, rearing back for another punch, but this time when he brought his fist down, she timed her counter perfectly. Swinging her legs up, she pivoted to one side and let his fist strike the granite beside her head. Isolating that arm, she snaked her right leg up over his shoulder and locked in a 'figure four' triangle choke.

He reared back, gripping his wrist with his free hand and, for a brief moment, it seemed like he would pick her up and spike her on her head in a potentially fatal move.

But to her surprise, he deigned to do so. A few seconds later, she was pulling his face down, unfortunately, toward her crotch, and squeezing both sides of his neck to cut off blood-flow to his brain.

He struggled for a few seconds, but it was clear he had no

idea how to extricate himself, and he soon went limp. She rolled him over without relinquishing the position, and once she was there, she cocked a fist and released the pressure with her legs.

He soon came to, and though it took him a few seconds, his eyes eventually fixed on her. When she had his undivided attention, she growled, "Do we need to tell the commander about this, or are we ready to get back to work?"

Ford looked up at her angrily, but mixed with that anger was something else. Something deeper, and considerably less confrontational.

If she didn't know better, she would have called it a glimmer of respect.

"Work," he muttered.

She nodded, standing and offering him a hand up, only realizing as she did so that her nose was bleeding profusely and had already ruined her undershirt.

He accepted the hand, and after he had regained his feet, the crowd, which had been silent for the last few seconds, erupted into approving applause.

"Did you have to cheap shot me to start?" Ford muttered bitterly, wincing as he adjusted his trousers.

"Come on," she replied with a withering look, ready to throw down again if he so much as flinched. "I'm not stupid. You may be full of cat piss, but you have fifteen kilos on me and greater reach. I'd have a hard time beating you straight-up."

He grinned, showing a mouthful of bloody teeth as he offered his hand. "Good fight, Lieutenant."

She was momentarily caught off-guard by the gesture, but eventually accepted his hand and gave it a firm shake while he made sure to let her know his grip was stronger. "Good fight, Ensign," she agreed, more than a little confused at just how quickly and severely his attitude toward her had changed.

The applause intensified before a booming voice called out

from the rear of the crowd. "All right, you knuckle-draggers," Sergeant Major Trapper barked. "Playtime's over, back to work!"

The crowd dispersed, and as it did so, the sergeant major met Xi's gaze, flashed a knowing grin, and tipped his helmet before turning and arrowing to the far side of the parking lot where a Pounder drew his attention and ire.

"What the hell just happened?" Podsy asked, staggering out of *Elvira* and coming to stand at her side. He was bleary-eyed after being interrupted from his well-earned bunk-time and appeared every bit as confused as she was, though clearly for different reasons.

"Honestly?" Xi boggled as Ensign Ford began directing crews to install the new mod components on *Elvira*, this time doing so at the more extreme angle, like she had initially ordered. "I don't have a clue."

TARGET ACQUISITION

"This is a lot harder than it looks," Podsy muttered as he guided their Owl-class drone across the glass-field in an ever-widening search grid.

"Tell me about it," Xi mocked, resting comfortably in her pilot's chair with a bottle of fresh water. It wasn't that recycled garbage, but direct-from-Fleet-sanitizers, honest-to-God mineral water which had mysteriously appeared beneath her bunk. Podsy had his suspicions about who had given it to her, and if those suspicions were correct, then he was ambivalent about what the gesture likely foretold.

"You're just lucky Strange Bed gave you twenty-four hours of strict bedrest." Podsy smirked. "Otherwise, you'd have to do some actual work." The truth was that she had been pushing herself too hard, and Podsy had surreptitiously gone to Doc Fellows seeking precisely such an order on her behalf. Her fingers bled from unbroken hours of manually controlling *Elvira*. She needed downtime, and there was no other way to get her to take it.

"I think he probably meant for me to serve the sentence under *his* watchful eye, not yours," Xi quipped.

"Oh, he's not so bad," Podsy played along, "especially since the drugs make you forget pretty much everything."

"Sometimes a girl wishes all you clowns would be so considerate."

He laughed, losing this particular round of their ongoing game of one-up-man-ship. "Dammit, Xi, have you no shame?"

"None."

"Or mercy," he added, knowing that would get a rise out of her.

"What do you mean by that?" She sat bolt upright as he gently turned the Owl drone and guided it into another leg of its high-altitude search.

"A knee to the ghoulies right off the bat?" he explained. "That's low, even for a chick. And I saw you try to hit that leg-lock—you were going to break his leg."

She paused before knocking back another mouthful of water. "Maybe I was."

"That wouldn't have done anyone any good," Podsy explained. "Least of all you."

"He's a loudmouth asshole who had it coming and then some!" she protested before slinking back into her chair. "Besides...all that sexual threat crap was uncalled for."

"Probably," he admitted, "but the truth is men and women don't mix seamlessly in combat situations. He probably didn't know how else to express his insecurity."

"Insecurity?!" she blurted. "The asshole threatened to rape me."

"He didn't threaten to rape you any more than you actually like the idea of being drugged unconscious and sexually assault-ed," he said dismissively. "Ford didn't know who you really were until you two threw down. After you did, he finally saw you as more than a shapely figure with a chip on her shoulder and he's accepted you as a warrior and his superior officer."

She was silent for a moment before sighing. "I'm trying to

understand, but it just doesn't make any sense to me. It seems like machismo run amok."

Podsednik chuckled. "Maybe it is, but it's how we've done it since cave-times. Until you showed him you knew the difference between a real fight and a power struggle, and that you were capable of winning either, he couldn't trust you enough to follow you into battle."

"What makes you think I know the difference between a fight and a power struggle?" she asked challengingly.

"It looked that way, toward the end at least." He shrugged as the Owl finally picked up something which caused him to focus its sensors on the patch of ground in question. "You didn't rip his shoulder out when you easily could have, and to return the favor, he didn't smash your skull on the rock."

She seemed unconvinced. "I didn't want my platoon to be down a Jock. He could pilot *Forktail* without his leg, but he needs both arms for manual controls if his neural link goes down."

Podsy whistled appreciatively at what he found on the scanners, forwarding the feed to Styles in *Roy* before replying, "Well... I wouldn't go telling him that was your reasoning. Because from the crowd's perspective, you earned a lot of much-needed respect."

Styles' reply came back with confirmation: Podsy had found what they were looking for.

"Looks like we've got a target," Podsy declared as he guided the Owl back to the barn.

"Really?" she asked in surprise, hopping up from her seat and moving to his side where she could see the monitors. Nodding in approval, she handed him the half-full bottle. "What would I do without you, Podsy?"

He knocked back the bottle's whole contents in a single go before sighing contentedly and replying, "Power tools?"

She slugged him in the shoulder, signifying that he had won that round.

"Ladies and gentlemen, we've found our hole," Jenkins declared, sweeping the battalion's assembled Jocks who had crammed into *Roy*'s main cabin. As he spoke, Styles threw the Owl's recon images onto the viewers flanking him. "Surface characteristics, thermals, EM interference—it paints the picture of a near-surface nexus."

"Why don't we just follow one of the attack tunnels down after the biters, sir?" Ford asked.

Sergeant Major Trapper scoffed. "Son, the rock-biters know more about tunneling when they hatch than you'll ever learn in a lifetime. They collapse those passages as soon as they retreat down 'em. My last time on this rock, we wasted days chasing after them on their terms and lost a lot of people doing it."

"And even if we wanted to, we don't have the resources to repeat that mistake," Jenkins agreed. He brought up a video log of the last engagement, when the rock-biters fell under Styles' spell and ceased their relentless assault. Hoots and cheers filled the cabin as the assemblage made their appreciation of Chief Styles' efforts clear, and Jenkins allowed the moment to stretch on before continuing. "Chief Styles, our de facto intelligence officer, discovered a way to temporarily sleep the rock-biters. He used the drones to relay a signal that, put simply, knocked them out long enough for us to elbow ourselves some breathing room. When they came to, they retreated en masse to their spider-holes."

"How many of these fuckers are down here, Commander?" asked Nakamura, one of 5th Platoon's Jocks.

"We have no idea," Jenkins replied heavily, sweeping the room with his gaze before deciding to relay what Trapper had told him, "but this rock is important to the Arh'Kel offensive—important enough that, six days ago, they came through the wormhole in force and took down five of our dreadnoughts trying to reach this rock."

A hushed silence fell upon the room, just as Jenkins had expected it would. He let that silence hang for a long while as his people came to terms with the magnitude of the situation.

"How's Fleet holding up at the gate, sir?" Xi asked, but the truth was Jenkins didn't know.

"I left on a slow-rider three days after the initial attack," Sergeant Major Trapper interjected grimly. "The yachties were holding their own last I checked but couldn't spare a carrier to come here and properly reinforce y'all."

"So the sergeant major," Jenkins put in dryly, "thought that if we couldn't get reinforced with a ten-pack of Marines, like originally planned, the next best thing would be for him to grace us with his ugly mug while delivering the good news."

Nervous laughter filled the cabin as Trapper drawled, "You Armor kids are almost as cocky as Marines. And you smell worse."

Even Jenkins chuckled as the mood lightened. "Chief, break it down for us." He gestured for Styles to take his place at the head of the table.

The de facto intelligence officer nodded and stood, gesturing to the looping video feed of the rock-biters being temporarily KO'd. "You're probably thinking we'll just keep using this trick," Styles said, raising his voice to be heard over the short-lived laughter which soon died down, "in which case, no problem. The rock-biters get close enough, we put them to sleep and mop up. The problem is it took me twelve hours to modify these receivers —" He held up a fragment of the rock-biter cybernetic implants. "—in such a way that they're no longer vulnerable. If I could do it, knowing next to nothing about this tech, the enemy will be able to make better modifications faster."

The mood sobered. And even Trapper seemed displeased by

the latest news. A dark cloud had descended on those who heard Styles' assessment.

"That's the bad news, but we've got two pieces of good news to go along with it," Styles continued confidently. "The first is that I knew exactly what I did in order to disrupt them, which means I have a head-start in figuring out a way to block it. But it's already been two days, so it's possible that the rock-biters who retreated have already made the necessary modifications. If I had to bet, I'd say they haven't worked it out—yet—but it's just a matter of time."

"That's the *good* news?" Captain Murdoch blurted, speaking for the first time since the meeting had begun.

"It is," Styles said without missing a beat, "but it's not all the good news. The rest is that, working with Lieutenant Xi—" He gestured to *Elvira*'s Jock. "—I've devised a way to take functional control of every rock-biter on Durgan's Folly."

Hoots and cheers erupted throughout the command center, but Jenkins knew that the next bit of Styles' presentation was likely to dampen the suddenly hopeful atmosphere. The intel dweeb's penchant for taking the battalion's leadership on an emotional roller coaster ride chapped Jenkins' ass.

"The catch—" Styles raised his voice, barely able to make himself heard as he repeated at the top of his lungs. "The catch—" He held up his hands, quieting the crowd enough to be heard over the din. "—is that we have to find an Arh'Kel nest and position *Roy* no further than fifty meters from five hundred individual rock-biters to make it work."

Predictably, the positive energy was sucked from the room.

"Their troop density is rarely that high, even in a full charge," Trapper mused.

"What about using the Vultures?" Ford ventured hopefully.

Styles shook his head. "We've run the simulations tens of thousands of times. The drones don't have the transceiver wattage, and even if we ginned them up to spec, there's no realistic way they'd get close enough to do the job before they got shot down."

Jenkins stood beside Styles and made brief eye contact with each of his Jocks. "*Roy*'s the only mech in the battalion with thick enough armor to pull it off. Even *Elvira* and *Flaming Rose* are too vulnerable to wade into a mass like that, but we'll need all three of those mechs to breach the junction if we're going to make this work."

"You're not taking the whole battalion, sir?" asked Falwell, *Preacher*'s Jock.

"No, we're not," Jenkins confirmed. "We'll have a lower seismic footprint if we take as few units as possible, but we'll need your MRMs to help crack this junction open."

"We've got six hot missiles ready to launch on your order and two more that could be loaded onto Vultures to be dumb-fired point-blank," Falwell said confidently.

"Good," Jenkins said approvingly, glad to hear that *Preacher*'s crew had managed to partially salvage two of their last eight MRMs—mid-range missiles. Every last round would be important where they were going.

"Commander..." Captain Murdoch leaned forward skeptically. "The chief says we need to draw five hundred Arh'Kel infantry within fifty meters of *Roy*. Even with the latest—" His lips twisted distastefully. "—*modifications* to our heavies, how the hell can we hope to pull that off? It only takes six rock-biters with cutting torches to cut a light mech down in ten seconds. I know *Roy*'s a beast, and that both *Elvira* and *Flaming Rose* are tough nuts to crack, but we're looking at...what, a minute of survival time at most?"

Xi smirked. "And that's only if we sneak in before they turn a dozen railguns on us." It was clear she wanted to say more, but after making brief eye contact with Jenkins, she opted to stow it for the time being.

"The latest mods will buy us at *least* a minute at knife-range,"

Jenkins assured his jittery company captain. "But let me be clear: we're going to have to go there cycling our anti-personnel guns so fast their barrels melt. It's the only way we can ensure enough of them flood the cavern."

"All right…" Murdoch sent a resentful look Xi's way. "So, we go in guns blazing. I still don't see what's so important that we can't just hole up here and wait for Fleet to arrive."

"We're bingo ordnance, *Captain*," Xi snapped. "If the rock-biters figure out how to block Styles' disruption method, you can bet your ass they'll storm this rock in force—and when they do, I might not have enough ammo to cover your back. *Again*."

"Lieutenant Xi—" Murdoch rounded angrily on the young woman.

"That's enough!" Jenkins barked. He sent each of his ill-behaved officers looks of dire warning before unimaginatively saying, "Save it for the rock-biters. We roll in twenty minutes. I want *Preacher*'s two dumb-fires loaded onto Vultures and airborne in one hour. We're going to hit them hard, fast, and right where they live. This is no joke, ladies and gentlemen," he said, setting his jaw grimly, "there are probably enough Arh'Kel on this rock to wipe out every human in the Terran Republic if those fireships break through our Fleet's blockade. I'm not going to sugarcoat it: this is a high-risk, high-reward operation. If we succeed, we neutralize an existential threat to the colonial way of life. And if we fail, we're looking at New Australia all over again —only this time on *every* colony in the Terran Republic."

Judging by the expressions around the table, his invocation of New Australia had done the trick of refocusing the group. New Australia was the worst slaughter in the history of the Arh'Kel Wars and had become a universal rallying cry for Republic soldiers. Ten million humans, most of them civilians, had been wiped out by Arh'Kel shock troops before Fleet could scrub New Australia—officially recognized as Terra Australiana—clean of the rock-biter plague.

"Any questions?" he asked, receiving nothing but shaking heads in reply. "Good. Dismissed."

Xi was just about to board *Elvira* and prep her for departure when she heard a now-familiar voice call from her back. "Lieutenant, a moment?"

She turned to see Sergeant Major Trapper striding toward her. "Yes, Sergeant Major?"

He grinned in reply, but behind his thick, handlebar mustache, the expression looked more like a bemused smirk. "I was hoping you'd agree to an unusual request," he explained with a mischievous twinkle in his eye.

She couldn't help but snicker. "If this is going where I think it's going…"

"Depends on where you think it's going," he chuckled before gesturing to the top of *Elvira*'s hull. "Between those dual fifteens is a pretty good spot for a nest, and you'll need all the close-in fire support you can carry down that hole."

She turned and looked up, studying the space between *Elvira*'s dual fifteen-kilo cannons, and nodded. "It looks like you could squeeze a couple Pounders up there with machine guns."

"I was thinking RPGs and hand grenades, mostly. I've got a couple boys lined up for the job if you don't mind," Trapper explained, though that mischievous grin never left his lips.

"I'm not going to lie," she said seriously. "I'd appreciate the extra close-in firepower, but it's a suicide mission even *inside* a heavily-armored mech. Riding on top of one?" She shook her head adamantly. "I couldn't ask anyone to do that."

"Good thing you're not askin' for it, then," Trapper drawled. "Wouldn't want to mix signals, would we?"

"Sergeant Major…" She did her best to screw her face up into a look of disapproval. "Are you offering fire support or hitting on me?"

"I'll let you be the judge of that," he chuckled. "But if you want me and my boys up there, we need to get set up on the double." He gestured to a small team of Pounders assembled nearby.

She was more than a little intimidated by the battle ahead of her, and she knew that every bit of support would help her focus on the task at hand. "I'd appreciate that, Sergeant Major," she said with genuine feeling.

"Please," he said, gesturing for his people to begin working on the makeshift nest atop her mech, "call me Tim. The only people who refer to me by my rank are my men and my father."

She cocked an eyebrow. "That last bit sounds like a story worth hearing."

"Might just share it with you after we get back, Elvira," he said, tipping his helmet before joining his people atop her mech.

He was a dozen paces away before she realized he had called her 'Elvira.'

CARBON VS. SILICA

Fifty-two kilometers from HQ, the trio of mechs had drawn within spitting distance of their target. *Roy*, *Elvira*, and *Flaming Rose* looked like props straight out of a post-apocalyptic blockbuster, with jagged spikes and other, more sinister-looking equipment having been hastily welded, bolted, and even cemented onto their hulls in preparation for the attack.

Jenkins activated the P2P comm-link, routed through their lone remaining Owl drone. Maintaining radio silence had been critical to this point, but now it was time to do their thing. "All right, people, this is it," he declared as *Roy* drove toward the hidden subterranean nexus beneath the glassy surface. "*Preacher*, make a hole."

Thanks to *Elvira* and her Owl, they knew where it was without having to see it.

"Copy that, Commander. Six Defiance birds inbound: ETA twenty-one seconds," Falwell replied promptly. "Good hunting, *Roy*."

Jenkins grinned as a particular phrase leaped to the front of his mind. "To paraphrase our very own *Elvira*," he intoned as the impact clock wound down toward zero, "it's time to send these assholes back to the Stone Age."

Six Defiance-class MRMs slammed into the ground before the mech trio, sending a geyser of rubble hundreds of meters into the air. Head-sized rocks clanked against *Roy*'s armor as the formation, led by *Elvira* and *Flaming Rose*, bore down on the impact site.

When the dust cleared, it was obvious the hole was too small.

"Vultures inbound," Styles reported as the two airborne drones' icons sped across the tactical plotter. "Time to engagement: eight seconds."

The mechs slowed to half-speed as Jenkins ordered, "Chaps, hit that hole with everything we've got."

At less than six hundred meters, *Roy*'s fifteens would be hard to put on the target, but Chaps proved his mettle as he managed to send a pair of HE shells within a dozen meters of the bulls-eye. Rockets tore loose of *Roy*'s launch tubes, slamming into the ground mere seconds before Styles declared, "Dumb-fires away!"

Another geyser of rubble erupted upward from the impact site as two more Defiance-class MRMs struck the ground.

Elvira and *Flaming Rose* added their weight of fire to the effort, and this time when the dust settled, there was a hole large enough to fit a single mech through at a time.

It was far from ideal, but it was what they had to work with.

"*Elvira*, you're up," Jenkins commanded. "Give 'em hell."

"Roger," Xi replied eagerly. The makeshift nest atop *Elvira*'s armored carapace sprang into action as six Pounders, led by Tim Trapper, laid RPGs over their hastily-assembled nest.

The Scorpion-class mech surged into the hole just as a pair of railgun bolts burst out, and Jenkins knew then that what he'd said in the pre-mission brief had been true.

This was for all the marbles.

Elvira II breached the hole, revealing an underground chamber remarkably similar to the one Xi and Podsy had fallen into in the original *Elvira*.

And this one was *crawling* with rock-biters.

Xi's flank-mounted machine guns sprayed hundreds of rounds per second into the cavern, laying waste to rock-biters even as a pair of railgun strikes narrowly missed her hull.

"You want the new mods online?" Podsy asked, ever the calm voice in the midst of chaos.

"Not yet." She winced as a third railgun struck her head-on, causing her to nearly lose the mech's footing on the scrabble. She recovered and sprayed depleted uranium rounds into the cavern as fast as her machine guns could cycle, while Podsy sent a fifteen-kilo slug into an enemy HWP on the far side of the cavern.

The shell tore the railgun mount apart, causing its wreckage to explode in a fireball that took out a dozen nearby rock-biters.

Elvira's machine guns ripped into the horde, but the carnage did nothing to dissuade the Arh'Kel as they hurled themselves at the death-dealing engine of war. Never before had Xi felt so in control of her mech, not even when the neural link had worked in the old *Elvira*. Seconds ticked by as she let herself ride the wave of inputs, reacting on hard-trained reflex rather than over-thinking things.

A pair of rock-biters leaped down from a nearby ledge, and she pivoted *Elvira* to sweep through them. They were torn apart mid-air, with roughly equal halves of their six-limbed bodies falling lifelessly to the cavern floor.

One Arh'Kel managed to get beneath her carapace, and without planning it, Xi splayed her mech's legs just enough that she actually *heard* the eminently satisfying crunch as her eighty-ton mech crushed the rock-biter. *Oyster vs. sledgehammer.* She smirked.

Just as she recovered the mech's footing, a wave of rock-biters surged up the scrabble, clearly intent on slowing her progress so the railguns could get another volley off.

A half-dozen explosions erupted from the rock-biter line as a swarm of RPGs tore the Arh'Kel troops limb from limb. She silently thanked Sergeant Major Trapper and his people as she continued crawling down the loose rubble toward the cavern floor.

They were halfway down the two-hundred-meter-long slope before it became clear that the rock-biters were closing in faster than she and the Pounders could clear them. Arh'Kel slammed into her hull and snuck inside her machine gun arcs before she could cut them down. She knew it as only a matter of time before they started doing serious damage to her systems.

"All right, Podsy," she decided, "activate the mods."

"Mods online," he acknowledged, and *Elvira*'s cabin was filled with a terrifying sound as a hundred motors whirred to life outside.

A mixture of circular saws, wire saws, and honest-to-God *chainsaws*—some of which were five meters long—sprang to life on *Elvira*'s hull. A dozen Arh'Kel were cut down by the mostly-diamond-tipped cutting devices in the opening seconds, their vital fluids decorating *Elvira*'s armored carapace in a macabre mix of purples and blues.

Looking and sounding like something that would have given Salvador Dali lifelong nightmares, *Elvira* waded into the Arh'Kel with her new anti-personnel mods picking off the few Arh'Kel her machine guns missed. For good measure, Podsy sniped another railgun mount before it could fire.

As the saws did their gruesome work, Xi heard Podsy cackle maniacally at her back.

"What's so funny?" she demanded, her focus temporarily broken by his mirthful outburst.

"Diamond-tipped saws," he declared gleefully before cackling even harder than before. "Carbon vs. silica…get it? It's this whole war boiled down to right here, right now. And guess who wins?!"

Xi couldn't help but giggle uncontrollably as she swept her machine guns through a particularly thick cluster of Arh'Kel soldiers. "You're a sicko, Podsy. But you're my kinda sicko."

After that, even with *Flaming Rose* finally adding its guns to the mix while making its way down the scrabble, the Arh'Kel were holding their own and gaining. It would become a race against time. Would the mechs run out of ammo before the enemy ran out of infantry?

A pair of previously unseen railguns spat fire, with one taking *Elvira* in the left flank and the other striking *Flaming Rose* on its heavily-armored prow. One of *Elvira*'s two left-flank machine guns was scrubbed by the hit, and with single-minded purpose, the Arh'Kel began to flow toward that gap in her defenses.

For a moment, Xi was concerned that the Pounders riding on *Elvira*'s back had been killed by the superheated tungsten, but when a fresh barrage or RPGs ripped into the approaching Arh'Kel, she knew they were still with her.

For now.

She noticed that *Flaming Rose*'s anti-boarding saws were already whirring, filling her with disgust at Captain Murdoch's perpetual skittishness. Had he waited until he was in the thick of the enemy before activating the saws, they could have done more damage. As it was, the Arh'Kel near his mech quickly targeted Murdoch's saws with small arms fire. With the same methodical precision they had displayed in every other engagement on Durgan's Folly, the rock-biters focused their fire on a few small areas. Slowly but surely, they opened gaps in *Flaming Rose*'s last line of defense.

Suddenly, *Elvira* lost power to her left legs. It was all Xi could do to keep the mech from tumbling down the scrabble as she fought to keep its still-functioning right legs pinned to the boulder pile. "Podsy!" she cried in alarm.

"I've got an electrical overload in the left main bus," Podsednik replied, undoing his harness and making his way to the rear of the cabin. "We've got a coolant leak that shorted the thing out and tripped the breaker. I'm on it."

The blast doors behind her slammed shut, causing her to demand, "Podsy, I need an update!"

"Keep fighting, LT," Podsy replied tersely. "I'll have the main bus back up in a few seconds."

She continued pouring machine gun fire into the surging Arh'Kel as *Flaming Rose* came up beside her vulnerable left flank. Covering her, Captain Murdoch's mech unleashed a swarm of rockets into the two railguns that had appeared moments earlier. The enemy mounts exploded, leaving a single railgun on her tactical board.

A handful of Arh'Kel had managed to crawl up *Flaming Rose*'s right side, which now faced *Elvira*. Trapper's Pounders scratched Murdoch's itch with a combination of small arms fire and hand grenades, sending the boarding Arh'Kel lifelessly off the *Rose*. As they did, Xi couldn't help but think that Murdoch had been less concerned with covering her vulnerable flank than he was with scraping rock-biters off his own hull.

There was an audible pop from the rear compartment, followed by a flickering of the onboard electrical systems before *Elvira*'s left legs were once again at her command.

"Good work, Podsy," she said, unable to keep the concern from her voice as she spoke.

"Nothing to it," he replied, but she had spent enough time with him to know that Podsy was hurt. Bad.

There was nothing she could do for him now except keep fighting in the hope that they could clear a hole for *Roy* to come down and do its thing. If she wanted to help Podsy, she needed to survive this nexus. That meant fighting her ass off, even if she had to claw at the Arh'Kel with her bloody fingertips.

So that was exactly what she did.

BALLAD OF METAL & MEAT

"Punch it, Chaps," Jenkins ordered after *Elvira* and *Flaming Rose* faltered near the base of the rubble-strewn slope.

Chaps drove *Roy* down the slope, easily traversing the loose surface as the battalion's most advanced mech stormed the cavern with coilguns spraying across the churning horde of Arh'Kel.

The four-legged *Roy*, half-rolling and half-walking down the treacherous path, paused its descent for a half-second as Chaps sent a pair of fifteen-kilo shells across the cavern. The railguns Chaps had targeted flew apart in a spray of shrapnel as *Roy* formally announced its arrival.

Jenkins saw that the junction contained far more rock-biters than they had initially expected. True to form, his people had done good work in thinning that number with a constant spray of depleted-uranium slugs. Muzzle flashes illuminated the dimly-lit cavern, making the Arh'Kel look even more terrifying as their bizarre cartwheeling movements brought them ever-closer to the mechs.

The roar of the other mechs' machine guns was now complemented by the high-pitched whine of *Roy*'s coilguns, and as the battalion's command vehicle neared *Elvira*'s rear, the Scorpion-class mech finally made it to the cavern floor.

Flaming Rose pulled to the left, its makeshift anti-boarding devices whirring and slicing through whichever Arh'Kel were unfortunate enough to get too close. From *Elvira*'s back, Trapper's Pounders launched RPGs at rock-biters clinging to the *Rose*'s rear. Arh'Kel plasma torches had already cut deep into the *Rose*'s rear left leg assembly, and it looked like the limb could not withstand much more abuse.

Unfortunately, one of the Pounders' RPGs went low and finished the job the Arh'Kel had started. Down one leg out of eight, *Flaming Rose* spun defiantly, spraying the cavern with roaring chain guns and sending AP shells into one of the tunnels through which rock-biters continued to pour.

Elvira stomped to the right, wading into the rock-biters and crushing several beneath her six-legged frame while her machine guns tore deep into the Arh'Kel line.

But as much as he liked to see his people lay waste to the rock-biters, Jenkins knew that there wasn't enough ammo on the planet to stop the horde.

"Get ready, Styles," Jenkins said as *Roy* moved between *Elvira* and *Flaming Rose*, and together the three mechs advanced in a mutually-supportive triangle formation. *Elvira* pivoted, angling her prow toward the mouth of the cavern while *Flaming Rose* and *Roy* took position at hundred-twenty-degree offsets. All three mechs' sterns pointed to the center of their triangular position, and together they waded into the cavern while the tide of rock-biter horde grew steadily in size and ferocity.

Small arms fire hammered at *Roy*'s armored hull, scraping away at the surprisingly effective anti-boarding systems that Xi and Styles had seen installed on the three mechs. But those systems still claimed dozens of Arh'Kel lives, while the wounded were trampled by their fellows as they surged toward the trio of mechs.

"Four hundred in range..." Styles called out just as a railgun bolt struck *Roy*'s prow. "Four twenty..."

Even with the three mechs' anti-personnel weapons cycling at maximum speed, splattering rock-biter gore across the cavern floor until the stone was slick and purple, the press of Arh'Kel bore down on the advancing mechs.

"Four sixty," Styles declared as *Flaming Rose* was struck by a high-velocity projectile. For a moment, it looked like the hit had killed the mech outright when it halted and its guns went silent. But after a few tense seconds, Murdoch's vehicle stirred to life and resumed its place in the triad, though it was clear from its uncoordinated movements that the *Rose* was struggling.

The deeper they moved into the cavern, the more convinced Jenkins became that they could achieve their objective. In the face of overwhelming odds, and even in spite of shaky morale caused by insubordinate and inflexible officers, Jenkins' people had finally come together in a way he had doubted possible as recently as a few days earlier.

Win or lose, this push represented the greatest success that Lee Jenkins could have hoped for. He had overseen the birth of an armor unit that had done more damage to the rock-biters in a shorter span of time than even the vaunted Marines had managed during their first engagements.

"Five hundred!" Styles declared, executing the command and sending the high-gain signal out into the crowd of silica-based warriors. For the briefest moment, the throng of rock-biters paused. Styles had actually done it!

But the moment was short-lived, and the Arh'Kel resumed their assault on the mechs with renewed vigor. Whatever Styles did had pissed them off, and they were looking to vent whatever passed for a spleen in their peculiar physiology.

"Try again, Chief," Jenkins encouraged, knowing that it was all down to a second try. *Roy*'s coilguns were already half-depleted, and the command vehicle had only been down the hole for half as long as *Elvira*. Guns were going to start running dry, and when they did, the rock-biters would swarm and the mechs would die.

"Five forty," Styles said shakily, and a quick look showed sweat streaming down his nose and cheeks. "Re-programming the signal...executing now!"

Jenkins held his breath and, again, the horde of Arh'Kel paused in unison. They were clearly being affected by Styles' takeover attempt, but just as before, they quickly shook it off and resumed the attack.

Plasma torches tore into *Flaming Rose*'s hull, cutting deep gashes into the armor protecting her main leg joints. *Elvira*'s machine guns swept across Murdoch's mech, sniping a few of the rock-biters while even more clambered aboard to take their place.

Roy was rocked yet again by railgun fire, causing warning alarms to scream across the mech's status boards. Chaps returned the favor with a pair of fifteen-kilo slugs that wrecked the offending HWP, but plasma torches soon tore into *Roy*'s armor, causing more alarms to wail.

Roy lurched to the right as Trapper's Pounders sent RPGs into the command vehicle's flank, scrubbing a handful of boarders off the hull. The grenades missed the transceiver array—the key piece of equipment if Styles' plan was to work. Jenkins knew that array would take mere seconds to destroy once an Arh'Kel went to work on it.

"Trying again," Styles said weakly, sending another virtual signal out into the cavern.

Again they paused, and again they charged. Rock-biters clawed atop *Roy*'s hull, and the hiss of their plasma torches filled the cabin.

Just as Jenkins was about to lose hope, something completely unexpected happened:

Elvira slammed into *Roy* with enough force to jostle everyone against their harnesses.

More importantly, it knocked the clambering rock-biters off the command vehicle's hull.

"Good thinking, Xi," he whispered, knowing this battle was about to end.

One way or the other.

"Hang on!" Xi yelled, hoping that the Pounders weren't so deaf they couldn't hear her warning over the line. Raising *Elvira's* front legs up, she struck them down on *Roy's* stern, digging the sharp points of her legs several centimeters into the command vehicle's white-hot armor.

Thankfully, Chaps seemed to understand what she was thinking. After a few seconds' work, she managed to climb her mech halfway up *Roy's* badly-battered stern where the all-important transceiver array was located.

Elvira's machine guns rotated, firing down on the encroaching rock-biters as they surged forward. Dozens clambered aboard the Scorpion-class mech and were quickly repelled by Pounder hand grenades and RPGs. Xi had just sentenced the Pounders to death by shielding *Roy* with *Elvira's* armor, but at this point, she didn't see a choice.

The only thing that mattered was protecting Styles and that transceiver, so that was exactly what she intended to do.

And if someone had seen tears running down her cheeks as she thought about the fate that would soon befall the Pounders who had fought so hard to protect her, she wouldn't have been ashamed to admit they were real.

Two railgun strikes slammed into *Elvira*, which shielded *Roy* from a full third of the cavern as her pilot threw herself on top of the command vehicle to buy it precious seconds.

"Seven fifty," Styles said tremulously. "Transmitting…"

The horde stopped its movements, and at this point, Jenkins was so numb that he honestly didn't care if it worked or not. He wanted victory so badly he could taste it, but the past few minutes had been more intense and terrifying than a human being was designed to cope with. Like any soldier caught too long in the clash of metal and meat, he felt disconnected from events around him, more an observer of his own actions than their author.

Whatever happened, happened. All he could do was focus on his job, which at that instant meant staring at the screen as Styles' latest takeover swept across the nearby Arh'Kel.

Then they moved again, and he felt his heart sink.

The Arh'Kel within the fifty-meter perimeter churned, with plasma torches igniting and cutting into metal as they seemed set to resume their bloody work.

But then some of the plasma torches cut out. Some reignited, only to cut out a few seconds later. Then Arh'Kel outside the fifty-meter perimeter began milling around, apparently aimless as the unthinkable occurred before their very eyes.

"Styles…" Jenkins whispered. "You've done it!"

Styles' eyes were wide as he sat, frozen mid-motion with his attention completely fixed on the displays.

The reverie was broken by an explosion from *Flaming Rose*, which began spewing fiery fuel across the nearby rock-biters. The Arh'Kel turned toward the explosion, but without the machine-like unity that made them such an indomitable force. Still, hundreds of them moved toward Murdoch's mech, plasma torches igniting as they made clear their intention to finish the crippled vehicle off.

"Open fire, Commander?" Chaps asked, a rare note of uncertainty in his voice.

Jenkins was torn. He hadn't anticipated a situation where the rock-biters might be partially pacified, but still dangerous enough to destroy one of his vehicles. But if they continued to ignore *Roy*, it might buy Styles enough time to fully complete his takeover which, at this point, appeared to be only partially successful.

"Negative," he said, knowing it was one of the rare moments in his life that he would remember for the rest of his days—no matter the outcome. "Hold your fire. Styles…" He gently placed a hand on the chief warrant's shoulder. "How do you finish this?"

Styles was frozen, incapable of responding or even acknowledging Jenkins' query. Jenkins squeezed his shoulder firmly, causing the other man to snap out of it.

"Styles…" he repeated, keeping his voice low and steady.

"Right, right…" Styles exhaled several times before nodding. "Finish… Okay, I've got a few ideas," he said, and his fingers were soon moving across his console.

Precious seconds passed as the rock-biters tore into *Flaming Rose*, which had either already died along with its crew or was playing dead in the hope of avoiding further bloodshed. Plasma torches rent the mighty mech's legs off at their main joints, its guns were slagged, and its rocket launchers were cut into tiny bits of scrap as the rock-biters methodically tore the vehicle apart.

But before they breached the *Rose*'s cabin, Styles said, "Let's try this."

As soon as he sent the signal, the rock-biters turned into silicon-based statues.

Styles looked at a second display, which showed a real-time feed of an implant he had plugged into the system to better monitor the effects of his inputs. He had been fairly clear that it would be easy to overload the system, just as he had done back at

HQ, and had convinced Jenkins to set up the 'control' unit right there in *Roy*'s cabin.

"I think…" he began hesitantly, audibly swallowing a dry knot in his throat before he said, "I think I've put them to sleep."

"How long will that last?" Jenkins pressed.

"Arh'Kel can hibernate for decades, Commander," Styles replied, though his tone wasn't exactly filling Jenkins with confidence. "The problem is I don't know enough about their nervous systems. The sooner I can take active control of them, the better. They might stay under like this for a few minutes, hours, or possibly even days."

"We don't have days, Chief," Jenkins warned.

"I'm aware of that, sir," Styles assured him, "but I think…I might be able to do this. Just…back off. Sir," he added belatedly. "I need some space."

"You've got it." Jenkins nodded, and for the next hour, he did his best not to interrupt the talented technician as he worked frantically to re-shape the course of the Arh'Kel-Terran Wars.

A KEY ASSIST

"Podsy," Xi said, trying and failing to override the blast door that sealed her off from the rest of the cabin, "open this door. Now!"

"Just hang...tight," he said, his breathing labored as he spoke to her through the mech's intercom system. "I can't seem to...get the thing...unlocked."

She wanted to do something to help him. He had obviously been hurt in the fight, but as the minutes ticked by, it became clear those wounds would prove fatal if he didn't get help. Fast.

Deciding that enough was enough, Xi broke open the emergency toolkit beneath her chair and took out the miniature plasma cutter. It would take a few minutes to cut through the door with it, but she couldn't sit here doing nothing for another second. Her Wrench, her best friend, was dying on the other side of that door.

As she ignited the torch, another thought came to her, which filled her with a nearly overpowering sense of guilt that remained lodged in the center of her consciousness:

I can't let him die alone.

She cut into the door, just as Podsy had shown her, and after a few minutes' work that came over Podsy's protests, she managed to cut a narrow window through which she could barely squeeze.

Ignoring the burns on her hips and sides, which had gone straight through her enviro-suit where she had touched the freshly-burned metal, she crawled into the rear cabin and found Podsy sitting beside his station.

The left side of his face was black from burns, and his legs were a ruined mess. It took her a few seconds to realize what had happened, but when it did, she couldn't keep the tears from coming. The coolant system must have sprayed hot liquid all over his legs, covering them with second and third-degree burns before an electrical discharge had charred half of his face.

"Podsy, you stupid bastard," she cried. "Why didn't you say something?"

He smiled weakly. "I didn't...want you to...worry."

His breathing was hoarse, and in his hand was a partially-opened emergency tracheotomy kit from the mech's medical supply cabinet.

"Only you would think you could do something like this yourself," she said, fighting to steady her bloody fingers as she worked to open the damned kit. Screaming in more frustration than pain, she finally managed to rip the lid off the small polymer box, scattering its contents onto the floor.

"Just...it's okay..." he said, placing a hand on her wrist.

"Like hell it is!" she snapped as she snatched up the scalpel. "I've done this on dummies a hundred times, so I've had plenty of practice," she said, fighting to keep her voice steady. "Now lie down and shut up."

"Who are you...calling a...dummy?" he wheezed as she laid him down on the deck.

She wanted to laugh but couldn't force herself to do it. "All right, this is going to hurt," she said before taking the scalpel and pressing it against his neck, "but you'll be able to breathe better afterward."

"You always...poke holes in...everything I do," he said before a short-lived laugh turned into a coughing fit.

"Shut up!" she snapped, hesitating as she held the scalpel in the ready position. "I'm... I mean..." She failed to find the right words to apologize if she inadvertently severed his vocal cords.

"It's okay, LT," he croaked. "That whole...pop-star phase... I'm past it."

This time she laughed, in spite of her anxiety, and went about the grisly task of opening up his airway so he could breathe long enough to get back to HQ.

During that hour, the team learned that Captain Murdoch, though badly wounded, had survived the attack. Unfortunately, the rest of his crew had died.

Podsednik was also in critical condition, having suffered extensive burns and requiring a field tracheotomy performed by Lieutenant Xi. Both Podsy and Murdoch were stable enough to collect with the Vultures. The surviving Pounders, including Sergeant Major Trapper, helped load them onto the drones for medevac to HQ.

The humans carefully wove their way through the Arh'Kel, who towered over them like stone statues as the soldiers took great care not to touch them while evacuating the worst of the wounded.

But in all that time, Styles had come no closer to solving the problem of completing his takeover of the Arh'Kel network.

"I'm learning a lot doing this," he said in frustration, "but I'm running out of ideas, Commander."

"What can I do to help?" Jenkins asked staidly. If Styles couldn't do this, they were as good as dead, so there was no point antagonizing the man. Most soldiers could be motivated by a swift kick in the ass or a public upbraiding, but in Jenkins' experience, techs and intelligence officers were different. They required a more cerebral engagement, and for obvious reasons, he was highly motivated to provide that at this particular moment.

"I just…I don't know." Styles shook his head in exasperation, but then his eyes lit up. "Get Xi in here!"

Jenkins eyed him warily before nodding to Chaps, who disconnected from *Roy*'s neural link to carry out the silent order.

A few minutes later, Xi came into the cabin. "You wanted to see me, sir?"

Styles beckoned without looking in her direction. "Sit down and help me with this. I'm trying to run our code fragments, but they keep getting rejected."

Xi gave Jenkins a questioning look.

"Do it," Jenkins urged, swiveling the chair to face her.

She sat down and pulled up a series of command interfaces before saying, "You know I'm not half as good at this as you are."

"You don't have to be half as good," Styles said dismissively. "I just need a fresh set of eyes. Tell me what I'm missing," he said, transmitting the logs of his recent attempts to her station.

She pored over the data feed in silence for several minutes before cocking her head, and even in *Roy*'s dimly-illuminated cabin, Jenkins could see that her cheeks were covered in dried tears.

Frankly, he didn't blame her. It sounded like Podsednik was circling the drain. But they were all on borrowed time if Styles couldn't make this work.

"Did you try a trinary introduction sequence?" she asked.

"Yes, I did," Styles replied. "Along with a quaternary, binary, and even an inverted Sokal technique."

"Okay," she mused as she tapped away, calling up feeds and isolating specific fragments before sending them back his way. "Do you see it?"

He shook his head in irritation. "No, I don't. If I saw it, I wouldn't have called you—"

"Look again," she urged patiently, but firmly. "There's a response pattern here. It's symmetrical..."

"But inverted..." He nodded, gritting his teeth angrily. "That's it. I wasn't hitting the whole thing simultaneously. It's not the code that's wrong, it's how it's being processed and rejected."

"Like Yin and Yang." She nodded approvingly. "You've got to make sure the process is balanced from the start, or the individual units will reject it and the code won't propagate."

"Virtual harmonics," he hissed irritably while his fingers flew across the console. "Thanks, Xi. That might be the break we need."

"Do you want me to set up a feedback block in case it doesn't take?" she asked.

"No time." Styles shook his head firmly. "We've got to try this."

"But if it doesn't work..." Xi said cautiously.

"Then we're all dead," he said, tilting his chin toward a third monitor, "but those input patterns are becoming unstable, and some of the rock-biters are starting to twitch. It's now or never."

Xi seemed like she wanted to object, but Jenkins put his hand on her shoulder and waved her off.

"Okay." Styles exhaled sharply. "Here goes nothing..."

He struck the execute glyph and, to Jenkins' eye, nothing happened. Streams of data continued pouring across the displays and the rock-biters didn't budge.

A few seconds later, Xi and Styles leaped out of their chairs and pumped their fists victoriously. "That's it!" Styles said in mixed triumph and disbelief. "We've got control of the whole system!"

"I told you!" Xi beamed, high-fiving the chief. "Yin and Yang!"

"Virtual harmonics, baby!" Styles declared, but Jenkins was only cautiously optimistic that they had, in fact, achieved their goal. "Look at that, will you?" Styles strutted, gesturing to the monitor that showed the control unit's status. "Have you ever seen something as sexy as that?!"

"Back up." Jenkins made a 'slow down' gesture with both hands. "How do you know you did it?"

"It's the same pattern we saw in the models," Styles replied matter-of-factly. "We've achieved balance. Our code fragments have been accepted into the distributed architecture, which means that we can send any command to them that we want!"

"Once we figure out how to actually *craft* commands," Xi said pointedly.

"Details, details." Styles waved dismissively as he sat back down at his console with renewed vigor. "Never bother me with the details."

"Some say that's where the Devil lives," Xi observed.

"Focus, people," Jenkins grunted, "we're not out of the woods yet. Or are we?"

"That's true," Styles agreed half-heartedly, "but we can see the tree line and daylight's a-peekin' through! Let's try the first batch of commands, one by one, using the same harmonic introduction technique," he said, and Xi nodded in agreement before they went about the unthinkable task of seizing control of an entire planet's population of enemy soldiers.

Twelve hours later, Xi and Styles had improbably completed the task to Jenkins' satisfaction.

"We can't puppet these things," Styles explained. "Whatever programming it was that let them function as a single-minded unit is beyond us. But what we *have* managed to do—" He gestured to a live video feed of the cavern. "—is upload the equivalent of general directions into small sub-groups."

"The virtual architecture is *very* basic," Xi agreed, "which is unexpected, but it's the only way this takeover was even possible."

Styles nodded enthusiastically. "It's like whoever initially programmed these things had no idea that someone might try to do what we just did. It's almost like the possibility never occurred to them."

"Arh'Kel psychology's different from our own," Jenkins mused. "And you said yourself that this type of interconnectivity is totally new as far as we can tell."

"We've never encountered rock-biters using anything like this," Styles allowed. "But whoever developed this system—"

"Or *adapted* it," Xi said pointedly, to which Styles nodded vigorously.

"—had to have known that something like this was possible," Styles completed, and Jenkins was both impressed and slightly concerned at the ease with which the two were finishing each other's thoughts.

"Our best guess," Xi explained, "is that this wasn't considered battle-ready tech. It's possible that it was installed early on in this crypto-colony's development and that some kind of design flaw or oversight was missed. Whoever made the initial installation was unable to make adjustments for some reason."

"It does seem like," Styles said carefully, "one of this system's primary purposes had to be to keep the Arh'Kel from following their standard model of behavior. Instead of congregating into centralized groups and building infrastructure in the typical fashion, they've remained more dispersed than is normal for Arh'Kel and only built a few relatively minor pieces of large-scale infrastructure, like the anti-orbital guns."

"Can you use this system to see how many Arh'Kel are on this planet?" Jenkins asked, having waited the better part of a day to get the answer to this all-important question.

Xi and Styles shared concerned looks before Styles nodded. "We're confident it's between three and five million."

At hearing that, Jenkins' worst fears were realized: *millions* of rock-biters were lurking beneath this planet's surface. It was nothing short of a holocaust waiting to happen. The main reason his armor battalion had been so devastating to the enemy was that he had specifically selected mechs which could stand up to Arh'Kel infantry long enough to deliver their payloads. Combined with their strange, unprecedented mob-like behavior, the body count he and his people had racked up was nothing short of astounding.

But his battalion was in shambles, with less than a company's worth of mechs currently battle-ready and no more than that many more salvageable even under the best circumstances. There were currently no dedicated armor production facilities anywhere in the Republic, and the Marines' power-armor was still badly depleted. In short, the Terran Armed Forces were woefully inadequate to the task of dealing with such a large-scale invasion.

Three million rock-biters, he thought grimly, briefly closing his eyes as he considered the havoc they could wreak on the relatively unsuspecting worlds of the Terran Republic.

"But that's only counting Arh'Kel that carry these implants," Xi pointed out. "It's possible there are even more than that which aren't connected to the network."

"They can't be allowed to get off this rock," he said, his eyes snapping open as he came to terms with the magnitude of the situation. "What are our options?"

"First," Styles said, "we've segregated the three thousand Arh'Kel here in the cavern and in adjacent tunnels."

"We've formed four groups," Xi explained, "since there are four major tunnels leading out of this nexus."

"We think that sending off groups of that size will flip whatever smaller ones they encounter over to our protocols," Styles agreed. "Eventually, these groups should grow to several thousand apiece, so when they reach other nexuses—"

"They'll flip those." Xi nodded eagerly, once again easily stepping into Styles' sentence. "And we'll write a general directive command which breaks them up into smaller groups that go off and repeat the process."

"That's...ambitious," Jenkins said skeptically. "And it sounds too good to be true."

"If I was a betting man—" Styles leaned forward, lowering his voice conspiratorially. "—and we all know that I am, I'd stake everything I own that these rock-biters were dormant when we arrived, which is why their tactics were so simplistic. I think they're plugged into some variant of the One Mind network which has short-circuited their higher reasoning. I think they were waiting around, reproducing and building nothing but defensive weaponry, with the plan of getting picked up and taken to one of the colonies where they can wage war on us the way they always have. I think what we're doing is, essentially, what the implant's designers intended." Styles jabbed a finger down on the desk emphatically. "We just happened to get here first and lucked into finding the backdoor before they overran us."

Jenkins took Styles' meaning plainly enough. He was suggesting that the Solar humans had played a part in this particular Arh'Kel crypto-colony's development, and somehow coordinated with the main Arh'Kel government to have this huge stockpile of Arh'Kel infantry picked up and taken across the Terran Republic. Once spread across the Seven Colonies, there would be no way the Terrans could hold on without requesting help from their Solar cousins and finally submitting to their dominion.

The Terran Fleet had held the Arh'Kel fireships off at the wormhole gate, which was a testament to the Republic's fast-growing space force. Still, the Arh'Kel had managed to destroy five Republic dreadnoughts in a single engagement, when not a single dreadnought had fallen in over thirty prior engagements.

They had stepped in something *big* here. This was far more

than just his unit's fight for survival. He had suspected, but the cold reality of it slapped him upside the head.

"All right," Jenkins said, fixing them both with a heavy gaze, "everything we just discussed *must* remain compartmentalized. Nobody, and I mean *nobody*, outside this mech learns the details of this until I've had a chance to think it through."

"You don't think Fleet Command is somehow in on this, do you?" Styles asked warily, causing Xi's eyebrows to shoot up in alarm.

"I don't know what to think." Jenkins cocked his head dubiously. "All I know is this kind of thing doesn't happen by coincidence. There's a decades-long plan at work here, and I'm not clever enough to see through it. What I do know is that we need to get off this rock ASAP. How long until you're ready to send these groups off to start the domino effect on the rest?"

"We should have the code cleaned up in another hour," Styles said confidently. "We might even be able to get a rudimentary surveillance system that gives us locations and force breakdowns of the various pockets as they flip to our new program."

Jenkins set his jaw grimly, hesitating before bringing up the nearly-unthinkable. "I hate to ask this…"

"I can't, even if I wanted to." Styles shook his head firmly. "Maybe if I had a month, a dreadnought's computer core, and a team of thirty people as talented as Xi—" He nodded deferentially to the young lieutenant. "—it would be possible. But ordering these Arh'Kel to self-terminate or start fighting each other is way beyond anything I could do right now, Commander."

"Could you order them to congregate into a single location?" Jenkins asked pointedly, and for a long moment, Styles regarded him impassively.

But when the answer came, it was the one Jenkins was looking for. "Yes, sir. I've already included that protocol in the package. Once they've run out of fresh communities to flip, they'll gather at a point eight hundred kilometers from here."

"Good." Jenkins nodded. "I don't like it any more than you do, and frankly I'm glad the decision won't be up to us, but this planet represents an existential threat to the Terran Republic. If Fleet brass decides to eliminate that threat, I'd like to give them an option that doesn't require more human blood to be spilled on this God-forsaken rock."

"Agreed, sir." Styles nodded.

"Agreed," Xi said. The idea rested in their guts like week-old, chow-hall Swedish meatballs.

"Good work," Jenkins said, sinking back in his chair feeling nothing short of amazed. "We may have just saved the Republic. The bitch of it is, we probably aren't going to be allowed to talk about it."

"Not talking about it is a low price to pay for surviving," Xi suggested.

"Good." Jenkins returned the nod, standing to attention and prompting them to do so. He raised his hand in a salute, which they returned before he released his own. "Outstanding work, you two. Now let's finish this and head back to the barn."

Three hours later, the rock-biters had left the cavern, making their way into the labyrinthine tunnels that connected the staggeringly vast subterranean network. When the last Arh'Kel had gone, *Elvira* and *Roy* secured what little remained of the unsalvageable *Flaming Rose* with demo charges, which went off as soon as they reached the surface. Afterward, the battered war machines limped back to the plateau.

WOUNDS

"Lieutenant..." a male voice nagged, as it always did when she had finally managed to shut her eyes for more than two consecutive seconds.

"Go away," Xi grunted.

"Lieutenant," the voice insisted.

"Leave me alone!" she groaned.

"There's been an update," he explained, and Xi was beginning to suspect it was Strange Bed himself who was harassing her—though thankfully not in the manner for which he was notorious. "The commander wants to see you."

"What is it?" she demanded, rolling over in the horribly uncomfortable cot beside Podsy's bed. She opened her eyes and saw the now-familiar monitor displaying his vital signs. All normal.

"He didn't say," Fellows shrugged, "but frankly, there are people that need this cot more than you, so if you could get up—"

"Touch this cot and I'll rip your balls off, grind them into burger, and stuff them up your nose with a fountain pen," she snarled.

"My, my, at least *someone's* feeling better around here," Dr.

Fellows deadpanned. "I must be doing something right for a change. Though you might want to get that 'raging bitch' gland looked at. I hear they cause a lot of trouble later in life...just ask my ex-wives."

"I can't understand what would make a woman think you were husband material in the first place," Xi retorted, "but divorcing you was easily the smartest thing the four of them ever did."

"No," the doctor scowled, "making me sign a prenup was the smartest thing they ever did."

She shot him a withering look before breaking down and giving an obligatory chuckle. "Fine, fine...I'll go see the commander."

She stood and stretched before looking down at Podsy, who hadn't moved since Fellows had put him into a chemically-induced coma three days earlier.

"He's stable," the doctor assured her, giving her an expectant look and shooing her away. "The commander's expecting you."

"I meant what I said about the cot," Xi warned, eliciting an eye-roll and mock gesture of surrender from the doctor before she left the field hospital and made her way to the battalion's command center.

Things had been relatively quiet since the takeover, though Commander Jenkins had compartmentalized the results of their wildly successful takeover. Patrols continued as before, and Pounders and mech crews saw to their wounded. Complaints persisted regarding the low-quality ration packs and, more disgustingly, the necessary consumption of recycled dark water.

Fortunately for Xi, sealed bottles of fresh water continued appearing in places she would find them. She had little doubt who was giving them to her, but she was confused as to their meaning. Ordinarily, she would have suspected such gestures to be sexual advances and would have publicly spurned them. But this time around, she found herself perplexed so she had avoided a confrontation with the most likely suspect.

As she approached *Roy*, the first thing she noticed was that the command vehicle's receiver dish was deployed. This only happened during scheduled links with orbital forces, which meant the commander was probably on the line with Fleet at that very moment.

Quickening her stride, she walked up *Roy*'s boarding ramp and heard Commander Jenkins' raised voice.

"Copy that, Wolf Three-Niner," Jenkins said in mild exasperation. "The area is secure; you are clear on all approaches. I say again: you are clear on all approaches."

When the static-laden reply came, it was filled with disbelief. "Wolf Three-Niner requesting you repeat your last, *Roy*."

Jenkins briefly met Xi's gaze and a wry, victorious grin spread across his face as he declared, "This is *Roy*. Allow me to rephrase, Wolf Three-Niner: we've already cleared this rock. We've even rolled out the beach blankets and are working on our tans. Why don't you guys come down and join us? The weather's perfect this time of year."

Xi couldn't help but laugh at the commander's quip—tidally-locked planets with negligible axial tilt didn't experience seasons. As she resumed control of herself, she noticed Sergeant Major Trapper had clambered up the ramp behind her. They made brief eye contact before both focused on the conversation taking place. It was clear that Commander Jenkins was every bit as proud of what they had done as she was and, for the first time since joining this ragtag group of convicts and misfits, she felt like she actually belonged among them.

"I've already forwarded copies of all thirty-eight anti-orbital gun placements," Jenkins continued, "but I say again: those guns are cold. You're clear on all approaches."

A lengthy delay followed, which was finally broken by a

different voice from the first. "This is Wolf Leader. Is that you, Leeroy?"

"Leeroy Jenkins, in the flesh." The commander grinned. "It's good to finally hear a familiar voice, Johnny. I thought Fleet Ground was coming. Didn't expect the Marines."

"We're on direct approach, ETA six minutes," Wolf Leader 'Johnny' replied, "and assuming this isn't some kind of payback prank for that regrettable latrine incident a few years back, it sounds like you people just set a record for the swiftest conclusion to a planetary siege in Republic history. On behalf of Fleet Command and everyone in Wolf Company, I'd like to congratulate you all on a job well done."

Jenkins turned to face those in his command mech. He pointed to each and nodded in silent celebration of their hard-fought and costly victory. The feeling of belonging, of purpose, and of camaraderie crystallized in that moment as she celebrated with her fellow servicemen. If she could have, she would have made that moment last forever.

"We appreciate that, Wolf Leader. We've got wounded down here," Jenkins continued, raising his voice above the celebratory din. "How soon can we expect priority medevacs?"

The mood dampened considerably, and Xi's thoughts immediately went to her comatose partner.

"The *Paul Revere*'s in geostationary orbit over the plateau," Wolf Leader replied. "As soon as my people have confirmed the area's secure, they'll start shuttling your wounded up."

"Roger, Wolf Leader." Jenkins nodded approvingly. "I'll start prepping the most critical cases for transfer. *Roy* out."

Xi's thoughts were now solely of Podsy, and she brushed past Sergeant Major Trapper before running toward *Elvira*. She needed to get Podsy's things ready for transfer and, if possible, she would accompany him. He had bled for her down there, and Doc Fellows seemed less-than-hopeful about his chance at recovery.

If he was going to die, she couldn't let him die alone.

———

The Terran Fleet Marine Corps was the unrivaled pride of Republican ground forces. From their rigorous physical and mental performance standards to their incredibly effective power armor, they were the undisputed cream of the crop in the Terran Armed Forces. Deployed by their advanced dropships, which could maneuver like void fighters and take direct hits from everything but the biggest naval guns, there was no stopping them from reaching their targets and eliminating them with unrivaled ferocity. While other branches joked at the Marines' expense, everyone in uniform knew the truth: everything about the TFMC invoked respect and fear from friend and foe alike, and they deserved every bit of their hard-earned reputation.

When Wolf Company's command dropship, the *Geralt*, appeared in the sky above the plateau, all eyes were there to witness its arrival.

Its monochrome matte-black, sharply-angular hull was broken only by the fierce, white wolf's head emblem representing the company's mascot. That emblem was emblazoned upon the side and rear doors of the vehicle, as well as the vehicle's underside. A command dropship like the *Geralt* was more valuable than a company of Jenkins' best mechs, and the power-suited Marines it carried were each worth more than *three* mechs.

The *Geralt*'s engines roared, gently lowering the vehicle to the ground beside *Roy*. No sooner had the landing gear touched down than all three doors opened to reveal fully-armored Marines.

Those superhuman warriors disembarked the Geralt with such precision they might as well have been pre-programmed machines. Armored boots touched the granite plateau as a dozen

Marines, three full squads, filed out and formed a perimeter around the dropship.

The total time from disembarkation to setting their defensive formation was just under three seconds, and Jenkins knew he was not alone in being awestruck by the display. A quick glance around at his fellows showed that even Sergeant Major Trapper, standing beside Jenkins, was unable to hide his appreciation of their precision.

An unarmored man came walking down the right-side ramp, wearing a Marine field uniform normally reserved for deployment in non-combat zones. Unlike his men, who were armored and ready to engage the enemy, Colonel Johnny Villa strode confidently past his peoples' perimeter toward Jenkins and Trapper bearing nothing but a sidearm and the unshakable air of a man who had stared death in the face and laughed.

Marines weren't known for taking other branches at their word or putting their safety in the hands of others, so it was that particular gesture, more than any other, which filled Jenkins with a sense of accomplishment and recognition for what he and his people had done on Durgan's Folly.

"Commander," Colonel Villa greeted after coming to a stop before Jenkins and Trapper, "Sergeant Major."

"Colonel Villa," Jenkins said, standing at attention while the majority of his people did likewise. "Welcome to Durgan's Folly."

Villa swept the command plateau with a critical eye before raising his voice. "This has got to be the sorriest-looking excuse for a military outpost I have ever seen in my life." He turned a slow circle, eyeing everyone nearby as he finally cracked a grin and boomed, "Which, in my military mind, makes what you Monkeys and Pounders did one for the history books!"

The plateau erupted in approving cheers, and the Marines at Villa's back stood up from their battle-ready crouches and fired their wrist-mounted autocannons in an arc over the desert. A few even launched short-range surface-to-air rockets high into the air, where they exploded with palpable *whumps*.

Villa clasped Trapper's hand, grinning as he said, "Trapper, you old bastard. You're not dead yet?"

"Doing my best." The sergeant major returned the grin. "Just can't seem to get over the hump."

Villa chuckled and turned to Jenkins before shaking his head in wonderment. "I don't know how you did it down here, but you're right: this whole rock's quiet as a Sunday service. I need you to confirm the coordinates of those anti-orbital guns so I can call down airstrikes to neutralize them. There's nothing like a space-based barrage to brighten one's day."

"I wouldn't do that if I were you, Johnny," Jenkins said firmly. "Send teams with demo charges to secure the guns locally. We've pacified the rock-biters down here, but my tech says it wouldn't take much to stir them back up. Orbital strikes could jeopardize our control of the situation."

"Did I read your strength estimate correctly, Lee?" Villa said in a lowered voice as the celebrations continued all around them. "You think there are four *million* Arh'Kel down here?"

"That's our best number." Jenkins nodded gravely.

Villa whistled appreciatively. "In that case, we need to get off this rock ASAP." He turned and snapped a series of commands into his wrist-link. When he had finished, he said, "I've sent teams to clear out the anti-orbitals in this sector. Once they're offline, we'll start bringing you and your gear up. In the meantime..." He gestured to the sleek, black-hulled *Geralt's* open doors. "Let's get your wounded aboard."

"I appreciate that, Colonel," Jenkins said with feeling, knowing that Villa was bending over as far backward as he could to accommodate Jenkins' circumstances—from the non-combat fatigues to turning his command vehicle into a medevac shuttle. Jenkins activated his wrist-link and raised Dr. Fellows. "Doc, start transferring your patients."

"I'm sorry, Lieutenant," Dr. Fellows reiterated tersely as he helped roll Podsy's gurney out of the mobile hospital. "This flight is for critically wounded only."

"But I need to stay with him," Xi insisted. "I'm only seventy-three kilos, Doc—each of the Marines' backup hydro-packs weigh more than that!"

"I've never heard a woman boast about weighing a buck sixty," Strange Bed muttered. "But no amount of whining or bulimic purging is going to change the fact that you're not getting aboard that dropship."

"But, Doc," she pleaded, causing him to stop and take her by the shoulders.

"Listen, Lieutenant," he said forcefully before relaxing and lowering his voice earnestly, "I've never seen someone as loyal to a crewmate as you've been to Podsy. You've spent nearly every second at his side since he was wounded and now I'm telling you, as a professional who deals with this kind of thing every hour of every day—" He patted her shoulder lightly, and somehow it didn't come across as condescending, unlike every other interaction she'd had with Strange Bed. "—you've done more than enough, kid. It's time to step back and let him get the care he needs."

She was taken aback by his apparent sincerity, and against her better judgment, she relented. "Just do everything you can for him, okay?"

"Of course." Fellows nodded. "I know Doc Turney, the *Revere*'s CMO. She's the best," he assured her. "I'll make sure Podsy gets top priority. You have my word."

Xi nodded, and at that, Fellows and his team wheeled Podsy out of the hospital toward the waiting Marine dropship.

A few minutes later, all nineteen of the worst-wounded were aboard, and the black-hulled *Geralt* rose from the plateau amid the high-pitched whine of its engines. Mere seconds after its gear was up, it rocketed into the sky, soaring ever-higher until it was a speck against the dome of perpetual twilight.

For the first time since landing on that rock, Xi felt completely rudderless. Podsy had become more than a crewmate to her during their training and deployment. He was family. He had looked out for her when no one else did, and now she was unable to reciprocate that commitment and devotion.

More than that, she was alone.

Wiping the tears from her face, she turned and headed for *Elvira*. She needed to sleep, to put the day behind her, and Doc Fellows had ordered her on strict non-physical activity to help heal her still-badly-blistered fingers.

When she arrived at her mech, she was immediately struck by just how empty it felt without Podsy.

Then she noticed it wasn't empty at all.

Hunched over her pilot's chair was none other than Tim Trapper. He had a bottle of fresh water in one hand and a slip of paper in the other.

He looked up at her and sighed. "I was hoping to slip the last of these in before you got back. My apologies... I must be getting old."

"Why?" she demanded a bit more irritably than she would have liked. "Why have you been slipping me bottles of fresh water? Is this some sort of courtship ritual for you?"

Trapper chuckled. "You couldn't be much further from the truth."

"Then what?" she asked, less upset than she expected to be during this understandably tense exchange.

"The truth?"

"What else matters," she agreed.

He sighed again. "The truth...is you remind me of my kid sister."

Xi recoiled in surprise, "Oh..." She couldn't think of anything else to say, which only served to embarrass her more than she had thought possible.

"It's all right," he assured her. "She was a dropship pilot assigned to the Marines. She enlisted because it's something of a family tradition, not so much because it's what she wanted to do."

Xi nodded, slowly realizing the significance of his speaking in the past tense about his sister.

"What happened to her?"

"Arh'Kel anti-orbitals while she was coming down to this very rock," Trapper replied matter-of-factly. "Managed to emergency-deploy half of her Marines before her ship went down. She was a good pilot…and a better person." He fixed her with those intense, diamond-hard eyes. "She might not have died if she'd been a little better at strategically dropping her guard and making friends… or if my old man hadn't pulled strings to get her strapped into a dropship before she was ready."

Xi had not expected this level of blunt honesty, or to hear him recount such intensely personal details. "I'm not your sister," Xi said pointedly, again unable to think of anything better to say.

"No," Trapper agreed, "but you remind me of her. You're both sharp as a tack and prickly as a hellspawn cactus, with more determination to excel than the good sense to stop and enjoy the moment. If there's one thing I could have gone back and said to her, it would have been this…" He drew a deep, steadying breath. "Sometimes it's better to drop your guard and risk being hurt than to live like this fuckin' plateau: alone, perpetually ready to engage, and surrounded on all sides by the endless sea of things that might do you harm."

She nodded before gesturing to the water bottles. "If you've got a few minutes, I'll share those with you while you tell me a little more about her."

He chuckled. "That sounds like a good idea, Elvira."

"You people have been through a lot down here, Lee," Colonel Villa said after reviewing Jenkins' logs. "I'm amazed you survived, let alone pulled off this takeover. You should be proud."

"I am." Jenkins nodded guardedly. "What about you? I thought you were on the *Descartes?*"

"I was." Villa nodded grimly, briefly eyeing the unopened whisky bottle atop Jenkins' shelf. He refocused on Jenkins and set his jaw. "When the Arh'Kel came through the wormhole, it was like nothing in Fleet history. The rock-biters moved with such intensity, such ferocity…three dreadnoughts were down before we could properly respond, but the *Descartes* lasted a little longer."

"How did they hit us?" Jenkins leaned forward intently.

"Mass drivers, hyper-kinetic warheads, limpet mines, fire-ships…" Villa leaned back in his chair and grimaced. "You name it, they threw it at us. We even got to repel boarding actions, which is the only reason my company's still intact. Most others weren't so lucky."

"Void boarding actions?" Jenkins asked in disbelief. Marines drilled anti-boarding actions as a matter of course, but not *once* had the Terran Fleet actually experienced such an engagement.

"First time for everything." Villa smirked. "We held our own and then some, scraping those sandy bastards off the hull as fast as they punched into it. Not *one* Arh'Kel breached the *Descartes'* interior on Wolf's watch," he declared with grim satisfaction. "But she was the only mobile dreadnought to survive the first wave of fire, so it was only a matter of time before the rock-biters bracketed her and finished the job."

Jenkins sank back into his chair in disbelief.

"Thankfully," Villa continued, "Sixth Fleet was on standby and responded in time to hold the gate and keep the Arh'Kel off this rock. And after reviewing your logs, it's pretty clear why they were coming here."

"This was going to be their beachhead," Jenkins said knowingly.

"For a *major* offensive." Villa nodded. "My guess is there's enough ordnance buried beneath this planet's surface to supply a ten-year war, and more than enough rock-biters standing ready to replace whatever losses such a conflict would entail. All they had to do was get the ships through this star system's gate, at which point they'd attack Terra Americana from Durgan's Folly and take complete control of the New America System. From there, it wouldn't be tough to break through the rest of the wormhole gates, but losing this star system would cripple our military infrastructure."

"And isolate the second-most populous star system in the Republic...before eradicating every human in it." Jenkins grimaced. New America was his home star system, and it lay just one jump gate beyond Durgan's Folly. Each of the Seven Colonies was located two gates distant from the central League Nexus System, which was the beating heart of the Illumination League. Hundreds of star systems directly linked through individual, two-way gates, and it was this network through which the League controlled the local galactic region.

"They knew where to hit us," Villa agreed. "Take out New America and there's only one star system in the Republic capable of mounting a protracted defense against the rock-biters."

"Terra Han." Jenkins nodded, shuddering at the thought of the most-populous star system in the Republic. The similarities between Terra Han and Sol, in terms of mindset and method, were too striking to ignore. But despite those similarities, Terra Han had been a crucial part of the Terran Republic—without their unflinching support, the Arh'Kel would have overwhelmed the Republic decades ago. "Why didn't the League stop them at the Nexus?"

"The League?" Villa snorted. "The only thing the Illumination League is good for is issuing binding resolutions that do fuck-all to stop Arh'Kel 'unlawful encroachments' into our territory. Those 'illuminated' aliens care more about staying on Sol's good side than they do about anything resembling justice or the rule of law out here. The League's official statement went something like, 'due to the human colonies' unwillingness to acknowledge and accept a formal relationship to Sol, the IL, having accepted and recognized Sol as a member state, cannot legally intervene on the human colonies' behalf until such a relationship can be ratified between Sol and its colonies.'"

Jenkins snorted. "Even after two centuries of standing on our own two feet, they insist on calling us 'human colonies' rather than the Terran Republic."

"They don't recognize our sovereignty out here." Villa nodded in agreement. "And since our wormhole gates are self-policed on our side of the Nexus, the League turns a blind eye to Arh'Kel offensives so long as they don't fire a single shot on the Nexus-side of the gates. It's a clusterfuck, Lee, and has been since the moment we stepped off Earth," Villa growled. "The rock-biters are just doing their best to take advantage of the situation."

"You sound like you admire their efforts," Jenkins commented.

"Hard not to admire an enemy as committed and efficient as them." Villa shrugged. "Besides, they're basically all we've ever fought out here. Aside from a few brush-ups against Vorr and Jemmin forces in what is nominally human territory, the only non-humans the Republic has ever engaged are the Arh'Kel. After a while, you get so used to fighting them that you can't imagine not doing it. And until the politicians back home see fit to iron something out with Sol and the League, I expect nothing much will change on the Arh'Kel front."

Jenkins sighed. "Politicians...the peak form of human bureaucracy."

"May they forever rot in hell." Villa grinned.

"Hear, hear."

"But you, my friend—" Villa suddenly turned serious. "—are going to have some serious explaining to do once you go wheels-up and leave Durgan's Folly behind. If my read on the brass is right, some are going to want to pin medals to your chest while others are going to want to stuff you into a faulty airlock. Are you ready for that?"

Jenkins was nowhere near 'ready' for any such thing, but he had spent the last few days drumming up a few lines of action which he hoped to soon put in motion. "I've got a few tropes and gambits set up," he replied stoically.

"Good," Villa said solemnly, "because, with our depleted strength, the Marines don't have as much pull at the big table as we once did. Fleet was glad to have you and your people pull some wrecks out of mothballs, spend some centuries-old-ordnance, and get your crew of convicts and castoffs wiped off the books the old-fashioned way, but I don't think any of them were prepared for what ended up happening down here. You need to find some cover—fast—or the gears of the Terran war machine will chew this unit of yours up and relegate it to the round-file of history. And from one warrior to another, it'd be a shame if this little experiment of yours didn't continue for at least a little while longer."

Jenkins flashed a lopsided grin. "You mean you'd like me and my people to keep doing the heavy lifting."

"Fuck you, Leeroy," Villa laughed. "Marines don't need help from *anyone*. That's the official line, and I'm toeing it like the good little party member that I am. You'd do well to follow my lead, at least until you've got your feet back under you."

"I appreciate the candid advice, Johnny. It won't go to waste."

"See that it doesn't," Villa said pointedly before standing and gesturing to the unopened bottle. "If you didn't crack that thing open down here, after the shit you went through, I'd bet everything I own that you never will." He offered a salute, which

Jenkins returned as his longtime friend nodded approvingly. "Hell of a job down here, Commander."

The Marine colonel stepped off *Roy* on his way to inspect the plateau.

"She sounds like quite a woman," Xi said after hearing Trapper spend a half-hour speaking of his long-dead sister. "And you sound like you have the worst daddy issues I've ever heard about for a fifty-year-old man," she added with a smirk before taking a long draw from the water bottle.

Trapper smirked. "Have to agree on both counts." His wrist-link chimed, and he abruptly stood from the chair. "I need to go. Your commander needs my help, and the *Geralt* will be back soon."

She cocked her head dubiously. "He needs your help...with what?"

"The commander thinks things are about to get all kinds of dicey for your battalion," he explained. "Leeroy is hoping I can help him outflank trouble before it knocks y'all out of the saddle."

Her brow lowered resentfully. "I have to admit, the politics of surviving an overwhelming victory are beyond me at present. I thought surviving was good enough."

"Sometimes the most dangerous enemies aren't the ones on the other side of the field," Trapper observed grimly. "That's why I need to get out of here on the next flight, which should be leaving in about eight minutes."

She stood from her pilot's chair. "Will you be returning? Between you and me, I'd much rather have your Pounders assigned to the battalion than Piper's people."

"Nothing would make me happier," he assured her, "but my coming here wasn't exactly sanctioned by the chain of command. Your commander isn't the only one whose ass is on a collision course with a sling, which is partly why I've got to get out of here before I find myself in the brig." He proffered his hand, fixing her with a look that conveyed sincere respect. "Whatever happens, I'm glad I came down here. I'd fight alongside you any day, Lieutenant."

Xi reached out and grasped his hand. "Likewise, Sergeant Major. It was an honor taking the field with you."

"The feeling's mutual," he assured her before hesitating. "And…thanks for letting an old man unburden himself."

"Thanks for the water," she replied with a lopsided grin.

"Any time, Elvira." He returned the expression before donning his helmet and leaving *Elvira*'s cabin.

A few minutes later, he was aboard the *Geralt* as it made its second trip to the orbiting Terran Fleet Carrier, *Paul Revere*.

DEBRIEFING & DEATH'S DOOR

"This is Rear Admiral Corbyn," the officer at the head of the table announced, turning slightly toward the recording pickup as he spoke, "presiding over this informal inquiry into the events which transpired at the dates listed on planet EO-1162, also known as Durgan's Folly. Captain Chen, Commanding Officer of the *Paul Revere*, and Colonel Farbright, Commander of the 243rd FGF, in attendance. Commander Lee Jenkins providing testimony to supplement official logs and records to be cataloged in full at a later date. Good morning, Commander," Admiral Corbyn greeted with all the warmth of an icicle.

"Good morning, Admiral," Jenkins acknowledged the assemblage in turn. "Captain. Colonel."

"Now, you understand," Corbyn continued in his droll accent, "that this is a purely informal inquiry, correct?"

"I do so understand, Admiral." Jenkins nodded, gesturing to Chief Styles at his side. "As you can see, I've brought my secretary, Chief Warrant Officer Third Class Jamie Styles, but have not secured legal counsel at this time."

"The goal of this proceeding," the rear admiral droned on in his bizarre accent, "is to clarify certain elements of your preliminary after-action report, which this board has already reviewed in detail. Again, you are under no legal obligation to answer any of these questions as this is an informal inquiry. I feel it is important to make this point absolutely clear, Commander Jenkins."

The temptation to reply as his people did, with the quip 'clear as a Solarian's conscience,' was stronger than he expected it to be. But Jenkins refrained and acknowledged, "Crystal clear, Admiral."

"Very good." Corbyn nodded, his jowls shaking as he shuffled a stack of polymer sheets containing what Jenkins assumed were pertinent details of his operation. "Now, on the twenty-fourth day of your deployment on Durgan's Folly, you encountered a significant concentration of Arh'Kel infantry and heavy weapons platforms. Is that correct?"

"That is correct, Admiral." Jenkins nodded. "Upon arrival, we immediately began executing a grid patrol of the area surrounding our field HQ, during which we encountered only light resistance until day twenty-four."

"At which time," Corbyn continued, "one of the vehicles in your battalion, hereafter referred to as *Elvira I*, fell into a subterranean transit junction filled with Arh'Kel troops and weaponry. Is that right?"

"It is."

"Now *Elvira I*'s crew was isolated after authorizing her detachment of FGF infantry, under the command of Major Pete Piper, to rendezvous with Captain Terrence Murdoch. Is that correct?" Corbyn asked, and here they came to the first of what Jenkins assumed would be many points of possible contention.

Murdoch had survived his injuries, and clearly done his level best to submit an account of events which looked favorably on him at the expense of the rest of the battalion. Normally, Jenkins would have objected to the board's mischaracterization of how those troops came to be with Murdoch instead of *Elvira*, where they belonged, but Jenkins knew this was going to be a hard-enough slog without getting bogged down in nonessential details.

"*Elvira*'s infantry were duly-transferred to support Captain Murdoch's position," Jenkins agreed, though the words tasted like ash as he spoke them. He felt dirty for hanging Xi in the wind, after all she'd done.

"At that time," Corbyn said after the briefest of delays, suggesting he had expected resistance on the previous point, "*Elvira I*'s crew authorized the deployment of a strategic-grade weapon, specifically a P-92-Z pulse missile. Did you authorize the deployment of that system, Commander Jenkins?"

"I authorized Lieutenant Junior Grade Xi Bao to deploy her arsenal in accordance with protocol, Admiral," Jenkins replied firmly.

"Perhaps I did not make myself clear." Corbyn peered over the old-style spectacles which were perched so far down his nose it was a miracle they didn't fall off. "Did you specifically authorize the launch of that particular P-92-Z pulse missile?"

"The admiral is no doubt aware," Jenkins said, unwilling to throw Xi any further under the bus, "that operational authority in a combat zone often requires some command decisions be made in the field and without prior consultation. I had previously authorized Lieutenant Xi to deploy her arsenal, which I was aware included a P-92-Z pulse missile, as she saw fit, so long as that deployment was consistent with the rules of engagement as put forth by the Terran Republic Military Code initially ratified in 2072 and amended on the subject of Arh'Kel engagement in 2235."

Corbyn made a point of removing his spectacles. "As Commander Jenkins is no doubt aware, I was a contributing member of the board which ratified those rules of engagement in 2235. As such, I do not require any clever reminders as to why those rules were modified to permit the field deployment of strategic weapons against Arh'Kel targets."

Jenkins had gotten under the admiral's skin, just as he had hoped. But as those eyes peered across the table at him, he couldn't help but feel the gravity of the situation he was about to plunge head-long into.

"Of course, Admiral." Jenkins nodded, careful to keep his features neutral.

Corbyn replaced his spectacles and resumed. "How did your battalion come to possess a P-92-Z pulse missile, Commander Jenkins?"

"We horse-traded for it, Admiral," Jenkins replied unashamedly.

"Come again, Commander?"

"Like much of the equipment in the battalion, that particular P-92-Z pulse missile was donated by a private security force, which did so on condition of anonymity," Jenkins explained. "The pulse missile was acquired for other, similarly donated materials in a manner consistent with my program's charter. The paperwork was filed at Terran Armor Corps HQ on New Britannia, in accordance with my program's trial charter. If I'm not mistaken, Admiral Corbyn was part of the admiralty board overseeing my program's inception."

"You're getting on my nerves, Commander Jenkins," Admiral Corbyn said in a casual but dangerous tone.

"That was not my intention, Admiral," Jenkins lied. He absolutely needed to get that piece of information on the transcript of this meeting.

"We'll table the matter of the pulse missile," Corbyn grunted, "and proceed to the issue of your assault on the underground facility hereafter referred to as Junction One, located several hundred meters below the surface of Durgan's Folly. Vehicle recorders show that you split your two companies, commanded by yourself and Captain Terrence Murdoch, respectively, and engaged the enemy with just half of your mechs while the other half was still more than a kilometer from the engagement zone.

You even, if the records are to be relied upon," he added off-handedly, though Jenkins knew this was merely the first of what would be many attempts to discredit the myriad logs his people had gathered during the operation, "pulled 2nd Company's CO, Captain Murdoch, from his post to have him support 1st Company's attack. Not only did this result in 1st and 2nd Companies being cut off after a cave-in, but that separation put the lives of your entire battalion at risk. A lot of good men and women died in Junction One, possibly as a result of questionable command decisions made by you, Commander Jenkins. At this time, we will examine those decisions in detail in order to better determine your project's viability and, to be blunt, its commander's fitness to oversee it. Again…" He smirked over his spectacles at Jenkins as he reiterated, "I feel obliged to remind you that you need not answer any of this board's questions, as this is a purely informal inquiry."

Jenkins swallowed the hard knot in his throat. Admiral Corbyn was clearly looking to ruin his career, discredit his people, and probably cover up—or steal credit for—the tremendous victory he had scored on Durgan's Folly.

It was tempting to refuse to answer the questions, and he could all but hear Captain Chen and Colonel Farbright pleading with him to do that very thing. They knew what he had done down there, and under other circumstances would have done everything they could to see him receive the recognition he—and, more importantly, his people—deserved. The safe play would be to fall back, regroup, and wait for reinforcements to arrive.

But Lee Jenkins hadn't gotten his callsign by playing it safe, so without breaking eye contact with Admiral Corbyn, he said, "I'm prepared to continue, Admiral Corbyn." He felt his spine stiffen at that moment as he added, "In my opinion, we've demonstrated what armor can do in the ongoing Arh'Kel Conflict, and this trial program's time's up." He allowed himself a shark-like smile as he finished with gusto, "We are ready to take the war to the enemy."

"Lieutenant Xi?" asked a woman with a beautifully-accented, staccato voice. Xi stirred from her short-lived nap, and before looking at the woman who had roused her, she checked the medical bed beside her.

Podsednik was still there, his body mostly wrapped in regenerative foam while a handful of pipes, hoses, and tubes stuck out of various parts of his battered body. In spite of the macabre imagery, his vital signs looked all right, so she gave the woman her full attention.

She was stunningly beautiful, with black hair, light brown skin, and eyes that almost looked feline. She wore a lab-coat, and a quick glance at the embroidery revealed her to be Dr. Turney, the ship's Chief Medical Officer.

"I'm sorry," Xi apologized, standing from the bedside chair in the cramped sickbay.

"It's quite all right," Turney assured her. "I'm making my rounds but thought you might have a few questions I could answer while I did?"

"Please." Xi nodded, having waited two full days since arriving on the *Paul Revere* to speak with its CMO.

"I understand you and he are teammates," the doctor said as she led Xi away from Podsy's bed.

"Since we transferred into the battalion," Xi confirmed. "How is he?"

Turney gave her a patient, sympathetic look that sent chills down Xi's spine. She'd seen that look before—it *never* heralded good news.

"Mr. Podsednik suffered extreme damage to his legs, Lieutenant," the doctor replied. "In fact, and I know this is not what you want to hear right now, I'm going to have to amputate them if we want to save his life."

"Amputate…" Xi was stunned. His vital signs had been getting weaker, but she had thought that with the latest round of medicine they'd given him, he'd start pulling around soon.

"I'm afraid so," the doctor said seriously. "And even after we do that, his liver and kidneys are all but shut down. Now, the renal function I can simulate until we get him a prosthetic, but the liver—"

"Wait, back up, lady," Xi snapped. "First you tell me you're going to have to cut his legs off, and now you're saying his kidneys and liver are shutting down?"

"They're almost completely gone, Lieutenant," Turney said firmly. "And I understand this is a difficult time for you, but you must understand that there are thousands of badly-wounded men and women in this fleet following the attack at the wormhole gate, and for reasons beyond my ability to divine, we are dangerously short on support ships to evacuate them. I've kept Chief Podsednik alive here as a personal favor to Nick, but without surgery and a willing liver donor, I've got no choice but to triage him out of that bed."

"A liver donor?" Xi repeated.

"Yes." Dr. Turney nodded. "As I said, I have enough external dialysis systems that we can keep him connected, but all of my synthetic kidneys have been used. I'm going to need a liver donor, and it would make things go a lot faster if you—"

"Of course," Xi interrupted anxiously. "Cut me open, rip out whatever bits you need, just don't let Podsy die!"

Turney smiled, this time more genuinely. "Nick was right about you."

"Who the hell is Nick?"

Turney laughed. "That's right, he told me about that horrible nickname you all gave him. Nick is, or was, my husband," she explained, but Xi was still drawing a blank. "Dr. Fellows?" Turney rolled her eyes expectantly.

"Strange Bed?" Xi blurted before shaking her head in disbelief before appraising the woman from head to toe. "There is no way Strange Bed convinced *you* to marry him. What are you, twenty years younger than he is?"

Turney laughed. "Got you all fooled, hasn't he? Good for him."

"Excuse me?"

"Nothing," Turney said dismissively. "Let's get some paperwork filled out so I can operate—on both Mr. Podsednik and you. I understand you have each other's power of attorney, which will expedite things greatly and might just save his life. He's lucky to have you, you know?" she said in all seriousness.

"No," Xi said with conviction. "I'm the one who's lucky to have him."

"Do you have anything else you'd like to add, Commander Jenkins?" Rear Admiral Corbyn asked after eight hours of grueling interrogation.

"Nothing of substance, Admiral," Jenkins replied. "I stand by the contents of my logs, vehicle recorders, and testimony here today. But what happened down on Durgan's Folly was a unique situation in the history of the Terran Republic. I don't know if I made all the right calls, and I'm certainly not qualified to stand in judgment on that account. What I do know is that my people exceeded the high standard required of this Republic's armed forces personnel, and they deserve to be recognized for their contributions on behalf of the Terran Republic's safety and well-being. All command decisions were mine and mine alone, and the people under my command executed my orders in a manner consistent with the good order and discipline of the Terran Republic Fleet."

"So noted," Corbyn acknowledged. "Oh, there is one more thing," Corbyn added, as though it was of little consequence, "are you aware of the whereabouts of one Sergeant Major Tim Trapper, Jr.?"

There it was. The most critical link in Jenkins' plan to weather this bureaucratic storm had just been publicly recognized by the rear admiral, which meant that Jenkins' worst fears about this proceeding had just been confirmed with the equivalent of an exclamation point. Jenkins didn't know *where* Trapper was because he pointedly hadn't asked. He had, however, made clear to the sergeant major that the future of his battalion was on the line, and that he had nowhere else to turn for help in clearing an exit path should things come down the way they just did.

Shaking his head firmly, Jenkins said, "No, Admiral Corbyn, I do not know Sergeant Major Trapper's present whereabouts."

Corbyn fixed him with a thousand-meter stare for too long before turning to his left, where Captain Chen sat. "Do my compatriots have anything to add?" he asked, giving both Captain Chen and Colonel Farbright expectant looks, to which they shook their heads. "Then this inquiry is concluded. Off the record, Commander Jenkins..." Corbyn removed his spectacles, laced his fingers together, and leaned his forearms against the table. "You people survived a harrowing ordeal fraught with all manner of obstacles, including being outfitted with substandard gear, having your roster filled with personnel of questionable ability and makeup, and being cut off when the Fleet was forced to postpone your reinforcements. You made your share of mistakes down there, and then some," he added markedly. "But at the end of the day, you survived and dealt a major blow to the enemy. Irrespective of the admiralty's decision regarding your trial program, or your worthiness to lead it, I want you to know that you did well for yourself down there."

"Thank you, Admiral," Jenkins said, barely able to keep from sneering at Corbyn's lackluster characterization of their victory as a 'major blow.' It was nothing short of a turning point in the Arh'Kel Conflict, possibly even the single-most significant turning point. Anyone with half a brain could see that.

But throughout the inquiry, one thing had been made abundantly clear to Commander Lee Jenkins: he had precious little in the way of support within the Terran Republic Fleet, and if his fate was truly in their hands, then he couldn't rule out a protracted stay inside a prison cell in the near future.

As he and Styles gathered their things and left the conference room, he knew that his battalion's hope and, possibly, its peoples' very freedom rested on Sergeant Major Trapper's secret mission.

"That went well," Styles muttered, nervously wiping the sweat from his brow after they had walked in silence for nearly a minute.

"We're not out of the woods yet," Jenkins assured the other man.

"I have a snarky reply to that, but I'll refrain," Styles allowed, "but we can see the tree line and there's daylight peeking through."

"It's either daylight," Jenkins said sourly, "or the headlamp of an oncoming train."

Now, perhaps more than ever, he was tempted to crack open that bottle and climb as far down it as possible. But somewhat perversely, his people needed him at his best if they were going to get through this mess.

"The operation was a success," Dr. Turney said as soon as she came to Xi's bedside located near Podsy's. "He's not completely safe yet, but if we make it through the next thirty-six hours, he should be on the road to recovery."

"Thank you, Dr. Turney," Xi said, surprised and more than a little guilty at how pain-free she felt following the extraction of over half her liver. Her liver was apparently larger than normal, especially for a woman, and the more she gave, the better Podsy's chance of survival.

"You need to rest here," Turney said seriously, "and if I even suspect that you're getting out of that bed to do anything but visit the head, I'll restrain you—physically or chemically. Do we understand each other?"

Xi scowled at the other woman. "Looks like I'm not the only one with an overactive 'raging bitch' gland."

Turney threw her head back and laughed. "Tell Nick he's missed...by all four of us."

Xi rolled her eyes in bewilderment as the doctor left her bedside, and in spite of Podsy's grave condition, she looked over at him with renewed hope and whispered, "Don't die on me, Podsy."

For his part, he remained blissfully unaware of his surroundings in the deep, dreamless sleep of a chemically-induced coma.

And for a rare moment in her life, Xi almost wished she could join him.

DEVILS & THEIR DEALS

T*hree weeks later.*

"Thank you for coming, Commander," Rear Admiral Corbyn greeted upon Jenkins' entry to the same conference room where his 'informal' debriefing had taken place. "Please, be seated."

"Admiral," Jenkins acknowledged, noting that the rear admiral and he were the lone occupants of the room.

"The admiralty's preliminary review of the evidence, along with your testimony, has led us to some rather unusual and, to be blunt, uncomfortable conclusions," Corbyn explained. "As you've doubtless noticed, this meeting is completely off-the-record for reasons pertaining to both information compartmentalization and Terran Republic security."

Jenkins had expected the old 'national security' bit, so he nodded. "Understood, Admiral."

"Pursuant to, and in addendum of, the conditional transfer of the men and women to your temporary command under the Terran Armor Corps, Fleet Command is prepared to execute its obligations to yourself and your people," Corbyn said, and Jenkins was acutely aware of the word 'execute' being included in the admiral's legal-sounding decree. "Effective immediately, every veteran of Operation Spider-Hole attached to your battalion will be formally transferred out of Armor Corps and onto Fleet rolls where their ranks will be normalized, and they will be promoted a full step. Or, if they so choose, they will receive an honorable discharge from active service with a pension commensurate with their total term of service, including any time served prior to incarceration. Additionally, all criminal records or other legal liabilities previously incurred will be expunged from their records, regardless of whether they choose to stay or leave active service. Posthumous pensions will also be served to the survivors of personnel killed in the line of duty, along with full-honors death benefits befitting their rank at time of death. If that rank was a field commission or other temporary placement, it will be formalized upon your acknowledgment of this document's authenticity," he finished, sliding a data slate across the table.

Jenkins deigned to look at the slate, instead studying the rear admiral's eyes before finally saying, "Admiral, you're clearly versed in the linguistics required to craft such a comprehensive agreement. I'd appreciate if you could break it down in terms I'll understand."

Corbyn smirked. "Put simply, Commander Jenkins, you agree that every data recorder in your battalion was corrupted by Arh'Kel interference, and that there were numerous errors in your logs and the logs of your people. Logs which, it so happens, were lost in the shuffle between the surface and here. You also agree, under the most severe penalty under military law…" He let that last bit linger for a long, tense moment before continuing, "That you will not divulge any account of what took place on Durgan's Folly, nor will you recount the events or operational details of Operation Spider-Hole to anyone but your immediate superior or, if you feel it prudent to bring it to their attention, to the Joint Chiefs themselves in a formal, secure setting. If I haven't made this clear enough, let me spell it out for you…" He leaned forward, and actually relaxed his hard-edged façade as he spoke with open frustration and, somewhat shockingly, a trace of fear. "The details of Durgan's Folly, if leaked to the press, could shatter the Terran Republic. The fear of Arh'Kel crypto-colonies lurking under the noses of every world in the Republic would be devastating for morale among the citizenry, and frankly, Durgan's Folly makes Fleet look bad. This happened on our watch, son. Yours and mine. And with a potentially catastrophic Arh'Kel invasion looming, the last thing we need is for the colonies, let alone Sol, to learn about this SNAFU. Fleet is humanity's only lifeline out here, Commander Jenkins. If faith in Fleet goes…"

"Understood, Admiral," Jenkins said agreeably. "I will, of course, stipulate to all of this, Admiral Corbyn. I've spent my life in service to the Republic, and I'm not about to stop now. If this is what the admiralty thinks is best, I will absolutely toe the line as you've just described it. But I need to know one thing, Admiral, and if you'll forgive me for being forward, I need you to answer me frankly and honestly."

Corbyn scowled before making an inviting gesture. "Go on, Commander."

"What's going to happen to my unit?"

The rear admiral eyed him, rhythmically drumming his fingers against the table as Jenkins awaited the reply. And when it came, it genuinely surprised Jenkins. "You've proven to my satisfaction that armor has a place on the battlefield, especially against the Arh'Kel. Unfortunately, the political will just isn't there to adopt a restructuring of the scale needed to move forward at this time, especially since the details of your outstanding performance on Durgan's Folly will be sealed for the foreseeable future. I've been in on the meetings with the Joint Chiefs, and I've testified before the Armed Forces Committees, Commander," he sighed. "The system is too set in its ways to change course in your proposed direction. The Marine Corps is the most devastating, efficient, and finely-tuned sub-branch of the Terran military and *everyone* knows it, which is why we were able to wrestle enough funding to get the power-suit production facilities back up after the Arh'Kel recently tore them down. For better or worse, we're riding that horse into battle. But let me be clear—" He emphatically put a finger on the desk. "—your work down there *will* revolutionize the way we fight the rock-biters, and possibly everyone else."

"Just not today," Jenkins concluded, making no attempt to hide his disappointment.

"Just not today," Admiral Corbyn agreed sympathetically. "Give it another decade, climb another few rungs up the ladder, and I'd wager you'll be asked to personally spearhead the development of a Fleet Combined Arms sub-branch to supplement the Marines. The bureaucracy takes time to make adjustments like this. You understand, of course."

Jenkins sat back in his chair, having learned one important thing that he hadn't expected to learn from the rear admiral: in spite of appearances, Corbyn seemed sympathetic to his entire situation.

"I appreciate your candor, Admiral, as well as what I expect will be your ongoing support. And I'd view it as a personal favor if you gave me the opportunity to break this to my people," Jenkins said.

"Of course, son."

"Thank you," Jenkins said before swallowing the dry knot in his throat and finally saying the four words he had dreaded from the moment he'd stepped aboard the *Paul Revere*. "Where do I sign?"

"Good boy," Corbyn replied in unveiled condescension. He nodded, and a few minutes later, the distasteful deed was done.

But the fight for Jenkins' command—and, more importantly, for the immediate resurgence of armor in the Terran military—was far from over.

"Lieutenant," Jenkins greeted after finding Xi and Podsy's place in the *Paul Revere*'s sickbay. "No." He held up a halting hand when she tried to stir. "Don't get up. That's an order."

Xi nonetheless propped herself up by adjusting the bed's posture. "What can I do for you, sir?" she asked.

He chuckled. "When I picked you out of a Terra Han prison last year, did you think it was possible you'd start *any* conversation with those seven words?"

She shot him an irritated look. "If you're here to gloat about pounding me into shape..."

"Far from it." He shook his head, pulling a chair between Xi's and Podsy's beds. "How is he?"

"He's going to pull through," Xi said with relief. "The doctor says he won't be conscious for another week at least, but it looks like the worst is behind him."

"I'm glad to hear it," Jenkins said with feeling. "You two were absolutely essential to our success down there," he said, letting his gaze linger on Podsednik's ruined body before turning toward Xi, "which is why I came to you first."

"Sir?" she asked guardedly.

"I just cut a deal with Admiral Corbyn," he said in a low voice. "Part of that deal was my agreement to have everything that happened down there be classified."

Her eyes went wide with anger. "Those assholes! After everything you did, after everything *we* did, they have the nerve to take it all away from you?!"

"Calm down," Jenkins said, and much to his surprise, she actually listened to him, though her face was now beet-red and he imagined steam pouring out of her ears. "You've got a choice, Xi. Option one is to sign out of military service, agree to never talk about Durgan's Folly again, and go back to Terra Han to start a new life. You're not even twenty years old," he said, marveling at that fact even as he stated it. "You've got your whole life in front of you. You'd even get a modest pension, and the right to wear dress blues at any and all formal functions," he snickered softly at that last bit.

She cocked her head in silent contemplation before asking, "What are you going to do, sir?"

"Option two," he continued without pause, "you stay on with Fleet, take a promotion to full lieutenant, and continue serving the Terran Republic with the same ferocity and commitment you've shown under my command. They need people with your abilities, Xi. I'd bet everything I own that you'd make dropship pilot inside of a year and carve a place for yourself in the Corps. Hell, I'd even put in the word with Colonel Villa and see to it you ended up in Wolf Company if that's what you wanted."

"What are *you* going to do, sir?" she repeated intently, her eyes as hard as granite.

"Me?" He cracked a mischievous grin. "I've never been too fond of binaries or of following the rules."

She returned the expression, and after hearing the details agreed to support his audacious plan on one condition.

He agreed and set about the task of informing the rest of the battalion of his high-risk plan, or at least, those members he wanted to include in it.

Later that day, Jenkins greeted the last member of his team who, like Xi and Podsy, was in sickbay.

"Captain Murdoch," Jenkins greeted, "a moment?"

"Commander," Murdoch replied stiffly. His wounds looked to have been largely healed, and to Jenkins' eye, he was fit to be discharged from sickbay. But the inveterate sandbagger was playing true to form, milking the situation for all it was worth in order to increase his personal comfort quotient as much as possible.

"First off," Jenkins said, turning a chair around before sitting in it, "I know you and I have had our disagreements, but you're a fine soldier. You played a key role in our victory down there, and I've been lucky to have your expertise and experience under my command."

Murdoch eyed him warily. "Thank you, sir."

"Fleet Command has given surviving members of the battalion a choice," Jenkins explained. "You can either sign out of the service or take a step up in rank and formally transfer to Fleet. Either way, your criminal record is expunged, and your jacket will read as clean as the day you signed up for service."

Murdoch nodded. "I'm taking the promotion."

"I expected as much." Jenkins nodded approvingly. "You've got a long career ahead of you. Fleet will be lucky to have you. Have you thought about where you'd like to be stationed?"

The captain shook his head. "Not really."

It was clear that Murdoch didn't want to go into any greater detail, so Jenkins said, "You've already spoken with Admiral Corbyn, so you know that the events of Durgan's Folly are classified. Correct?"

"Yes," Murdoch sneered, "I've spoken with the admiral."

"Good." Jenkins nodded. "Good. Then I just want to say that it's been an honor serving with you, Captain Murdoch." Jenkins proffered a hand invitingly.

"Permission to speak freely, sir?" Murdoch grunted without acknowledging Jenkins' outstretched hand.

"Granted."

"You're a loose cannon, sir," Murdoch sneered. "You put all our lives at risk with every single decision you made down there. We're lucky *any* of us got off that rock alive, and the fact that some of us are still breathing is due to nothing but dumb luck."

"Come now, Captain," Jenkins deadpanned, fighting to keep

his expression flat as anger slowly filled him, "tell me how you *really* feel."

"How do I feel?" Murdoch scoffed. "I feel like I just charged into the mouth of Hell, *Commander*, and that my CO's only concern was finding just how far down we could make it before that fiery maw swallowed us all."

"When you're going through Hell—" Jenkins smirked, quoting one of his favorite historical politicians. "Keep going."

"Is that what you'll tell him when he wakes up and finds his legs are gone?" Murdoch demanded, thinking of Podsednik's tortured body. "This is all some kind of game to you, isn't it? Or are you still obsessed with proving the merits of your precious armor experiment? What is it, some kind of catharsis for a life spent at the bottom of a bottle—a bottle that cost you everything you ever loved?"

Jenkins stood from the chair and looked down at the bedridden captain, doing his best to keep his voice from rising while rhythmically pumping his hands into fists. "That's enough, Captain Murdoch. You've made your point. Now I'll make mine. I meant what I said about it being an honor to serve with you. I don't have to like you to know that down there, you stood as tall as anyone when the shit hit the fan. Did we have our disagreements? Yes. But frankly, you'd still be busting rocks on a penal colony if I hadn't given you a chance to redeem yourself. And you did!" he snapped, unable to control himself any longer. "You *did* redeem yourself, just like I thought you would when I dragged your sorry, supply-stealing ass out of that cold, miserable cell. And if taking fire down there was enough to rattle you beyond the ability to conduct yourself with a little dignity, I hope Fleet finds a nice, cushy desk for you to hold down in some quiet, safe corner more to your liking than the cockpit of a combat mech. I also hope that, like me, you've learned the error of your former ways and choose to make the most of this well-earned fresh start. Men like us are rarely lucky enough to receive second chances."

He shook his head in disgust before turning on his heel. "Good-bye, Captain Murdoch."

No matter how brave a front he had put up, Murdoch's blow had struck truer than Jenkins wanted to admit. Maybe he *was* obsessed. Maybe it was nothing but some misguided quest for redemption for misdeeds of years gone by. He didn't care anymore, because after fighting down on Durgan's Folly, he had learned one crucial thing that transcended everything else.

He had found something he was *good* at: fighting armor.

And he had no plans to stop.

LIPSTICK ON THE COLLAR

"Attention on deck!" barked the *Paul Revere*'s XO, Lieutenant Commander Bashir, as the airlock began its final cycle.

Jenkins stood just behind the XO, having expected the arriving VIP since before stepping off Durgan's Folly.

The airlock opened, and a pair of figures stepped through, followed by Marines in dress uniform. The left figure wore a high-end business suit that probably cost more than a year of Jenkins' salary. He was pale-skinned, medium build, had a half-bald head of gray hair and quick, calculating eyes—eyes which immediately found Jenkins before scanning the rest of the corridor.

"Permission to come aboard?" asked the right-hand figure, an elderly man with deep brown skin and a brown dress uniform displaying more military regalia than seemed possible.

"Permission granted, General Akinouye," acknowledged Commander Bashir. "Welcome aboard the *Paul Revere*, sir. We weren't informed of your visit, or Rear Admiral Corbyn would have…"

"It's all right, son," the general interrupted. "What's the point of a surprise inspection if it's not a surprise? Where can I take my things?" he asked expectantly.

"We've assigned you a berth on D-deck," Bashir replied promptly. "I'll have my people take your things…"

"No, that's quite all right," General Akinouye—the oldest serving member of the Joint Chiefs of Staff—assured him before gesturing to Jenkins. "I'll have him collect my bags and show me to my quarters."

Bashir hesitated before nodding. "Very good, General."

"You do know the way, don't you, son?" Akinouye asked, and even at the ripe age of a hundred and ten, the general's commanding presence made Jenkins feel small as a mouse.

"Yes, General." Jenkins nodded, collecting the man's bags.

Akinouye turned to the ship's XO. "I'll conduct my inspection in a few hours. Traveling through wormholes takes a toll at my age."

"Yes…of course, sir," Bashir said, his eyes nervously flicking back and forth between Jenkins and Akinouye as he began to understand the nature of the general's visit.

"Good." The general nodded before looking around in mock bewilderment. "Well…don't you people have *jobs* to do?"

"Company," Bashir snapped, "dismissed!"

The assemblage quickly dispersed, and Jenkins wordlessly led the general to his assigned berth. Once inside, and with the hatch closed, he turned to the ranking member of the Terran Armor Corps and said, "General, I appreciate your taking the time—"

"Cut the bullshit, son," Akinouye interrupted. "I don't know how you did it, but you made the Senior and Junior Tim Trappers sit down and speak for the first time in two decades." He held up a pair of fingers. "Truth be told, I wasn't convinced you had the brains—or the balls—to do anything but get yourself killed riding one of our half-rusted-out mechs into combat against the rock-biters. And frankly, I'm still not," he admitted with an indifferent shrug before shaking his head in bewilderment, "but somehow, you made those two intractable sons of bitches actually talk to each other, so I thought to myself, 'this man might *actually* be more than meets the eye, and not the walking disgrace I've been repeatedly assured he is.' I trust you'll do your utmost to let an old man cling to that fleeting hope as long as possible?"

Jenkins had expected a prickly greeting, but he was still wrong-footed by the general's full-frontal assault. "General," he rallied, "as of two hours ago, I, and roughly half of the men and women under my command, collectively agreed to formally resign our current commissions—"

"Glad to hear it," the general interrupted. "The TAF needs as few cowards and sandbaggers as possible on the rolls. I trust you'll find a career in retail more to your liking…"

"Concurrently," Jenkins interrupted, "we've tendered a proposal for your review which, upon approval, would more than double the Terran Armor Corps' current active-duty roster with the only men and women in the TAF fit to crew mechs."

Akinouye grinned, and the expression was so savage it sent a chill down Jenkins' spine. "You arrogant son of a bitch. Appealing to my vanity, is that your angle? Playing on an old war dog's eroding sense of dignity rooted in the branch he's faithfully served for ninety-one years while, slowly but surely, it crumbled all around him as funding went to every leaf and twig of the TAF but his. You're about to promise me one last, heroic charge into the teeth of the enemy, riding mechs, singing battle hymns, and clearing guns that haven't seen proper use in decades. You aim to paint the picture of a romantic end or, dare one even think it, a new beginning for my beloved Armor Corps." He shook his head in disappointment. "Have I got it about right, son?"

Jenkins didn't hesitate. "That's precisely it, General."

The general regarded him critically, during which time Jenkins felt sure he shrank twelve centimeters, before finally chuckling. "All right, you're cool enough under fire. Walk me through this proposal of yours—slowly, though," he added, wincing as he carefully lowered himself to the dinette. "I feel like there's a pulsar in the middle of my brain. You wouldn't happen to have a drink, would you?"

"Nothing but water, sir," Jenkins said firmly, clearly taking the other man's meaning.

"*Good*," Akinouye grunted, and Jenkins proceeded to make his pitch.

Two hours later, after a thorough grilling from General Akinouye during the pitch, Jenkins made his way to the berth assigned to the second VIP from the shuttle.

He rang the chime outside, knowing that if the meeting with the five-star general had been difficult, this one would be even worse.

"Enter," came the calm, collected voice of the man on the other end, and Jenkins swung the hatch open to reveal the same pale-skinned, half-balding man who had been first off the shuttle. "Ah, Commander Jenkins," the intense, mid-statured man greeted with perfunctory courtesy while scanning the contents of a data slate. "I have to admit I'm more than a little surprised to receive your summons, especially now that I come to find the planet below is under strict military quarantine. Hardly what we agreed to, no?"

"My apologies, Mr. Durgan," Jenkins said with grave sincerity, "but that call was out of my hands…"

"Taking cover behind your superiors?" Durgan quipped. "That doesn't sound like the man who came to me eighteen months ago offering nothing but a tax write-off in exchange for the mechs in my war museums—" He tossed the slate to the bunk and finally fixed Jenkins with those cold, calculating eyes. "—along with a raw, unyielding passion for a project that no one—not even myself—considered likely to succeed. What's changed, Commander?"

Jenkins had anticipated this measure of candor from a man who served on the board of Durgan Interstellar Enterprises—acronym almost certainly intentional—and was prepared with the best he could possibly offer. "You misunderstand me, sir. I'm not hiding behind my superiors' decision; I agree with it one hundred percent."

"Betrayal then?" Durgan nodded in disdain. "Well, you've had your fun, got your free ride out of me in furtherance of a once-stalled career arc, and I'm sure in the process pleased a number of your superiors who are only too eager to trumpet this situation at my shareholders' expense. So if there's nothing else..."

"I didn't betray you, Mr. Durgan," Jenkins interrupted. "In fact, without violating the terms of an agreement I just signed on behalf of all my people—an agreement which gave me not a whit of pride to enter into, but as CO I felt it was my obligation to do so—the most careful and deliberate way I can describe what happened down there..." He drew a steadying breath. "...is as the most important break Terran humanity has ever received in its war with the Arh'Kel."

"Truly?" Durgan said witheringly. "You are a changed man, Commander Jenkins, from the ambitious, if none-too-bright, officer who came to me in an hour of desperation. I admit..." His quick, cold eyes narrowed. "I'm ambivalent about the changes I see in the man before me. But to say that what happened on planet EO-1162 was the 'most important break' in the history of the Arh'Kel Conflict, well...you understand if I'm reluctant to take you at your word."

"You know more about my psyche profile than I do, Mr. Durgan," Jenkins said bluntly, "so let me ask you a question: am I the type of man given to fits of hyperbole?"

Durgan cocked his head, seeming to study every pore on Jenkins' face before finally replying, "No, Commander, you are not particularly prone to hyperbole. But you will agree that without some evidence to corroborate your alarmist claim, I can hardly act based solely on your word."

"I understand that, for a variety of reasons, I'm not the most trustworthy source on this issue," Jenkins said, pushing past the wave of shame he felt as those reasons flitted through his mind. He then produced a data slate with an order originating from one of the Joint Chiefs himself. "But do you trust General Akinouye's judgment on the matter of EO-1162?"

Durgan glanced down at the slate and scoffed. "He wasn't privy to the details upon arrival. I know, because he and I have a clear line of communication," he added pointedly. "Unlike certain other officers with whom I've previously transacted."

"I understand that your security clearance gives you access to certain details of highly-classified operations—" Jenkins nodded, holding the slate unwaveringly as he spoke. "—which is why the general thought you might want to see this. It contains every bit and byte of intel your level of clearance permits you to access regarding the operation below, previously code-named Operation Spider-Hole."

Durgan glanced down at the slate once again before, somewhat reluctantly, plucking it from Jenkins' fingers. "I sincerely hope you have not wasted my time, Commander. My sudden disappearance has already cost my shareholders point-three percent of their stock valuation," he said, flicking a look Jenkins' way that sent chills down his spine. "I dislike answering for losses incurred for actions not resulting from my decisions. Doing so vexes me," Durgan said casually before finally reviewing the slate's contents, "and I can assure you I'm unpleasant when I am vexed."

Jenkins knew that to speak further would only dig his own grave, so he kept his mouth shut as one of the most powerful private citizens in the Terran Republic perused the sparse contents of the slate.

"No mention of troop strength beyond the engagement body counts." Durgan snorted in disdain. "No itemization of Arh'Kel material assets encountered, not even a prospectus detailing future FGF deployments. Everything of value on this slate is redacted!" he snapped, tossing the device to the deck with a clatter. He held up a warning finger. "You are testing my patience, Commander Jenkins."

"That was not my intention, Mr. Durgan."

"Perhaps not," Durgan snarled, "but it is your *achievement*, and it is perhaps the last one of note in what might have been a productive career in service of allies who know how to repay their debts, of *all* varieties."

Jenkins clasped his hands behind his back. "Consider for a moment the level of security clearance required to redact that information even from you, Mr. Durgan. Your company provides more arms and armaments than any other private entity in the Republic; you've built every APC and dropship in TAF service today, and Durgan micro-fusion generators power nearly every mobile platform in the Republic, be it military or civilian. Your company's contribution to Terran security and prosperity have been rivaled only by the contributions made by the various military branches which ride and carry your weapons to war in defense of humanity."

"Get your tongue out of my ass, Commander," Durgan seethed, "and make your point. Quickly."

"General Akinouye personally redacted that document, Mr. Durgan," Jenkins said simply. "Check the distributions markers..." He stooped to collect the slate.

"Stop," Durgan snapped, freezing Jenkins mid-motion where he remained, half-stooped, for a long moment before the businessman finally, and with great deliberation, moved past him to collect the slate off the deck.

Jenkins resumed an upright posture while Durgan scanned the slate's file headers. After a moment, Durgan's eyes narrowed significantly before a glimmer of realization seemed to dawn. "This was addressed directly to me..." he mused.

"Correct, Mr. Durgan," Jenkins agreed. "For your eyes only."

"But without any of the relevant information—" Durgan shook his head, though Jenkins suspected the other man already knew the answer he clearly expected Jenkins to provide. "—of what use is it to me?"

"It indirectly tells you how grave the situation was down there, sir," Jenkins replied promptly, "and it tells you that General Akinouye wanted you to understand the gravity of Operation Spider-Hole, even though you cannot know the specifics."

"As the local ranking officer, Corbyn knows..." Durgan mused, his eyes snapped back and forth in calculation, "and clearly the Joint Chiefs, represented by General Akinouye, are authorized to receive the operation's details. But redactions at this level have only been issued once before..."

"At New Australia." Jenkins nodded grimly. "The public didn't learn the full truth of Terra Australiana's fate for three full years following the massacre. In all honesty, I'd be surprised if Spider-Hole is *ever* fully revealed to the public."

Durgan nodded slowly before handing the data slate back to Jenkins, who took it and clasped his hands behind his back while the other man paced. He moved across the deck two dozen times, from one end of the relatively large berth to the other, before finally stopping and facing Jenkins.

"I agreed to support your experimental project for a variety of reasons, and tax write-offs, while a somewhat quaint angle to employ during your initial approach, was not among them," Durgan said pointedly.

"I understand, sir."

"If you do, then tell me why I agreed to help you in the first place." Durgan fixed his diamond-hard gaze on Jenkins. "Because right now, you're asking me to throw good money after bad, a habit I have not formed in my eighty-three years."

"The chief reason you agreed to support my project," Jenkins said steadily, "was to clear your family's name from EO-1162. You consider the past failure to colonize EO-1162, and its ensuing official designation, a stain upon your family name. It's become an obstacle to your company's continued expansion into adjacent industries, like exo-colonization, terraforming, and even biotech."

Durgan quirked a brow. "My, my...you're better informed than I suspected. Not many know of our burgeoning bio-tech department. I clearly have a leak that needs aggressive plugging."

"No leak, sir." Jenkins shook his head. "General Akinouye filled me in a few minutes ago."

Durgan seemed genuinely surprised at that. "Ben must be more invested in your project than I thought."

"He is, sir," Jenkins agreed, "but I'd be lying if I said we could do it without your support."

"I assume you mean to indicate that the support I have *already* provided is no longer sufficient." Durgan smirked.

"An accurate assumption, Mr. Durgan."

Durgan pursed his lips thoughtfully, and Jenkins decided to leap into the proverbial breach. "We rode substandard gear into this fight," Jenkins said passionately, "much of which was generously donated by you, but some of those platforms were older than the Republic. Some even ran on diesel engines, sir, and they frankly didn't fare well."

"You want fusion generators and capacitor banks for your depowered mechs," Durgan stated flatly. "But you and I both know that Fleet will never let those cores fall through their fingers and into your lap. They'll divert them long before they ever make it into your battalion—a factor which, you'll recall, played no small part in my reluctance to hand them over the first time we had this little chat."

"I've addressed that obstacle, Mr. Durgan," Jenkins said confidently, allowing a grin to spread across his lips. "All I need from you is a verbal agreement to supply those power cores, along with cores for the rest of the vehicles you've got in storage," he added pointedly. "I intend to put them *all* to good use as soon as humanly possible."

Durgan cocked his head skeptically before realization suddenly dawned. For the first time since Jenkins had met the man, the business tycoon actually cracked a smile. "I underestimated you, Commander Jenkins. I rarely do that. Are you sure you can weather the storm?"

"We wouldn't be talking if I wasn't," Jenkins said with conviction before adding, "and I didn't come to you until *after* getting the general's support."

"At least your threat assessment skills are on point," Durgan grunted with mild approval. "Fine. You've got my verbal agreement that if you can sidestep Fleet's involvement, you'll get your mechs and the cores to power them. What about crews?"

"That's high on the agenda, sir," Jenkins assured him, "and I've already got a few moves lined up."

"Specifics, Commander."

"The extra-orbital population of Terra Australiana is my first stop," Jenkins explained. "I expect I'll pull thirty to fifty qualified, near-combat-ready personnel from there to help fill out my Wrench and Monkey rolls. But getting combat-ready Jocks is going to be hard. There are two more max-sec prisons, both civilian, that I can scour for link-equipped pilots. Combined with my current roster of holdovers, it should give me enough pilot-ready personnel to field the battalion."

"Which puts you roughly back where you were when you started Spider-Hole," Durgan said sourly.

"Barring additional personnel transfers, that is correct, sir." Jenkins decided not to argue before observing, "Though our gear will be significantly upgraded following your pending generosity, and our support will be as well."

"Well...even before arriving, I was aware that you and your

people brought EO-1162 into compliance," Durgan said, making a point, as always, not to refer to the planet as 'Durgan's Folly.' "It was clear before I set foot on this ship that you had done outstanding work with the limited means provided you. With better support and gear, I expect you'll do nothing but improve your record. I intend to leverage that improvement for the benefit of my shareholders."

Jenkins felt his throat tighten at that, but he knew that added scrutiny was a small price to pay, so he nodded in agreement. "Of course, Mr. Durgan."

Durgan also nodded. "Very well, Commander. You'll have your gear. Now it's time for you to go."

"Thank you, sir," Jenkins acknowledged before turning and exiting the room.

When he was outside, with the hatch sealed behind him, he could not help but enthusiastically pump his fist in victory.

This was finally going to happen!

The pieces were in place, and all relevant agreements had been made. He had successfully navigated the viper's pit of military politics, secured private support for his project, and would soon be able to regain the field at the head of a column of combat-ready mechs.

Now the only thing left was to get his people, and their gear, the hell off this ship before Fleet wised up to his plan and threw them all in the brig.

Podsy's eyes fluttered open, and immediately shut again when the bright lights stabbed into them.

"Hey," the familiar voice of Xi greeted his ears, "you're awake."

He didn't hurt much, but he was weak and unable to sit up for some reason. "Where..." he croaked, and soon a drinking straw was pressed to his lips. He took a meager gulp of the sweet water, licked his lips, and tried again. "Where are we?"

"We're aboard the *Paul Revere*," Xi replied, her voice taut with anxiety. "Doc Fellows said you couldn't be moved until you regained consciousness, so I told the pervert to dose you up with enough stims to send an elephant through the roof."

Podsy smiled, glad that she was putting on a brave front for his sake. "How bad...is it?" he asked, finally able to crack his eyes open enough to see the faint outline of the sickbay around him.

"You didn't lose anything we can't grow back," she replied.

"That wasn't...my question," he said as his throat suddenly began to scratch with every word. He coughed, but fortunately another sip of water mostly quelled the would-be fit.

"You lost both legs, your kidneys, and your liver," Xi replied tremulously, and it was the first time he had heard her sound anything but brash and over-the-top.

"Is that all?" He closed his eyes, having suspected his legs were a lost cause minutes after suffering his wounds on *Elvira*. A proper medical facility would have almost certainly saved them, but in a field hospital as poorly-outfitted as theirs, he was glad just to regain consciousness, even if only for a few minutes. "How long...do I have?"

"Doc says you're going to make a full recovery," Xi assured him, and he was surprised to hear nothing but confidence in her voice. "Fellows and Turney installed your new artificial kidneys yesterday, and it looks like with a little gene therapy, your liver transplant will be good long-term as well."

"Liver transplant?" he repeated warily. "What seventy-year-old drunk do I have to thank for that?"

He felt a sharp impact against his shoulder, and despite the sudden pain, he couldn't help but laugh as he realized why she had punched him.

"Oh." He nodded, his eyes finally adjusted well enough to

focus on her. "I get it. You decided while I was asleep...that you'd slip a little piece of yourself into me. Is that it?"

"Asshole," Xi snapped, but her eyes were filled with tears as she gripped his hand gently in her own.

"I may be mistaken," Podsy continued blithely as Dr. Fellows came to stand at the foot of the bed, "but I doubt that's the ideal point of entry for a liver transplant."

"It isn't?" Fellows asked with mock confusion. He rolled his eyes as Xi chuckled with nervous laughter. "Huh...learn something every day in this business." He then turned serious. "Podsy, I hate to push this, but we're under something of a time crunch here. Moving you is extremely risky, but it's the only way we can guarantee your freedom."

Podsy's eyes widened at that. "What'd you guys do while I was out, assassinate the president?" Judging by their non-reactions, the joke clearly fell on deaf ears.

"I need your consent to transfer you to the *Bonhoeffer*," Fellows said gravely. "I'm not going to lie, it's a bad idea for a lot of reasons, so if you want..."

"Where do I sign?" Podsy interrupted. "I'd rather die with you guys than live without."

Xi happily wiped her tear-streaked cheeks. "You mean you're not going to discharge?"

He shook his head firmly, having arrived at that conclusion a few minutes before losing consciousness in *Elvira II*. "No. Though I have to admit..." He looked down at his missing legs, surprised to feel little, if anything, as he did so. "I doubt I'll be much good in my current state."

"I'll make sure we fix you up, Podsy," Fellows said solemnly as he handed him a medical release form. "You have my word."

Podsy signed the form, and Fellows made his way to a nearby access panel to log the document.

Meanwhile, a commotion arose across sickbay as a woman doctor consulted with one of the patients there.

"As you requested, Captain Murdoch," the woman doctor said with forced patience, "and per your rights under TAF regulations, I have brought in Doctor Xiahou for a second opinion. Doctor?" She gestured to a second doctor.

"I concur with Doctor Turney's analysis," the second doctor, of medium build and clearly from Terra Han. "You are fit to be discharged from sickbay, effective immediately."

"I'm not sure either of you understands..." Captain Murdoch began to object, standing from the bedside to plead his case.

Xi and Podsy made brief, but knowing, eye contact regarding their least favorite captain. Podsy gave her an encouraging nod, and the younger woman set off with a determined look in her eye.

"My sickle-cell anemia is extremely volatile," Murdoch explained, "and highly interactive with environmental factors. I remain unconvinced that I am stable enough to be transferred—"

Announcing her arrival in the most emphatic terms possible, Xi uncorked a sharp right hand into Murdoch's face. Blood sprayed down his chest as he clutched his shattered nose, miserably failing to stem the flow. "That's it, Xi," Murdoch snapped as Dr. Fellows and a team of assistants began to roll Podsy's bed out of sickbay. "You're finished. Do you hear me?! Finished!"

"That's for pulling my infantry detail and forcing me to send a strike on my own position, Captain Asshole," Xi barked. "You want to press charges because you were clumsy and hit your face on the bedrail?" She raised her arms challengingly to either side. "I suggest you sue the bed's manufacturer. Or better yet, the company that supplied the non-skid beneath your feet."

"This isn't over, Xi," Murdoch fumed impotently while the medical personnel in sickbay gave Xi silent, thankful looks as she turned her back and took her place at Podsy's side. "Do you hear me?! This isn't over! Arrest her!"

"Now, Captain Murdoch," the female doctor soothed, "you need to lie down. I don't think you're hemodynamically stable enough to continue standing in your current state. We need to immediately administer coagulants, but we can only administer them if you lie down for at least another fifteen minutes…"

The last look Podsy saw on Murdoch's face was one of conflict as he visibly weighed the pros and cons of another day or two in the comfort of sickbay versus filing a likely-impotent complaint against Xi. Fifteen minutes would be more than enough time for them to disembark, and Murdoch knew it. Thankfully, he remained true to form and accepted the extra time in the comfort of sickbay in lieu of filing an immediate complaint.

"Good work, LT," Podsy muttered after they had left sickbay behind.

Xi looked down at him and grinned, and even Doc Strange Bed seemed to enjoy the frantic rush to the airlock. They reached it without incident, and soon transferred to the *Bonhoeffer*, where Podsy was installed in sickbay under Fellows' direct supervision.

NEW HOME

"In recognition of meritorious service," declared General Akinouye before the small crowd, "and in-keeping with the Jasper Act of 2156, it is my privilege, honor, and pleasure to formally recognize the induction of former Flect Officer, Commander Lee Jenkins—and the men and women at his sides—into the Terran Armor Corps. Consistent with the Jasper Act," he continued as a handful of hover-drones recorded the event for media dissemination, "all prior ranks are hereby normalized in accordance with standard transfer protocols between TAF branches. Mr. Jenkins," the General intoned, his booming voice easily filling the cavernous chamber of the *Bonhoeffer*'s empty port drop-deck, which was large enough to fit two full companies of mechs, "step forward."

Jenkins, sporting the deep brown dress uniform of the Armor Corps—a significant departure from the blues-and-whites of the Fleet he had served for his entire military career—snapped to crisp attention and parade-marched from the head of his people to stand before General Akinouye.

"After extensive consultation with branch leadership, and as the ranking member of the Armor Corps," Akinouye proclaimed as he affixed the silver regalia befitting Jenkins' new rank to his collar and lapels, "I am proud to confer upon you the rank of lieutenant colonel."

The faint clicking of camera shutters could be heard from the drones, while their media-minders hung back and remotely-controlled the recording devices via virtual interfaces.

"I am also pleased to report," the general continued officiously, "that, for service above and beyond the call of duty, you, Lieutenant Colonel Jenkins, are to be awarded the Medal of Honor, the highest honor which can be bestowed by the Terran Armed Forces upon one of its own."

As he pinned the exceptionally rare medal to Jenkins' chest, the newly-minted lieutenant colonel noted that the button, as it was affectionately known, was one of the few awards that Akinouye's impressive board lacked.

"Also," Akinouye continued, briefly eyeing Jenkins for apparently noticing the lacking medal, "for exceptional courage under fire and bravery in the face of overwhelming odds, cut off from support and operating behind enemy lines, every member of your unit present is to be awarded the Eye of Jupiter."

He pinned the blazing red eye-shaped medal on Jenkins' chest, and by now, Jenkins was more than a little self-conscious as the drones subtly shifted their focus from the general to himself.

"And finally," Akinouye announced, picking the third ornate medal from the podium and displaying it to the pickups, "the Silver Comet, awarded for engagements requiring conspicuous valor and cunning in the Arh'Kel Conflict. This is only the third time a unit has received this high honor, Lieutenant Colonel," Akinouye said with a glint in his eye as he pinned the medal to his chest, "and, as you can see, the Armor Corps has been present for all three. You've inherited a proud tradition, Colonel. See that you live up to it."

Jenkins saw the pair of Silver Comets on Akinouye's chest and nodded. "Thank you, General."

Akinouye gestured to Jenkins' people. "I defer further ceremonial privileges to you, Colonel."

Jenkins snapped a picture-perfect salute, which the general returned, before the newly-made lieutenant colonel turned on his heel and barked, "Xi Bao, step forward."

Xi, looking far more professional than ever in her dress browns, stepped forward and came to attention before him.

Jenkins met her eyes, giving her a barely perceptible nod of approval before raising his voice. "In accordance with the Jasper Act of 2156, and pursuant to Terran Armor Corps tradition of rewarding conspicuously meritorious displays of leadership and discipline under fire—" Her eyes went wide in nervous surprise at that last bit, but fortunately, she kept her cool as he continued. "—I am proud to confer upon you the rank of captain." He pinned the silver bars to her collar, seeing her blush and struggle against the urge to squirm as he did so. After affixing the insignia to her uniform, he proffered his right hand. "Congratulations, Captain Xi."

She clasped his hand, and even after two weeks of rest, her fingers were still pink and slightly raw from the abuse suffered on Durgan's Folly. "Thank you, Colonel."

Thirty minutes later, after pinning a bucket-load of medals on his people—which included the Broken Tread for the double amputee, Podsy, who had miraculously survived his harrowing wounds—the ceremony was concluded, and the battalion personnel were dismissed.

"Way to go, LT," Podsy said from his wheelchair after clearing from the drop-deck and evading the watchful eye of the media drones hovering there. "Wait, make that, Captain, or 'Skipper,' if

I'm allowed to use the Marine nickname," he amended unabashedly.

"Way to go, yourself," Xi retorted, ripping her cap off and splashing her hair over her shoulders. She needed to get out of those clothes ASAP. She hadn't felt so self-conscious since her first teenaged tussle in the backseat of a car.

"Me?" Podsy scoffed. "I'm not sure what good I'll be to anyone. Ol' Strange Bed says it'll be a few weeks before he can calibrate my prosthetics and get me into physical therapy, and months more before we can even think about growing a new set of legs." His face scrunched up into a wholly uncharacteristic look of bitter resignation.

"Hey," Xi snapped, grabbing him by the chin and lifting his face up to meet hers. "None of us would have survived down there without what you did. Calling down that e-mag strike, and keeping *Elvira* on the line when you knew it would cost you... Nobody in that drop-deck—" She pointed to the closed blast doors at her back. "—would be alive if it hadn't been for you. We owe you, and none of us will *ever* forget it."

"Cold comfort while I'm riding a desk up here," Podsy said sourly, "and you guys are clearing guns on whatever our next mission ends up being."

She lowered herself down and met his eyes with a piercing look of her own. "Don't start feeling sorry for yourself now, Podsy. If scuttlebutt's anything to go by, we're about to be totally cut off from central supply lines. Fleet's pissed at what the commander— Sorry..." She bit her lip irritably. "At what the *colonel* was able to pull off behind their backs, transferring us to Armor Corps before they figured out how to screw us all right into the ground and lock us away somewhere cold and dark while they spun things to make themselves look good at our expense. We need a quartermaster with balls, Podsy, and frankly, nobody could be worse than Murdoch."

Podsy snickered. "Not exactly a ringing endorsement there, Captain."

"No," she admitted, "but it's the best I could come up with on the fly, and we both know it's true. Without creative supply acquisitions, like that bit of porn-swapping you pulled back on Durgan's Folly—" She twisted her lips in muted disgust before pushing on. "—we're going to find ourselves out of everything we need to keep the battalion rolling. And since that's exactly what Fleet wants, I say our best bet to deny them the satisfaction is by plopping your ass into that particular seat until you're ready to get back in a mech."

He sighed, "All right, all right...you win. You're right. I'm not *totally* useless."

"You're God-damned right I'm right." She nodded triumphantly. "Besides, as far as I'm concerned, *Elvira*'s not going anywhere without Lieutenant Andrew Podsednik aboard."

He shook his head firmly. "I appreciate the sentiment, but we both know that's not going to happen any time soon. It takes six months minimum to get combat-ready with prosthetics, and a full year to grow, graft, and train into vat-grown legs. I'm down for the foreseeable, Captain," he said, fixing her with a hard look, "but *Elvira*'s place is at the head of 2nd Company."

She wanted to argue, but the truth was they both knew he was right. Arguing would only serve to threaten his clearly-shaky self-esteem.

"I just..." She hesitated, uncertain how to express her feelings even after weeks to think about what words to use. "I can't imagine doing this without you, Podsy. You're like a brother to me."

Podsednik recoiled in mock alarm. "Wait, was that a legitimately tender moment that just whizzed past? Who are you, and what have you done with my Jock?"

"Podsy..." She glared at him, recalling Sergeant Major Trapper's advice. "I'm trying to open up here."

"I know, I know…" he said before he shifted awkwardly in his chair. "It's just… Doc told me that you never left my side…"

She flushed with emotion before shaking her head firmly. "I hit the latrine a few times."

He snickered. "And took a well-deserved break after I got lifted up to the *Revere*, from what I hear."

She cocked her head in confusion. "What are you talking about?"

"Rumors abound," he leaned in conspiratorially, "regarding a certain mech Jock and sergeant major spending a little 'quality time' together from the privacy of her mech."

Xi flushed with anger. "Nothing of the kind took place, and I'll rip the balls off whoever started spreading those rumors!"

"Methinks the lady doth protest too much," he chuckled.

"Look, nothing happened between Trapper and me…but if it had, at least *my* lays are still breathing when I notch them, Stumpy," she snapped hotly, rounding on him angrily.

"Aaaand she's back," Podsy declared with perfect timing, disarming her on the spot.

After a brief pause, the two shared a deep laugh that echoed through the *Bonhoeffer*'s corridors. It was the Armor Corps' lone combat-ready assault carrier, and they knew it would be their home for the foreseeable future.

But neither of them cared if they were aboard the *Dietrich Bonhoeffer*, the *Paul Revere*, some rust-bucket intra-system garbage-scow-turned-freighter, or hunkered down in a soaking-wet foxhole.

All that mattered was that they were together and that they were going to do great things. They had found a place where they fit in, far from the halls of civilized society. And after surviving the nightmare that was Durgan's Folly, they knew they would be able to deal with whatever the universe threw their way.

They were brothers (and sisters) in arms, and nobody, not the politicians back home, the bureaucrats who steered Fleet, or even the high-and-mighty Solarians could take that from them.

It was who they were, and realizing that fact filled her with a more profound sense of purpose and belonging than she had ever dreamed possible.

"It's good to be home," she said contentedly after the laughter had died down.

Podsy nodded. "It is indeed."

EPILOGUE - SEND IN THE ARMOR

"Colonel Jenkins," General Akinouye greeted, "thank you for joining us."

"Of course, General," Jenkins acknowledged, removing his cap in accordance with protocol. His recruiting drive had been cut dangerously short by the urgent summons, and he was none too pleased about it. He had only filled thirty of his battalion's forty-six Jock slots with qualified candidates prior to receiving the missive from Armor Corps brass. "What's the situation, sir?" he asked, pushing those thoughts aside.

"We've just received word of a highly unusual situation unfolding in a nearby star system," replied Major General Alice Chamberlain, the youngest of the Armor Corps' remaining brass, at the vibrant age of eighty-nine. "Fleet is otherwise engaged securing our wormholes against Arh'Kel throughout the Republic, and the Marines are engaged on four Republic worlds where rock-biter crypto-colonies were discovered, though thankfully none as significant as the one you dealt with," she added with the faint hint of a smirk, causing Jenkins to warily eye General Akinouye.

"One of the perks," Akinouye said with a humorless chuckle,

"of being the ranking member of the Joint Chiefs is that I get to play a little looser than most with classified information. I've briefed this room on the details of Durgan's Folly, Colonel, because I think it's important for everyone here to know the truth about the man whose hands currently hold the future of the Metal Legion." Jenkins had come to know that Armor Corps brass referred to their branch of the TAF by the nickname 'Metal Legion.'

Jenkins knew that Akinouye wouldn't have told them about Durgan's Folly without good reason, and he suspected it was to assuage their concern at having the 'future of the Armor Corps' in the hands of a recovering drunk and, as Captain Murdoch would say, a 'loose cannon.'

"Understood, General." He nodded to Akinouye before turning to Major General Chamberlain. "What's the situation, ma'am?"

"It's…unique in the history of the Republic, at least officially," she replied hesitantly, as all around the semi-circular table heads bobbed up and down in agreement. "It seems that the Vorr have established some sort of archeological dig site on EO-5293, a frozen planetoid in orbit of a gas giant in the Naga System."

"The Naga System?" Jenkins' brow furrowed in confusion. "That's Solar territory."

"Correct," a third Armor Corps general, named Pushkin, grunted in disdain.

"Under the Illumination League's most recent ruling regarding human interests," Major General Chamberlain explained, "the people of the Terran Republic are permitted to freely travel throughout human-designated territory, which includes star systems nominally assigned to Sol. As a result, certain forward-thinking Terran business interests have funded expeditions to star systems like Naga."

Jenkins nodded, suspecting he already knew whose interstellar corporation was involved.

"The Solarians—" Pushkin leaned forward irritably. "—have all but holed up in Sol for the last half-century. Few go in, fewer come out, and as a result, the non-League worlds have taken certain liberties with human-designated resources and territory which, of a right, ought to belong to humanity."

Jenkins was still confused, but he started to understand what they were saying. "The Vorr are unearthing something in Naga… How did the corporate interests in-system learn about the dig?"

"The Vorr *told* us they were doing it," Akinouye replied. "Specifically, they told the Terran Republic through secret back-channels which, officially, have never existed. These back-channels, officially-speaking, do not involve your friend, Chairman Durgan of D.I.E."

Jenkins nodded slowly. "Fleet can't afford the black eye if they officially investigate and the situation goes pear-shaped."

"It gets better." Chamberlain smirked. "The Vorr aren't the only non-human species in the Naga System."

Jenkins bristled. "The Arh'Kel?"

Akinouye gave a throaty laugh. "No, son. The rock-biters wouldn't have much interest in EO-5293."

His laughter infected the rest of the room's occupants, save Jenkins, who had no idea what was so funny.

"It is a species which the Vorr say they have previously encountered, but never successfully liaised with," Chamberlain explained. "The species is apparently known to the League, but the Vorr asked us to keep their presence secret and, at this point, the Republic is inclined to honor that request."

Jenkins finally understood. "This is essentially a first contact situation with a species we know nothing about, and our intro-duction is being facilitated by the Vorr, a recently-departed member of the Illumination League, who in turn are conducting some sort of excavation on a planet nominally under Solarian control. Should Sol learn about any of this, they'd be less-than-pleased to have not been brought in the loop on either the dig or the unknown species' presence. Whoever goes in there stands to alienate Sol, the League, the Vorr, and possibly even this unknown species if they cock it up, which is why Fleet's letting it slip to us. If we make a hash of it, they get all the ammo they need to shove us and what's left of the Metal Legion into a corner somewhere and run the clock out on us in the Armed Forces Committee when it comes time to dole out funding to the various branches. Am I missing anything?" Jenkins asked.

"Oh, she's not done." Akinouye smirked.

"Ma'am?" Jenkins asked in confusion, uncertain how it could get much more convoluted and dangerous than what he'd just outlined.

"Whoever goes to EO-5293," Major General Chamberlain explained, "will be accompanied by the press."

Akinouye snorted loudly. "Who, if the operation goes well, will be put under a gag order for national security reasons. But if things fall apart…"

"Will be ready to sink us with every image they bring back to the folks at home," Pushkin grunted.

"You knew the thunder you were calling down from Fleet when you transferred here, Colonel Jenkins," General Akinouye said matter-of-factly. "Well, you just saw the flash. As the commander of the only combat-ready battalion in the Terran Armor Corps, what do you think: do we pass on this, like any sane group of actors would?" He gestured to a data slate, presumably containing the mission's details. "Or are you ready to fulfill those bold promises you made to us before we brought you aboard?"

Jenkins knew this was one of those turning points in his life that he would never forget. But unlike every other moment like it, this time, he knew with absolute conviction what he needed to do. This was his chance to prove his worth not just to the Armor Corps brass and the politicians back home, but to himself and the people who trusted him to lead them.

He met the eyes of everyone at the table before turning to General Akinouye and clarifying, "So the question, General Akinouye, appears to be: what do you do when every other branch of the Terran Armed Forces passes on a mission because of tactical and political unknowns? A mission which is to be carried out in a star system well beyond the line, with the press in tow to record every misstep and error so it can be used against you at your court-martial should you come up short. Is that an accurate breakdown, sir?"

"Yes, son." Akinouye nodded gravely as all eyes scrutinized every centimeter of Lieutenant Colonel Jenkins' body. "What do *you* do?"

As Lee Jenkins placed his cap back on his head, his lips curled into a confident grin. And the next words to pass his lips were spoken with greater conviction and certainty than any he had uttered in his entire life.

"Send in the armor."

The End

Metal Legion, Book 1

If you like this book, please leave a review. This is a new series, so the only way I can decide whether to commit more time to it is by getting feedback from you, the readers. Your opinion matters to me. Continue or not? I have only so much time to craft new stories. Help me invest that time wisely. Plus, reviews buoy my spirits and stoke the fires of creativity.

Don't stop now! Keep turning the pages as Craig talks about his thoughts on this book and the overall project called Metal Legion.

AUTHOR NOTES - CRAIG MARTELLE
WRITTEN OCTOBER 28, 2018

You are still reading! Thank you so much. It doesn't get much better than that.

I love this series! I can't thank Caleb Wachter enough for doing the heavy lifting. I met him through Matthew Thrush and ours was a writing match made in heaven! Caleb brings the characters and the flow, an innate understanding of the characters, and how to keep the reader riveted. I bring the military experience and lingo to punch up the realism. I am blessed to have found someone with Caleb's talent to bring these stories to life.

We ran this one through two editors and a dozen different readers to catch any misalignments or inconsistencies. I think everything is on track. For those military aficionados out there, I know an org chart would answer a lot of questions. Maybe we'll publish one separately on my blog (which I don't update anywhere near as often as I should). TO&E would be cool, too – a table of organization and equipment so you can see directly which mechs are in which platoons and companies. Roles & responsibilities. All that good stuff we took for granted while we served. My TO (table of organization) weapon was an M16 when I was a second lieutenant. The colonel told me to get my TO weapon for a field exercise. I show up to hop on the five-ton, and everyone else has pistols. "Martelle, what the hell are you doing with that? Where's your pistol?" "Sir, my TO weapon is an M16," I countered. "The pistol won't get in anyone's way, and if you have to fire your weapon, we've already lost. Next time, get the pistol."

I just got off a podcast with Ramy Habeeb regarding our conference next year in Edinburgh. I'll be there from July 25 through the 31st with 250 of my writer friends. We're going to craft some great stories, do lots of Scottish stuff, and teach each other how to do better as self-published authors.

Changing gears back to today, it's dark a solid eighteen hours out of the day, soon to be twenty. By the time you read this, it'll be dark twenty hours out of the day. The sun will rise on the southern horizon, will barely get above it as it cruises along for a few hours, and then it'll set in the south. In the summer, the sun makes a big circle in the northern sky, not setting at all. Sun rises in the east and sets in the west for people in the south and only a couple months in the spring and fall here.

Phyllis' knees were bothering her so I had to take her to the vet for a new prescription of doggy ibuprofen. They have to do a blood test to make sure that nothing is going on as there is a remote chance that this medication will affect the kidneys. Phyllis has been taking a pill here and there for the last few years, so she's way good. No side effects for her. BUT, she was a shade overweight, up six pounds from our previous visit, so now she's on a diet, but it's a good lifestyle change for her. We add a cup of water to one cup of dry dog food along with a little homemade bone broth and plenty of green beans for maximum fill with minimum calories. She's lost at least three centimeters off her neck in less than two weeks. Good for Phyllis! She's limping less, too. If she keeps trimming down, her knees will be quite happy.

What else am I working on? So many new books coming. About one a week in 2019 from military science fiction to dragons in space to a cozy mystery series that is already shaping up to be spectacular. Or maybe spooktacular since this series is called Monster Case Files. It'll be all kinds of fun.

I have an epic fantasy trilogy coming, too. I hope you like that one, too – a journey of three sisters to save three kingdoms. Kill the kings, save the world.

No one goes on this journey alone. If it weren't for being surrounded by great people and the incredible readers who keep picking up my books, none of these stories would be possible.

Peace, fellow humans.

Please join my Newsletter (www.craigmartelle.com – please, please, please sign up!), or you can follow me on Facebook since you'll get the same opportunity to pick up the books for only 99 cents on the first Saturday after they get published.

If you liked this story, you might like some of my other books. You can join my mailing list by dropping by my website **www.craigmartelle.com** or if you have any comments, shoot me a note at craig@craigmartelle.com. I am always happy to hear from people who've read my work. I try to answer every email I receive.

If you liked the story, please write a short review for me on Amazon. I greatly appreciate any kind words, even one or two sentences go a long way. The number of reviews an ebook receives greatly improves how well an ebook does on Amazon.

Amazon – www.amazon.com/author/craigmartelle

BookBub – https://www.bookbub.com/authors/craig-martelle

Facebook – www.facebook.com/authorcraigmartelle

My web page – www.craigmartelle.com

That's it—break's over, back to writing the next book.

BOOKS BY CRAIG MARTELLE

Craig Martelle's other books (listed by series)

Terry Henry Walton Chronicles (co-written with Michael Anderle) – a post-apocalyptic paranormal adventure

Gateway to the Universe (co-written with Justin Sloan & Michael Anderle) – this book transitions the characters from the Terry Henry Walton Chronicles to The Bad Company

The Bad Company (co-written with Michael Anderle) – a military science fiction space opera

End Times Alaska (also available in audio) – a Permuted Press publication – a post-apocalyptic survivalist adventure

The Free Trader – a Young Adult Science Fiction Action Adventure

Cygnus Space Opera – A Young Adult Space Opera (set in the Free Trader universe)

Darklanding (co-written with Scott Moon) – a Space Western

Rick Banik – Spy & Terrorism Action Adventure

Become a Successful Indie Author – a non-fiction work

Enemy of my Enemy (co-written with Tim Marquitz) – a galactic alien military space opera

Superdreadnought (co-written with Tim Marquitz) – a military space opera

Metal Legion (co-written with Caleb Wachter) - a military space opera

End Days (co-written with E.E. Isherwood) – a post-apocalyptic adventure

Mystically Engineered (co-written with Valerie Emerson) – dragons in space

Monster Case Files (co-written with Kathryn Hearst) – a young-adult cozy mystery series

For a complete list of books from Craig, please see www.craigmartelle.com

69623468R10182